MURDER ON CATHEDRAL HILL

FIFTH PETE CULNANE MYSTERY

S.L. Smith

SIGHTLINE PRESS

St. Paul, Minnesota

ISBN-978-0-9964640-9-3

First Edition, December 2020

Printed in the United States of America

Cover photo by Matthew Gorrie

SIGHTLINE PRESS
St. Paul, Minnesota 55117
www.sightlinepress.com

For Gale, the best neighbor anyone could hope for, and a dear, kind, and generous friend taken way too soon.
You're greatly missed, Gale.

ONE

Fifteen-year-old Alyssa took control of her life when she boarded a Greyhound bus in Virginia, Minnesota ... or so she thought. In the process, she stripped her mother of the ability to make all the decisions—to smother her and squeeze the life out of her. After all, she reasoned, she was far too old to be under her mother's thumb.

She spent more than anticipated on her one-way ticket. For this small-town girl, Minneapolis, the largest city in Minnesota, held great promise. She remembered coming down to a Vikings game with her dad—the crowds, the traffic, the noise—like a huge party.

On the bus, she smiled every mile, confident of her path from the worst of times to the best of times. Years of bickering, arguing, and fighting over everything and nothing at all preceded the final confrontation with her mother.

Having conferred with the mothers of Alyssa's friends, her mother set up parental controls to lock her out of all kinds of websites. She discovered this late one night while completing a research paper for her humanities class.

After numerous failed attempts to circumvent her mother's efforts, out of desperation she woke her mother up at midnight. Her mother blew up. Alyssa did her best to civilly explain the things she could no longer access. She got nowhere. And her dad refused to contradict her mother. That was one of their cardinal rules. Alyssa got a D on that paper, and it counted as 25 percent of her grade. She'd never before had a C, much less a D.

She went freaking crazy when she got her grade. She spent hours devising ways to get even. Each idea hurt at least one person more than her mother. She gave up. That didn't change the fact she wanted to stop hurting. Escaping to Minneapolis became her mission. Smart enough to think ahead about food, she'd packed two peanut butter sandwiches, an apple, a banana, and four chocolate chip cookies for the trip. Her backpack also held the favorite clothes not on her back. That was as far as her planning had taken her. But she was equipped with a large dose of confidence that she could and would make things work. She'd done so repeatedly, but never at this level. She never doubted she'd succeed. Unfortunately, she didn't consider what this action ... or more accurately this reaction ... entailed.

Reality began gnawing at her excitement as she exited the bus in Minneapolis. For the first time, she wondered what to do next. Focused on getting to Minneapolis, she'd failed to think about the intricacies of life once there.

A handsome, well-dressed, great-smelling man opened the door for her as she exited the Greyhound Depot. He reminded her of someone. One of her dad's friends? She was too nervous to sort that out. They started talking.

Her newfound freedom quickly became a prison. She would soon learn how cruel and unforgiving life can be. She'd shifted her life from what she'd discover too late qualified as the best of times to something worse than her wildest imaginings. And this time there was no escape.

In the past, she'd loved reading about people her age in the world she knew, plus a few vampires and zombies thrown in for good measure. That was no longer true. She no longer found an escape in books. She couldn't concentrate enough to get into a book, any book.

After barely more than three months, which felt like an eternity, Alyssa, who was now known as Amber, knew she couldn't do this much longer. She found a degree of comfort in believing her dad would move heaven and earth to release her from this prison ... even though that wasn't possible.

If there were such a thing as hell, it couldn't be worse than this. And like hell, there was no escape. She brushed away a tear before it turned to ice and before JD saw it and delivered a reprisal. He dished it out in a surprising variety of ways. He delivered it for everything ... and for nothing at all. He was crazy, and he was getting worse. He no longer had a kind word. He was nasty and intolerant. Often downright cruel to her and the other girls, he constantly concocted new ways to make them feel lower than dirt. She, Ruby, and Pearl could handle it better than Opal. Despite constant reassurances from the other three, Opal couldn't ignore his perpetual criticism of her face and body. She was too sensitive, too insecure to realize that JD did it because he was evil and reveled in her pain. He hated women.

Amber longed to talk to her dad. Remembering the security once defined by his embrace always brought tears. How could she have been so stupid?

Tonight, the Red Bull Crashed Ice Competition, where racers skate on an elevated track with steep turns and high vertical drops, provided the venue. JD knew the crowds would provide both opportunity and invisibility.

Dressed to show off their wares rather than protect them from frostbite, he knew his girls could shatter the resolve of any normal guy. Tonight would be profitable, and it was just the beginning of a trail of opportunities for JD to line his pockets. In less than a week, he would take advantage of St. Paul's Winter Carnival. Then crossing the river, at the 2018 Super Bowl, his girls would pull in the dough. Life was good for JD. It was anything but good for his girls.

Amber sought refuge in memories. She thought about the good old days when she never missed watching a televised Vikings game with her dad. They cheered every yard gained by the Vikings, and they booed each penalty against them, and every inch gained by the opposition.

She thought about the jig they both did whenever the Vikes scored points. She'd started it as a little kid. Soon her dad began mimicking her. Before long, it became a tradition—had been for years.

In her former life, she was ecstatic whenever the Vikings got into the playoffs. Not anymore. This year, she silently asked her dad's forgiveness each time she rooted for the opposition. To avoid yet another winter venue, she prayed the Vikes didn't make it into any post-season games. *Sorry Dad.*

Tonight's windchill registered below zero. How far below she didn't know. There was a time her cellphone would have told her, but JD had stolen it and told her and the other girls that they'd be sorry if he ever caught them with one.

After the way she treated her mother and the life she now led, she doubted what lay ahead would be better than what she had now. At least it would be different. She heard once that hell was whatever you'd define as the worst thing possible. If so, did that mean JD and winter would define her hell? She groaned at the idea.

JD heard her and jabbed an elbow into her side. If it weren't for his thickly padded down jacket, he might have broken ... or at least cracked ... a few ribs.

Would she go to hell for what she was doing? Her dad believed everyone experienced their hell while on this earth. She tried to believe that. Had to believe it. It was the only thing that gave her hope. The only thing that kept her sane.

Amber stood alongside JD and Ruby near the St. Paul Cathedral. Back home, she'd hated going to church. Now she'd give her skimpy jacket to duck inside the Cathedral for even a few minutes. She had an ulterior motive—warmth. She was so cold.

Her long, thick mane of blonde hair helped some. Even so, she longed for one of the Scandinavian stocking caps her grandma knit. Pitted against these temperatures, her short skirt, leggings, and high-heeled boots provided little warmth. JD's one concession was her padded mittens.

The three of them huddled together. Amber shivered on JD's right, Ruby on his left. Someone selected Pearl at the beginning of the races. Opal left a short time later. *Was it luck?* Amber wondered, *or did tonight's crowd prefer short and tall conquests?* She estimated Pearl as about five-ten, using her dad as the basis for comparison, and figured Opal might reach five feet when she wasn't dragged down by the weight of their situation. She stood five-feet-five, and Ruby had a couple of inches on her. *Or perhaps the guys who buy our services prefer Pocahontas and Chin Chin to chocolate or vanilla? Is it coincidental the four of us are of such varied races and sizes? Did JD select us with that in mind, or was it coincidental?*

Amber worried about Pearl and Opal. Hoped everything was going smoothly. No surprises. No incidents. Just the disgusting same old same old. Each of them had experienced at least one night when they weren't that lucky. *Funny how much circumstances can change your perceptions*, she thought. Not long ago this same old same old would have made her want to puke. It wouldn't have been a relief.

Three months ago, Amber and the other girls were strangers. Now they were best friends, even though they had just one thing in common. And that one thing united them against a common enemy.

Previously, her best friends, like her, were of Scandinavian descent. Aside from a smattering of Germans and Italians, so were a majority of the people in Virginia, Minnesota. Her bond with the other three girls amazed her. She would never have wished this on any of them, but felt grateful they were as trapped as she. She wasn't strong enough to do this alone.

JD had hooked his right arm through her left and suddenly used that connection to pull her closer. Ordinarily, Amber railed at being this close to the sleazebag, but tonight she benefited a bit from the warmth afforded by his down parka.

Deafening roars and whistles greeted the beginning, middle, and end of each race, as four abreast the racers dropped 120 feet from the dome of the St. Paul Cathedral toward downtown St. Paul. While 90-degree turns were common, occasionally the turns approached one hundred eighty degrees. Amber wondered about the sanity of the racers. She wouldn't take on a course like this if it were on the flat. The time between races provided little respite from the noise. Despite a rip-roaring, cold-induced headache, Amber kept the smile JD forced her to wear on her painted face.

She'd heard the crowd was predicted to reach 120,000 but had concluded it unlikely, thanks to the weather. The estimate proved more accurate than her expectations. Minnesotans had to be crazy to be out here in this weather. Of course, judging from her predicament, who was she to criticize anyone?

Tonight's crowd, she thought, qualified as a mass. How appropriate, since they viewed an event that began at the Cathedral. At least all these bodies provided a bit of protection from the wind and kept her a degree or two warmer.

The throng provided so many opportunities. Why was she still here? Did Crashed Ice fans like plump girls? Did they seek warmth in some extra pounds? Did they prefer someone who provided more of a cushion? Did they like women, not girls? She knew anyone who cared to look through the makeup could tell she was under eighteen.

Amber could actually smell the cold. It smelled crisp. It smelled incredibly fresh. It failed to block the smell of alcohol bleeding from the pores of the woman on her right. The odor of the peppermint schnapps the woman drank from a thermos almost overpowered the mouthwatering smells of hot dogs and mini donuts wafting from the wagon of a nearby street vendor.

Under different circumstances and dressed appropriately, Amber would have enjoyed the excitement, the sounds, the colors of Crashed Ice. She said a silent prayer that she'd soon be delivered from all of this.

JD tugged her arm, then turned and pulled her away from their coveted spot to one less crowded. Apparently he'd decided their location wouldn't do. She assumed he'd decided they stood too close to the action to draw attention away from the races. He refused to allow a poor location to deter him from a strike in this goldmine. He had two hits but wouldn't be happy unless he was four for four.

Inching their way to the new location, Amber apologized to the people she unintentionally jostled on the way. She tried to concentrate on the races. Tried not to think about how cold she felt. Tried not to think about her family. She stood, shivering, wishing the night would end, wishing winter would transition into spring, wishing she didn't have to do this anymore.

Her thoughts were interrupted when someone rammed into JD. The collision rearranged all three of them. She didn't bother looking back. It wasn't the first time someone bumped into them tonight. It was unlikely to be the last, as long as she was here. Is that what this was about? Did some klutz move in close to strike a deal with JD?

When the person who plowed into him stayed put for more than a second, she couldn't help it. Keeping the plastic smile, just in case, she looked over her shoulder. A bulky guy dressed for the weather leaned into JD, slightly to the left of center, and close enough to be making an offer for her or Ruby.

Amber glanced at JD.

On impact, he'd gasped as if he'd had the wind knocked out of him by the force of the impact, and he muttered several expletives. Not surprising. He bore the brunt of it. Then a questioning look flashed across his face. He didn't turn and didn't utter another word.

She looked back, again. She saw the man disappear in the crowd. *How weird was that?* she thought. The fact JD didn't go after the guy surprised her. *Why didn't he knock the guy down?* she wondered. This was one for the books.

Seconds later, the umpteenth racers stepped onto the track. Simultaneously, JD's legs began to buckle. His weight dragged Amber down with him. He had to weigh nearly twice what she did.

"JD, I can't hold you up," she complained.

JD seemed oblivious to her and her words. He continued downward, taking her in the same direction.

Amber looked at Ruby who looked as puzzled as Amber felt. It seemed JD's hold on Amber and Ruby was the only thing keeping him from hitting the pavement. "What the hell?" Amber stammered.

"You got it girl," Ruby said.

Amber clenched JD's sleeve and pulled her arm free.

Noting the success and burdened with JD's full weight, Ruby did likewise.

JD's forehead bounced off the pavement. Thump. His stocking cap cushioned the blow, but hardly enough to matter.

Amber regretted permitting JD's crash to the pavement. There'd be hell to pay when he came to. She could guarantee it. She was so stupid. Why didn't she think before she acted? And what was with JD?

Did he drink too much? Did he OD?

TWO

Amber had no idea what to do. Should she give him CPR? With all the people around him, someone must know. Why didn't someone step up and help? Why did she care? Was she also supposed to be a nurse?

Ruby took a step back and stared down at JD. She looked as dumbfounded as Amber felt—too dumbfounded to scream. She contemplated her options. Not one idea seemed to improve her predicament.

Amber thought about taking advantage of the opportunity—about taking off. Almost did. Couldn't. Couldn't do that to her family. It felt like forever, but probably took only a few seconds before a man placed a hand on her shoulder and said, "I saw your friend go down. What happened?"

Both girls blurted out, "Don't know!" in unison. During their time with JD, they'd learned to say as little as possible.

The man shrugged and stepped forward. He crouched over JD for several seconds, then stood and said, "I'm not an EMT. Have no idea what to do." After looking at the girls, he yelled into the crowd, "We need a doctor, an EMT, a paramedic!" hoping for a response.

"Right here," a woman called as she fought her way through the crowd. "What happened?" she asked, rolling JD over on his back.

Eyes closed, his mouth hung open.

After looking at Ruby, true to form, Amber took the lead. "One minute he was fine. The next he went down. That's all I know."

While raising an eyelid to check pupil size and placing fingers on JD's throat, the woman glanced at Ruby, hoping for something more.

Ruby rubbed her neck and looked away.

"I'm a Richfield EMT," the woman said. "Do either of you have a phone? Don't want to stop what I'm doing to make the call."

Both girls shook their heads.

The EMT initiated chest compressions and yelled, "Hey people, you need to give us some space. This guy needs air!"

The crowd pressed in around her, the victim, the girls, and the man who'd shouted for help, drawn by this new attraction.

"Can you please push them back?" she asked the man.

After he succeeded, marginally, she said, "Now please call 911. We need police and a medic. Both should be nearby, I hope. I'm losing him. These girls need to get someplace warm ASAP. They look like they're just this side of hypothermia."

The man called 911. As he provided details to the 911 operator, he spotted two uniformed officers headed his way. Ignoring the operator, he let out an ear-piercing whistle, motioning frantically to the officers.

The circle of people staring at the ground, oblivious to the races, had already alerted the two St. Paul officers. They were two of many working overtime to cover this detail. The whistle that sounded more like a scream and the frantic waving of a man at the center of the cluster accelerated their pace.

The Richfield EMT called out, "Any sign of a medic van?"

"There's one coming up John Ireland Boulevard," one officer said.

"Can you push these folks back and give us some breathing room?" the EMT asked. "And please get these girls into a warm squad car before they succumb to hypothermia!"

One officer recruited some spectators to help push back the crowd while speaking into his shoulder mike, requesting a Central District officer to take the girls to headquarters.

Simultaneously, his partner rushed the girls to his squad car, keeping them in a tight little group, so neither could take off.

Amber and Ruby now huddled together in the back seat of his squad.

"It'll take a few minutes for the heat to kick in," he apologized. "At least you're out of the wind. That's a big plus. What happened to your friend?"

He wanted to ask what possessed them to go out in this weather dressed the way they were, but didn't want to irritate them. He figured he already knew.

As always, Ruby left the talking to Amber.

After a protracted pause, Amber said, "Don't know. One minute he was standing there. The next he was dragging us down with him. It was weird."

Amber had never imagined wanting to be in a squad car. *Funny how the situation affects a person's preferences*, she thought. She felt the blower's cool air transition to warm. After a few minutes of this, for the first time since they arrived at the Crashed Ice races, her teeth stopped chattering. Comparatively speaking, the squad qualified as heaven—even in the current context. In the last three months, she'd learned to appreciate every good thing in her life. So few remained.

Finally warm enough to think, Amber's mind raced. What now? She and Ruby couldn't just sit here. They couldn't permit themselves to be questioned by the police. Initially, she didn't think they'd have a chance of outrunning the cop while wearing their high-heeled boots. Then she realized the cop had to be wearing boots too. She and Ruby could set off in different directions before heading toward their apartment. Maybe at least one of them could escape.

Amber nudged Ruby's foot with hers, bent over far enough to be unseen by the cop, and pointed to both doors, hoping Ruby understood. With her hand still hidden from the cop, she counted down. One finger. Two fingers. Three fingers. Then she thrust her thumbs toward the back doors.

Both girls grabbed for the door handles. They prepared to pull, while simultaneously throwing their shoulders into the doors.

THREE

St. Paul Police investigators Commander Peter Culnane and Detective Sergeant Martin Tierney, Pete's fiancée Katie Benton, and Martin's son Marty stood on a corner in downtown St. Paul. They packed in tight to prevent frostbite and enjoyed the spectacle.

At age thirty-four, Martin couldn't understand anyone crazy enough to lace up ice skates, climb all those stairs, and step out onto the Red Bull Crashed Ice racecourse. *Sheer insanity*, he thought. He would never consider doing it upright on ice skates. Sliding down on his butt? Might be fun.

Pete, on the other hand, was thirty-eight and itching to give it a try. Just the same, he valued his relationship with Katie too much. It had withstood many last-minute cancellations and her nagging fear for his safety. Asking her to witness a foray into this test of agility and stamina came dangerously close to crossing the line. Was this, as Martin insisted, a test of sanity?

Pete permitted himself to take an imaginary run down the track. He felt the exhilaration of climbing the steps to the rose window of the St. Paul Cathedral and stepping out onto the course. He felt the burst of adrenaline as he looked at the 120-foot drop down the hill to downtown. He felt the wind in his face as he conquered the course. He felt his body react to the speed, tight turns, and bumps from his competitors. He felt the adrenaline rush and another adrenaline burst when strobe lights edged into his peripheral vision, breaking the spell.

Turning his head, Pete saw a medic van edging along John Ireland Boulevard toward the Cathedral. Despite the lights and occasional siren blasts, the crowd continued hindering its progress. Spectators resisted surrendering their hard-won spots ... even to an emergency vehicle. The vehicle won of course, even as some spectators flexed their muscles.

Pete elbowed Martin and tilted his head in the direction of the flashing lights.

Pivoting toward the right, Martin saw what the racetrack kept him from noticing. A medic van appeared over the crowd. He sighed. It was 9:30. The final race loomed, the reason they'd been on this corner for more than two hours. So much for that.

Bending in close to be heard over the crowd and pointing in the direction of the medic van, Pete said, "Katie, Martin and I need to check that out. If it takes a while, are you okay with driving Marty home?" He already knew the answer. "I'll call you as soon as I know more. Here are my keys, just in case."

Meanwhile, Martin explained the situation to Marty, waving his hand at the strobes.

Marty did an almost convincing job of hiding his disappointment.

"I hate doing this to you, son. Will you do me a huge favor?"

"Sure, Dad." The pace of Marty's answer conveyed his disappointment.

"Please memorize every twist and turn, every bump and spill, every change in leadership in the final race. I want you to give me a blow-by-blow account of that race, so I can experience it with you. Will you do that for me?"

"You bet!" A smile lit Marty's face.

"Katie, will you also do me a favor?" Martin asked.

Katie smiled and nodded.

"I planned to get Marty a souvenir. Will you take care of it and also get him something warm to eat?" Martin asked, handing her more than enough twenties to suffice.

"I'd love to." She nodded.

Those details covered, Martin and Pete headed toward the strobes.

Sticking with the norm, if for no other reason than his long-legged stride, Pete took the lead.

Ordinarily, Martin struggled to keep up. It felt like his partner was forever racing somewhere. Not tonight. Tonight's crowd had Martin wishing they could speed up.

He observed their mission take precedence over politeness. Pete pushed ahead, slicing a path through people reluctant to relinquish even an inch of the space they'd captured. With the final race about to start, people pushed closer together, attempting to better their view. It went against their grain to move aside for an interloper. For the time being, the overriding sentiment being they owned their space.

Martin stuck close on Pete's heels, slipping through the openings Pete created before the spectators swallowed them up. He marveled at the pace Pete sustained, as they fought for every inch of progress. It sometimes helped when Pete shouted, "Police! Let us through." But it seemed as many people challenged the claim as gave ground. In their defense, often the only way to make room was to huddle even closer together. With this crowd, there was no such thing as personal space. Everyone invaded the space of those around them.

Thanks to several blocks of jockeying for position, Martin felt exhausted by the time they neared their destination. Fortunately, the proximity to their target brought a burst of adrenaline.

Heightened awareness following events like the Boston Marathon bombing meant tonight's races drew not only spectators but police and their dogs. The plethora of police sought to short circuit any attempt to take advantage of the crowd to gain notoriety or a voice.

Despite lights and sirens and an assist from several uniformed police officers, the medic van continued edging its way to the scene. Within a stone's throw, Martin saw two crew members jump out of the van and, complete with satchels, push their way on foot to the victim. The number of people crowding around this second spectacle made it impossible to see the focal point.

Pete struggled through the remaining spectators separating them from the scene. Martin observed almost half of the people with their backs to the race. Distracted by the unexpected? Anxious to know what had happened in their midst?

Guess they decided to settle for a replay of the race, Martin thought.

The crew of the medic van took over lifesaving efforts for the Richfield EMT. A paramedic hooked the man up to telemetry, another continued the chest compressions, and an EMT examined JD's trunk and arms for any explanation for his collapse.

"Commander Culnane," said an officer helping to hold back the crowd. "Didn't expect to see you out on a night like this. Were you here for the races?"

Pete nodded then crouched down to hear the exchange between the medic van's crew and a woman who, judging from her attire, was here as a spectator. The continuing noise elicited by the races necessitated this. Pete got in place just in time to hear the supervisor say, "Stop the compressions, Kathy. The doc at Regions said he's flatlined."

JD was declared dead at 9:54 p.m.

The shoulders of the medic van's crew and the Richfield EMT dropped. They all sighed deeply and shook their heads. All looked deflated.

Pete said he'd call the medical examiner, and that completed the work of the medic rig's crew. They gathered their equipment, placed a blanket over the body, and thanked the Richfield EMT for her efforts.

Before leaving, Pete and Martin thanked each of them. Then Martin called the watch commander to request Commander Lincoln dispatch the Forensic Services Unit. Meanwhile, Pete called the Ramsey County ME Office.

"I assume there are still plenty of spectators," the on-call investigator said. "Can you provide an escort from Rice and John Ireland? I'll be there with a technician in about ten minutes."

While Martin called Katie, Pete asked a uniformed officer, "Did anyone see what happened?"

"I heard him let fly with a string of expletives," a man in the front of the pushed back crowd said. "Glanced over. Thought there was going to be a fight. Saw a guy pressed up against him. Assumed there was a collision. Assumed someone was texting or jockeying for position and accidentally slammed into him. Saw the guy who created the ruckus back away and melt into the crowd. A minute later, this guy went down. I stepped up to help the girls who were with him."

"My partner took the girls to our squad, so they could warm up," one of the many uniformed officers doing crowd control, and getting names and contact information said. "By now, someone from Central District's probably on the way to headquarters with them."

"Please ask the watch commander to have them put in separate interview rooms and have someone stay with each of them until we arrive," Pete told her and continued questioning the man who'd assisted the girls. "Look around," he told the man. "Do you see the person who bumped him?"

The man towered above the crowd, making the job easier. After doing a three-sixty, he shook his head.

"Describe him."

"First, I should qualify that. I assume it was a guy. The down jacket and facemask make it hard to know for sure. As best I could tell, under the circumstances, the person was about six feet and medium build."

"What colors were the jacket, facemask, and pants?"

"Black, black, and black."

"Anything make this person stand out?" Pete asked. "A limp, markings on the jacket? Anything at all?"

"I didn't notice anything."

"Was he or she holding anything?"

"Not that I noticed, but I can't rule it out."

Observing the arrival of the ME rig, Pete headed in that direction.

The ME Office beat the Forensic Services Unit to the scene, but not by much. Forensics had just closed out a case in the vicinity.

The investigator and technician from the ME Office greeted Pete and Martin by name and got to work. At the instruction of the investigator, the technician took numerous photos of the body. Then the investigator placed brown paper sandwich bags over the victim's gloved hands and used rubber bands to keep them in place. The mission? Avoid dislodging any evidence on the gloves, while transporting the body to the ME Office for the autopsy.

"When you finish there, Don," Pete said to the investigator, "Let's check his back."

"Great minds ...." Don smiled.

Forensics arrived in time for an officer to obtain photos beforehand and observe, along with her supervising sergeant, as Don and the technician rolled JD onto his stomach. Then they carefully pulled JD's jacket up over his head, watching closely to see if anything fell out. In the process, they exposed a bulky sweater.

All six observers spotted it simultaneously: A red patch covered the back of the sweater, top to bottom and side to side. JD's sweater, turtleneck, and jacket had kept the blood from providing a clue.

With gloved hands, Don and Marc, the technician, carefully rolled first the blood-soaked sweater, then the turtleneck up to the victim's head. With all three layers out of the way, Pete and Martin saw why the victim went down, and why efforts to revive him failed. A star-shaped bullet wound and a lot of blood stood in stark contrast to the man's pasty white skin.

"If his heart was the target," Pete said, "looks like the shooter succeeded. No sign of stippling on his back. Not surprising with all these layers. Let's check his jacket again."

Don and Marc carefully rolled the turtleneck, sweater, and jacket down over the victim's back. As they did, they, Pete, Martin, and Forensics watched for anything dropping out.

It didn't happen. Thanks perhaps to its bulkiness, nothing showed on the back of the jacket in the vicinity of the bullet hole in JD's back.

"Grab that side of his jacket, and I'll grab this side," Don told Marc. "We'll stretch it tight."

Their efforts provided the information he sought. They saw the hole in the back of the jacket. Pulling a mag light from his jacket pocket, Pete shined it on the hole. Barely visible on the Kelly green jacket, Forensics, the ME staff, Pete, and Martin saw the scant traces of gunshot residue.

"Based on the star-shaped wound, the shooter was in close proximity. Despite the crowd noise, they must have used a silencer, don't you agree?" Pete asked.

"Logical," the Forensics supervisor said. "Despite the noise, without one, people in close might have heard the gunshot. It's reasonable the shooter didn't risk it."

"Want me to call the watch commander? Tell her we're here and we agree to work the case? Ask her to contact Commander Lincoln?" Martin asked Pete, already knowing the answers.

Pete nodded.

Despite the ambient air temperature, and despite being pushed back 50–60 feet by the police, a crowd continued to surround the area.

That will change once Don and Marc remove the body, Pete thought.

"There were two girls with him," he told Forensics and the ME staff. "Hope they can add details. I'll get back to you after we speak with them."

Finding no exit wound, before placing the body in a body bag the investigator made one last attempt to find a bullet. He recruited police and forensics officers to light the area with their flashlights—just in case. Their efforts proved futile.

Meanwhile, additional forensics officers obtained the scant information currently available, secured the area, and searched for trace evidence. Locating the bullet casing, assuming it existed and was in the vicinity, took priority.

"Someone might have accidentally ... or intentionally kicked it, sending it flying when we cleared the scene," Martin said. "And it might have gotten caught in a waffle-soled boot. Lots of them around tonight, thanks to the weather."

"We talked to the people who were here when he went down," one of the police officers still doing crowd control said. "I have a list of the people in closest proximity when this happened ... at least those still here when I arrived. I also have several photos of the crowd. Several saw someone bump into him shortly before he went down. Their descriptions of that person run the gamut. With so many cellphones, thought maybe someone took a picture. If so, they didn't hang around."

"We've done all we can here," Pete told Martin. "Let's talk to the girls who were with him.

FOUR

I wouldn't be happy if they hung me with a new rope, Martin realized as he and Pete hoofed it to the squad for a ride to headquarters. *First, I felt frustrated because the crowd impeded Pete's and my pace. Now I'm frustrated because I can't keep up with him. Can't decide which I liked less ... or which is more stressful.*

He wondered about Marty and Katie. Where were they now? Eating? Definitely someplace warmer than his current location. Chasing after Pete provided one benefit. It got his blood pumping, warming his extremities a bit. He could almost feel his toes. Tonight he needn't worry about the caffeine he'd consume over the next several hours keeping him awake. Who knew if or when he'd get to bed? Besides, the way he felt now, drinking something warm was secondary to taking advantage of the warmth the mug would transfer to his hands.

Pete felt a blast of warm air as he opened the door at headquarters. He hoped the girls would be as welcoming. He wasn't naive enough to think that would happen. Walking toward the interview rooms, Pete tucked his gloves and stocking cap under his left arm and ran the fingers of his right hand through his thick, wavy hair.

A thread of jealousy flashed through Martin as he shook his head and followed suit. Pete now looked camera ready, while Martin knew he had helmet hair—at best.

"What do you think about splitting up and getting a feel for what we're dealing with?" Pete asked.

"Sounds like a plan." Martin waited before heading to the second interview room to observe Pete and learn a bit about the girl he'd interview. He also sought a heads up on what he might be up against.

After ensuring the audio and video recorders were operating, Pete entered the first interview room and thanked the female officer who'd kept the girl company. Then with an almost imperceptible tilt of his head, Pete told the officer he wanted to confer.

First, he sat across from a beautiful blonde, blue-eyed girl and said, "You look like you're still chilled to the bone. Can I get you a refill?"

The girl smiled and nodded.

"What are you drinking? Coffee? Hot tea? Hot chocolate?"

"I had coffee, but prefer hot chocolate, please."

To stay warm, Dad always filled a thermos with hot chocolate before driving down to Vikings games, she reminisced. *That was when he and his friends could afford tickets. Now he can barely afford to put food on the table.*

The forlorn look that flashed across her face told Pete something had triggered a memory. Something to do with hot chocolate? He'd do his best to get her to share it. He knew he faced an uphill battle.

"Sit tight. I'll be right back. Then we'll figure out how I can help."

Before getting the cocoa, Pete spoke with the officer who'd filled in prior to his arrival. He was disappointed but not surprised to hear the girls clammed up. The officer had nothing to share, aside from the fact the girl spent the entire time silently staring at her hands. "The only words she uttered were, 'I'd like coffee.' Unlike many, she said please."

How I wish this cop could help me, Amber thought. *The problem is, he can't. He can only make things worse.* That was one of the first things JD taught her. She angrily brushed away a tear. Crying wouldn't help. She couldn't let the cops see her cry. She had to convince them all was well, so she could go home.

And she had to let JD know they hadn't tried to flee from him. Had she and Ruby succeeded in escaping from the squad car, she wouldn't have this problem. They'd be back at their apartment, and JD would know their whereabouts. All things being equal, that would be bad. But all things weren't equal in her current world. Unfortunately, she hadn't realized the back seat of a squad car served as a prison since the back doors couldn't be opened from the inside.

She hoped as far as JD was concerned their night was finished, even though she hadn't made a cent. She was sure to hear about that. Ruby hadn't done any better. At least she wasn't the only one. At the same time, JD would be twice as angry twice as likely to make them pay. She refused to think how they'd pay this time. The possibilities were numerous, unfathomable, daunting. This was his only area of creativity, and it scared her. She pushed these thoughts out of her head.

Could they convince him tonight's spectators just weren't interested in girls like them? Would he be satisfied with the money Pearl and Opal made tonight? She said another prayer that they'd be okay—that they hadn't gone off with a couple of crazies. Amber pondered these things as the cop returned, carrying two steaming cups.

Pete set one cup on the table and handed the second to Amber.

She wrapped her hands around the cardboard cup. The warmth and smell triggered a smile.

Pete saw it and hoped he'd begun softening the shell sure to separate him from this young girl. He figured she was fifteen or sixteen. The makeup did a poor job of disguising that. Reaching deep in his pants pockets, he pulled out M&Ms, Oreo cookies, and a package of granola, then pushed them toward the girl. "Thought you might be hungry. Help yourself."

"Thanks, I'm starving." Amber smiled warmly.

Despite the cold outside and the warmth in here, despite the warmth she felt holding the cocoa, Amber wanted out of here. She was afraid of screwing up—of accidentally saying something she would regret in the worst way. Before the cop had a chance to ask anything, she put on her sweetest smile and asked, "Can I go home now, please? I'm really tired. Too tired to think."

Pete noticed she still had her coat zipped up to her throat and shivered frequently. "Feeling like you'll never be warm again? My jacket's like an oven. I'll loan it to you if you're interested."

Taken aback, Amber's eyebrows shot up. Wide-eyed she asked, "For real?"

Pete smiled at her reaction and nodded.

"That would be awesome." She tilted her head and smiled.

Pete transferred the contents of the pockets to his pants and handed her his jacket. She pulled it on over her sexy but skimpy, waist-length pink ski jacket. "Thanks! You're right. It feels like heaven." She pulled the zipper to the top.

"If you cooperate, this shouldn't take long. My job is to determine what happened tonight. I need to do that for both you and your friend who collapsed. What's his name?"

Deep sigh. "JD."

"Are those initials or is that his name?"

"Got me. That's the only name I know."

Having observed this much, Martin headed to the second interview room.

"Let's start with your name," Pete continued. "Mine is Pete Culnane. You are?"

"Anxious to go home." The girl took a long drink of the still-steaming hot chocolate and struggled to open the granola. Finally succeeding, she said, "They sure make it difficult, don't they? You'd think they wanted you to look at it, not eat it."

Trying to change the subject, Pete knew and permitted it, hoping she'd relax.

"It's an issue with modern packaging. My grandma has a terrible time opening some things. Jars and 'easy-open' cans are the worst."

"I know what you mean. My grandma hates them too."

"Are you and she close?"

"Very!" She smiled and nodded.

"Does she live near you?"

"She's ten or fifteen minutes from our house." Her reply started enthusiastically and trailed off as her head sank.

Pete figured this was prior to her getting mixed up with the victim. "Do you take the bus to see her?" he asked.

She shook her head. "No such luck. I have to depend on Dad and Mom."

So she didn't live somewhere with good bus service, such as the Twin Cities, St. Cloud, Rochester, and Duluth, Pete thought. "Do you see her often?"

"It's been awhile," she sighed, frowned, and rested her head on her right hand.

"I bet she misses you."

Moist eyes were her only response.

Pete gave her a few seconds before asking, "Were you named for your grandmother?"

"No. That would have been nice."

"What's her name?"

"Amy. I like that name."

"Me too. What's yours?"

Amber dropped her focus from Pete's eyes to her hands and stared silently at them.

"I don't get it. Why won't you share something as harmless as your name? Are you on the ten most-wanted list?"

That brought a smile.

"Thank goodness. I was hoping it wasn't going to be one of *those* nights."

"Okay," she sighed, "my name's Amber." For maybe a thousandth of a second, she thought about sharing her real name. She wanted to. She liked this cop. But the price? Way too high.

"Last name?"

"Anderson," she answered, still concentrating on her hands.

He didn't ask to see an ID, confident she had a fake one. At least for now, he wouldn't risk alienating her.

"Mighty cold night to be outside for hours, even when you're dressed for it," he said.

"I didn't realize it was so cold when I walked out the door."

"Under the circumstances, I'm surprised your friend permitted you to stay. The first responders worried about hypothermia."

"JD was so excited about being there. He wanted to see a Minnesotan win it three years in a row. He's going to be furious he missed the final race."

"I hope he doesn't take it out on you. Would he?"

Her eyebrows sought higher ground.

"Do you have any brothers?"

"One."

"What's his name?"

"Garret."

Must be his real name, Pete thought. *She didn't look away or pause to think before responding.* "How old is Garret?"

"Seventeen."

"Does he have a car?"

She chuckled. "Heck, Dad and Mom are in danger of losing .... Never mind. Not important." She shook her head and pulled back away from the table and Pete.

"Any sisters?"

"One. She's just a kid."

So are you, Pete thought. "How old?"

"Eleven."

"I'll bet she idolizes you. What's her name?"

"Madison."

"I need your help with some things."

"You've already asked a lot of questions. It should be my turn. Is JD okay?" She still wondered if he'd OD'd.

"I won't know for a while. Any idea what happened to him?"

"No, won't get my MD for a few more semesters," Amber said with a straight face.

Quick on her feet, Pete thought. *Wonder if that's kept her going.* "How long have you known JD?"

"About three months," she said, looking him in the eye.

"Where did you meet?"

Now Amber looked past Pete and tapped an index finger on her lips, carefully considering her answer. If she said outside the Greyhound Bus Depot, it might tell him too much. She played it safe. "Sorry, I don't remember. Three months is a long time. We've been so many places since then." *Unfortunately.*

"I need some details about tonight."

Amber wanted details about when she could go home, but kept her mouth shut. The cop had to know that. Why wasn't he interested in her, not just figuring out what happened to JD? She was both glad and sad about that. She wished she could get his help and escape this hell, but she knew that couldn't happen. She should be happy he wasn't pressuring her. She should feel relieved. Why didn't she?

"First," Pete continued, "how did you get to Crashed Ice? If one of you drove, you need to move the car or pay a fortune in parking or towing and impound lot fees. I assume neither you nor your injured friend wants that."

"JD has the keys. He may already have the car. He may be worried about us." *He may be wondering where we went and if we took off. By now, he should know better than to worry about that.*

"He won't be able to retrieve it soon enough. The paramedics looked through his pockets to find his medical insurance card. If he has the car keys, they didn't find them."

"He always puts them in the inside, zippered pocket of his jacket. The pocket is small, and his jacket is so thick they're easy to miss."

"If you tell me where to find the car, we'll be able to move it once we have the keys." *And hopefully get some helpful information about JD,* Pete thought.

Since the victim had no ID, the ME Office immediately fingerprinted him, and someone was called in to run the prints. The results could help get the investigation up and running, and enable notification of the next of kin.

This time, those efforts proved futile. They discovered the victim: JD, Jay D, Jay Dee, or some iteration thereof never served in the military, obtained a security clearance, or had a background check. And he was never arrested. Otherwise his prints would have been in the Integrated Automated Fingerprint Identification System (IAFIS), maintained by the FBI, and they'd know not only who he was but also his past. His prints told them just one thing. He didn't have a record.

"Why can't JD move it?" Amber rubbed her cheek and repeatedly rearranged herself on the chair.

"It doesn't look like he'll be out of the hospital in time. It should be moved right away to eliminate any potential problems."

"What's the matter with JD?"

"I don't yet have the details."

"Okay, fine." Amber let out a protracted sigh. "We parked in the State of Minnesota lot by the State Capitol and the freeway ... by Cedar and the frontage road north of I-94."

"Can you tell me the make and model? Unfortunately, the keys won't tell us all we need to know to find the car."

"It's a Toyota Highlander. Guess you might need to know the color, huh? It's black. JD said that's the best color if you ...." Amber shook off the rest of her response.

The best color if you don't want to draw attention? Pete wondered. *The best color if you want to melt into the background?* "Any additional details you provide could help."

"There's a St. Paul Saints sticker in the back window. I don't know the license plate number."

"How did you meet JD?"

"What difference does it make?" Amber snapped. "I'm tired of so many questions. When can I leave? When can I go home?"

"That's a lot of questions from someone so tired of questions." Pete smiled.

Amber's shoulders dropped a few degrees, and the corners of her mouth turned up.

"Why are you sensitive about where you met? Are you hiding something?"

"No." She shook her head a little too emphatically. "It's personal."

Pete leaned in, propping his chin on his right hand. "Tell me about JD's friends."

"I haven't met any of them."

"What about the girl who was at Crashed Ice with the two of you?"

"That's different." Pause. "Actually, she's more my friend than his."

"So she was there because of you?" Pete's timing left much to be desired. Amber was taking a drink of cocoa when he asked.

She coughed and began choking. "Down the wrong pipe."

Pete stood. "Anything I can do to help?"

Amber shook her head and continued coughing. It took a couple of minutes for her to stop coughing and catch her breath.

He already knew the answer, and she didn't use the opportunity to ask for help, so Pete moved on. "Where do you live?"

Amber gulped and looked at her hands. She didn't dare tell him. After thinking a few seconds, she blurted out, "In an apartment near Dale and

Grand." That was the best she could do. She knew there were lots of apartment buildings in the vicinity, but she had no idea of an address.

"Does the friend who came here with you live there too?"

"Yes." Amber nodded.

"Anyone else?"

"Yes, two other friends."

"Where were they tonight? Did they decide to pass on Crashed Ice?"

"They went, but left early."

"What are their names?"

"Opal and Pearl."

"Last names?"

"White and Lake, in that order." Amber shared the names on their fake IDs.

"And the name of the friend who came here with you?"

"I'm sure she already told someone."

"Sometimes people get nervous and fib about those things. Are you nervous, Amber?"

Amber rolled her eyes. "Wouldn't you be?"

"If I was your age? For sure."

"I'm older than I look. Mom says someday I'll be happy about that."

"How old are you?"

"Eighteen." Amber looked embarrassed saying that.

"What grade are you in?" Pete hoped she'd answer reflexively. Something she didn't do when it came to her age.

"I was a sophomore ... in college."

Permitting Amber to believe she'd spoofed him, Pete changed the subject. "Do you like the place where you live?"

"It's okay."

"Pricey, isn't it?"

Amber responded with a hands-up shrug.

Pete knew apartment rents in the area she mentioned ranked up there. "Are you going to school?"

"No."

"I'm surprised. You seem to have your head screwed on. Why did you quit?"

"I got tired of it."

"Hope you decide to go back. Where were you enrolled?"

"What difference does it make? Don't you believe me?"

Hoping to trip you up, Pete thought and said, "You grew up on the range, didn't you?" He'd detected an Iron Range accent.

Amber shook her head emphatically. Too emphatically again. She looked bored.

Pete worried he was losing her and decided it was time to give her a clear opportunity to ask for help, if she dared. "Based on the fact JD kept you out there despite the way you're dressed," he said, "it seems your health and safety aren't important to him."

Amber burst out laughing. She couldn't help it. JD care about her? That was ridiculous. She thought this guy was smart enough to know the arrangement between her and JD. Obviously she was wrong. Obviously she'd given him too much credit.

She scrambled to eliminate any suspicions triggered by her outburst. "Sorry. That tickled my funny bone. Reminded me of a story."

"How about sharing it? I could use a good laugh."

"Sorry, I just remember the punch line."

"You didn't answer the question."

"He wanted to see the races. He didn't want to leave before the end." *At least not while Ruby and I were still hanging around.*

"Were you scared when JD went down?"

"Surprised. Actually, shocked would be more accurate." Amber felt grateful he'd changed the subject.

"What happened from the time you arrived until JD went down?"

"JD wanted to grab a spot by the new jump over John Ireland Boulevard." *He was confident there would be a lot of traffic there.* "We would probably have had to claim a spot by midafternoon to get one of the best locations. Not even JD was up for that."

"Then?" Pete prompted.

When the races started, people concentrated on the part of the track we could see, the screen, and the announcements, trying to find out who won. That's what we were doing when this guy piled into JD. The end."

"Describe that person. How tall? Bulky or thin? What were they wearing?"

"I only saw his shoulders and head from the side. JD had his arm through mine and had me pulled in close, so I could only turn my head. I only glanced back over my shoulder. I know he had his hood up and wore a face mask. I think both were black, but I only saw him for a second. I didn't know the details would be important. I think he was about the same height as JD. About my dad's height. Five feet ten or so, I guess."

"Did you stay in the same location the whole time?"

"More or less. We were always in the shadow of the Cathedral. Not literally, of course."

"You said a guy piled into JD. He didn't just bump him?"

"Well, he bumped him pretty hard. He was probably concentrating on the jump and the racers."

"Was it a glancing blow, or did this person stand there before backing away?"

"He stood there for several seconds. I got the impression he was surprised and was trying to figure out what happened. What did he expect, moving around and not paying attention to where he was going in a crowd like that? Anyway, now you know it all."

"You've consistently referred to that person as 'he.' Are you certain it was a man? If so, why?"

"It could have been a woman, I guess. I assumed it was a man, because of the person's size. The down jacket looked like a man's, but I have a friend whose down jacket looks more like a boy's than a girl's."

"Did the person who bumped JD say anything to him or you?"

"No," Amber shook her head. "The crowd noise would have made them difficult if not impossible to hear. The person didn't back away immediately, so I expected to hear something. I did my best to hear them. JD swore as soon as he was bumped, but didn't say anything after that. If the person said something and JD heard them, he'd have responded. JD likes to have the last word."

"Did that bump occur at a critical point in the race?"

"Actually, yes. The racers were almost at the finish line. The crowd was screaming for their favorites. Like I said, I thought it happened because the person was watching the race instead of where they were going."

Pete rubbed his neck and said, "We'd both benefit from a break. I'll be back shortly. Can I get you anything?"

"Just a ride home. What else could you possibly need? Seriously, I answered all your questions. I want to go home. Now!"

"I know there's a lot you aren't saying, Amber. I understand your hesitation. JD told you stories so you'd clam up if you were ever questioned by the police, didn't he?"

Amber moved her hands to her lap and clenched her fists. "JD didn't tell me anything. Can we come back tomorrow? Once I get some sleep, I'll be much more helpful. How about if I meet you here at one o'clock tomorrow afternoon? I know Ruby is even more tired than me. She told me she was exhausted on the way here. We'll both return tomorrow. We can be here at whatever time is best for you."

Pete now had Amber's version of the other girl's name. Too bad she wouldn't disclose any important details. He knew she'd never show tomorrow. He couldn't let her go, regardless.

He thought about delivering a speech, telling her he knew Amber wasn't really her name, she wasn't eighteen, and he knew the relationship between her and JD. But he knew the lies guys like JD told their girls. They had to convince her JD lied. Until he and Martin accomplished that, she'd remain under JD's control, even though he was dead. They only had to reach one of the four girls. Would they succeed? Would Amber help them?

FIVE

Martin drove knowing you can't judge a book ..., Martin paused, looking through the window at the second girl. This attractive girl, whose coloring he'd describe as coffee with cream, clenched and unclenched her fists. Her ultra-short, kinky, black hair accentuated a beautifully shaped head, as did her large hoop earrings. Makeup highlighted her big, dark-brown eyes. Her outfit stressed her well-built, slender figure and large breasts.

In an attempt to start on a positive note, Martin entered the interview room bearing gifts. He'd looked for things that appealed to teenagers. Didn't they all like chips? If they were like his son, the answer was a resounding "Yes!"

He entered with hot chocolate, potato chips, Twix, and a granola bar. *All the basic food groups.* He smiled and placed everything on the table in front of the girl, sat down, and said, "My name is Martin Tierney. What's yours?"

"All for me?" she asked.

"Yup. Thought you might be hungry." Martin continued smiling, pleased with the apparent success.

"I am! Thanks so much." Like her friend, she took advantage of the warmth offered by the cup of hot chocolate. Unlike her friend, she wasn't shivering.

"What's your name?" Martin repeated.

He watched her give him the once over and decided he must have passed when she said, "Ruby." Then in response to Martin's silence, added, "Hansen ... with an *e*, not an *o*."

"How old are you, Ruby?"

"Eighteen."

Knowing there was no way, he tried to trip her up by asking, "What's your date of birth?"

He decided she'd memorized the answer, had answered this question before, or was good at math. She responded immediately with a date that would make her eighteen.

"Are you in school?"

"No. Hated school. So glad when I graduated, and Mom didn't force me to go to college."

"What do you do now?"

"Well ... you see ...," she stumbled, buying a few seconds. "I've always loved clothes. I was lucky enough to get a job at Target. Now I can use my employee discount to buy more than I otherwise could." Ruby smiled.

Martin thought the smile indicated satisfaction with the story she'd concocted, not with her discount. He doubted she purchased tonight's wardrobe at Target. "Do you have any brothers or sisters?"

"Yes, I have a twin brother."

"How old is he?" Martin asked, hoping he'd catch her this time. No go.

Ruby rolled her eyes. "I'm eighteen. We're twins. Two times eighteen is thirty-six, so he must be thirty-six, right?"

Martin liked this kid. She had moxie. "What's his name?" he continued.

Ruby crossed her arms and stared at Martin.

"So he has a criminal record, huh?"

Seething, Ruby placed both hands flat on the table and leaned in as close as she could get to Martin. "Of course not! Why would you say that? Because I'm Black?"

"Whoa, Ruby. I said that only because you're withholding his name. The color of your skin had nothing to do with it. I understand your reaction. Sorry I touched a nerve. Any brothers or sisters in addition to your twin?"

"A sister. She's twenty."

"Are you willing to share her name?"

"No, and she doesn't have a criminal record either." Ruby scowled.

Martin regretted the turn his questioning had taken and tried to get to friendlier ground. "Your sister must be worried about you," he said.

"No, why would she be?"

"When's the last time you saw her?"

"It's been a while."

"Have you spoken recently?"

"No."

"If you were my younger sister and I hadn't heard from you in a while, I'd worry."

Ruby's stare softened, and she shrugged.

"Do you live with your family?"

"No, with Amber."

"She's the girl you were with at Crashed Ice?"

Ruby nodded.

"Where do you and Amber live?"

"In an apartment with two other girls."

"What are their names?"

"Pearl and Opal."

"Are you attracted to people whose first names are precious gems or is it coincidental?"

Ruby rolled her eyes.

Martin had hoped his question would at least elicit a smile. No go. "Where is your apartment, Ruby?"

Ruby silently stared at him.

W hen Pete was outside the interview room and beyond Amber's hearing, he again contacted the watch commander. He provided the description and location of JD's vehicle. He asked to have a squad dispatched to get the VIN or plate number. With that information, they could obtain the owner's name, address, and any warrants.

Many people went to downtown bars and restaurants rather than home after the races, so the lot where JD parked might still be crowded. Knowing that pressing the panic button would quickly identify JD's car, he explained where they could get the keys. He knew Amber lied about several things, but believed the info about the car. He also requested the watch commander contact Commander Lincoln with the owner information, so Lincoln could obtain a search warrant. He asked for a text with the owner details, once Lincoln had been contacted. "One other request," he continued. "Media was all over Crashed Ice. Once you have the address, please dispatch a couple of squads to keep an eye on the car owner's home. I'd hate his friends to beat us to anything that could help the investigation."

After disconnecting, Pete called Commander Lincoln to explain why he was convinced the victim was trafficking young girls and why he was anxious to get a search warrant. He said the watch commander would provide the victim's name and address as soon as possible. He asked Lincoln which one of them should contact the FBI Violent Crimes against Children Section. "Maybe the FBI is tracking this guy. Maybe they have information about his clients and friends."

Lincoln said he'd handle it, so Pete headed to the second interview room.

Martin welcomed the interruption provided by a tap on the one-way glass. As he'd anticipated, it was Pete.

"How's it going?" Pete asked.

"I assume you stood here long enough to know I'm obtaining little to nothing of value." Martin summarized the questionable details garnered. I don't think she knows he's dead. Going any better for you?"

Pete shook his head. "They were well-coached, and they're scared. Starting with Ruby, let's try two on one. If we fail with both girls, I'll call Child Protection. Hopefully, Commander Lincoln will have a search warrant by then, and we'll attack it from that angle.."

SIX

Pete followed Martin into the interview room occupied by Ruby. "This is my partner, Pete Culnane. He has a few questions."

"The whole clown band," Ruby snickered, using her grandpa's pet phrase.

"Tell us what happened just before a person bumped into JD, setting his collapse in motion," Pete said. "Specifically, did anything about the situation strike you as strange or unusual? Did anything make you nervous, anxious, or worried?"

"No to all those questions." Ruby spit out her answer.

"Pretty good at playing the tough guy, don't you agree?" Martin asked Pete.

"I think she's Oscar material. Unfortunately, the competition is spending the night in juvie."

"How can you send us to juvie? We haven't done anything!" Ruby shouted and slammed both fists on the table.

"Nothing like cooperating, you mean?" Pete asked.

"About all I saw was the races. A lot of races. We stood there watching them. That's why we went," Ruby lied.

"Was the person who bumped into JD just before he went down the only one who bumped into him or you?" Martin asked.

"You're kidding, right?" Ruby's head bounced up and down. "Do you have any idea how many people were there tonight? Lots of them tried to improve their location each time a new race began and each time the skaters ran parts of the course we could see."

"I understand that last bump barely jarred JD," Pete said.

Ruby gazed skyward and said sarcastically, "Only if you call almost knocking him on his face barely jarring him."

"What's your take on it, Ruby? Was that bump an accident or intentional?"

"What difference does it make?"

"It matters if someone was trying to hurt him. That's what we're trying to determine," Pete explained.

"He's okay, isn't he?" Ruby gulped, eyebrows raised, fear splashing across her face.

"Last I heard he was still in the ER at Regions."

"At the time, I thought it was just an accident. Never occurred to me it could be anything but. Do all these questions mean it wasn't?"

"That's the million-dollar question." Pete rubbed his upper lip. "We watched the races from several blocks away. It was really crowded there. How crowded was it in the area you occupied? Say, for example, could you have packed in twice as many people?"

"No way." Ruby rolled her eyes. "There was barely breathing space between me and the people around me."

"Describe the last person who bumped into JD," Martin said.

"I felt the bump. Didn't look back. Thought it was more of the same. Kept watching the races until JD started dragging me down."

"Didn't get even a sideways glance at this person?" Pete asked. "Any details you provide could help more than you might think. For example, what they wore, their size, anything."

"Nope. I concentrated on the races. Like I said, that's why I was there."

"Unusual." Pete again rubbed his upper lip. "I was pretty absorbed in the races, but saw lots of things happening around me."

Ruby flipped her head back. "Guess that's the difference between you and me, huh?"

"Describe JD's personality," Pete said.

Ruby shrugged and said nothing. There was no way she could answer that question without getting them all in trouble.

"Okay, that may be difficult. Have you noticed a change in him over the last few days, weeks, or months? Has he been more demanding, nervous, anxious?" Pete asked.

Ruby opened her mouth to respond, then had second thoughts and shook her head.

"Stay here, Ruby," Pete said. "I'm going to check on Amber. Before I go, can I get you a refill or anything else to eat?"

"No," Ruby snapped through a glare that could turn hot coffee to iced.

"I'll check on JD and make a few other calls," Martin said. "I'll be back in a bit."

"Since you have other things to do, I should go?"

"Can't let you go before we get some answers," Pete said.

Martin followed Pete out the door and to the interview room where Amber sat, head propped on her left hand, impatiently tapping the manicured fingernails of her right hand on the tabletop.

Pete and Martin sat in the chairs opposite Amber. Pete introduced Martin, then said, "Something's been bothering me, Amber."

SEVEN

Amber's blue eyes stared questioningly at Pete.

"With so many people around you," Pete asked, "if the last person to bump JD did it accidentally, how did they get moving fast enough to jostle him so much?"

Amber looked thoughtful. "Good question. I never thought about it."

One point for Pete, thought Martin.

"How long after that bump did JD go down?" Pete asked. "What's your best estimate?"

"Less than a minute, I'd say. Right after the guy moved away, I felt JD's weight on my arm." She continued looking Pete in the eye. "Like I told you, JD had his right arm hooked through my left one. He also had his left arm hooked through Ruby's right one. As his legs buckled, he pulled us down with him."

"Did you see anyone you knew at Crashed Ice?"

"No, but with the way most people were dressed, I probably wouldn't have recognized my own dad." Her eyes moistened, and she frowned and stared into space. "Anyway, no one talked to me ... aside from the people I was with, I mean."

Pete caught the frequent referrals to her dad. *They're obviously close*, he thought. After several seconds, he said, "I'll bet your dad would come crashing through that door if he knew you were here." He directed his thumb at the interview room door.

Amber's head dropped. Her long blonde hair obscured her face.

Pete heard her sniff. He'd bet her eyes were again moist. He knew she felt lost. He wished she'd trust them and permit them to help. For now, all he could do was continue providing opportunities. "Where does your dad live?" he asked.

Amber crossed her arms and looked past the two investigators. Her mascara had run, leaving tracks down her cheeks.

Pete placed a large hand in his pants pocket, pulled out his cell, and faked an incoming call. "Better take this," he said. "Could be important. I'll be back in a minute."

Not sure how to interpret Pete's departure, Martin got Amber more hot chocolate and a bag of chips. *How does she stay so thin, while packing it away like that?* he wondered and filled the remainder of Pete's absence with small talk about the races. In the process, he confirmed what he already knew. Amber couldn't have been less interested in the races. That assured him he was right about the reason she and Ruby were there tonight. Vice wasn't his field, but he knew sporting events were popular venues for guys like JD.

Pete returned, saying, "That was the hospital. Sorry to have to tell you this, Amber. JD didn't make it."

A flash of despair darkened Amber's face, and she bit her lip. "No way! That can't be true," her voice went up an octave. "He was fine a second before he went down. What happened?"

"He was shot in the back. They couldn't save him. We need your help, Amber. Who would want to hurt him?"

"I have no idea. Like I told you, I don't know anything about his friends ... or his enemies."

"I understand not being able to come up with names. Can you think of any reason someone might want to hurt him?"

She answered with a hands-up shrug.

"Did he ever talk about his friends even if he didn't mention names?" Martin asked. "Did he talk about getting together or what they did when together?"

Amber shook her head, then started biting the nails of her shaking right hand.

"Scared?" Pete asked.

She nodded and tears rolled down her cheeks. *What now?* she wondered. *What are Ruby, Opal, Pearl, and I supposed to do? Where will we go? What will JD's friends do when they find out? They're sure to find out. Will they blame us?* Tears welled up and overflowed.

Pete's heart melted. He and Martin worked homicide, not vice. This was their first child trafficking case. Knowing what was done to these girls sickened him, but he had to mask his reaction. He couldn't permit the girls to see how cases like theirs angered him and dragged him down. He wanted to put an arm around her and assure her they could help—if she let them. He had to settle for handing her a box of tissues.

Eventually, Amber composed herself enough to blubber, "He was always impatient and intolerant. I don't know if he got worse." She knew he'd gotten worse the last few weeks, but thought it was because he'd grown impatient with them. She took the easy way out and lied.

After composing herself, she asked, "Can we go now, *please*?" and added. "I told you everything I know."

"Anyone we can call for you?" Martin asked.

"No!" she said louder than intended, then whispered, "Thanks."

"We need to contact JD's family," Pete said, extracting a notepad and pen from the back pocket of his jeans.

Amber looked questioningly from Pete to Martin and shook her head. "I don't know anything about his family." She accentuated it with a hands-up shrug. "He never talked about family. Maybe he doesn't have one. Maybe they all died."

"Or maybe he ran away," Pete said, providing another nudge in hopes of getting Amber to share a few details now that her nemesis was out of the way.

"He wasn't that stupid!" Amber shot back, closed her eyes, and shook her head.

Pete suspected she'd just called herself stupid. "That's an interesting assumption about runaways, Amber," he said. "It's also way off base. Intelligence has nothing to do with it. Things like a person's fears, problems, living situation, and relationships are important contributors."

"If you ever thought about running away, you'd know that. I ran away when I was a kid. Thank goodness my uncle found me and told me what a mistake I was making. He told me my parents were a mess because I took off. He said they'd give anything to get me to come home. I thought he was crazy. I thought they were happy to have me out of the way. I thought, if anything, maybe they missed the chance to order me around. I missed them. I wanted to go home. By then I'd have been happy to have them order me around. Both Mom and Dad cried when they saw me. It's the only time I saw my dad cry."

Pete continued piling it on, hoping he was hitting the mark with some of his assumptions, hoping something he said would hit home with Amber. "In order to survive, I did things I'd never share with anyone. Somehow, Mom and Dad found out. It didn't matter. All they cared about was having me home."

"My situation wasn't unusual," Pete continued. "Lots of kids who run away want to go home, but don't know how to go about it. Most families would do anything to get their kids back. I mean anything in their power and then some. Do you think that might have happened with JD?"

"You were lucky," Amber said. "Sometimes it isn't that easy." Her eyes were still moist.

"Usually there are lots of people who would like to help. People like Martin and me. We'd like nothing better. Right, Martin?"

Martin nodded. Amber longed for his help, but couldn't ask. Her family would pay if she did. She couldn't risk it. She said what she had to say." The thing is, I'm not a runaway. I don't need help." She stood and announced, "I'm out of here. Too tired to do this anymore."

"Before you go," Pete said, "since you can't provide names of any of JD's family, we need a list of friends and their contact information."

"Can't help you. I already told you I don't know any of them, much less how to reach them."

"Are you his friend?"

"Oh, yeah. Of course. I thought you meant *other* friends. Friends besides Ruby, Opal, Pearl, and me," she stammered.

"No family and only four friends," Pete shook his head. "You have to feel sorry for someone like that, don't you?"

"Of course he has other friends." *I wish he didn't,* Amber worried. *They will make us pay if we screw up. JD was clear about that. They may make us pay for being here. Do they know we're here? Please, no.* In a flash of brilliance, she asked, "Don't you have his phone? He must have a list of contacts on his phone."

Pete took one more run at getting her to talk. If they failed, he had no choice. He had to turn her over to child protection. "Amber, I know JD was trafficking you and your three friends. I also know traffickers hold onto their girls, keep them from running, by lying about what will happen if they run. You had lots of opportunities to run, didn't you?"

Shoulders hunched, Amber stared down at the table.

"I'd be surprised if JD didn't say he'd find and kill your family, except for Madison. He probably told you he'd force her to take your place. Sound familiar?"

How does he know? Amber wondered.

"He also said if something happened to him, his friends would do these things for him, didn't he?"

That's exactly what JD told Ruby, Opal, Pearl, and me. This guy must know of cases where those things happened, she thought.

"You're doing an outstanding job of playing the role of one of those girls ..., including buying the stories, the lies JD told you," Pete said. "I'll bet your dad would give his life to find you. There's no need. We'll protect your family. I understand you being too scared to risk it. I'm right aren't I, Amber?"

"No way." Amber continued staring at the table. The emotion-free answer told another story.

"Talk to me, Amber. Don't trust JD. He relied on cooperation through fear. His game plan was to paralyze the victims with convincing and often repeated threats."

Amber flexed her hands nervously.

"JD isn't the first trafficker to do this. He had to. You know that, don't you? Otherwise, why would you stay? Why put up with him and the way he treated you? You had plenty of opportunities to escape but didn't. Correct? He victimized you. He promised things he had no intention or ability to provide. It's not your fault. He was a pro at selling the line he gave you. Now he's gone and you can escape, return home, start a new life. JD's no longer in the driver's seat. My partner and I want to help. We want to free you from a life you were forced into and help you make your way toward the kind of life and opportunities you deserve."

While he said those things, Amber's face turned red, then scarlet. "I have no idea what you're talking about."

"Martin and I would like nothing better than to help your family find you."

Martin nodded. "Please, let us help you and your family."

Amber's head dropped.

Pete took advantage of the potential blip in Amber's resolve, saying, "If you cooperate, you could be reunited with your family in the time it takes them to get here."

"And be guilty of murder?" Amber murmured. "No thanks."

"I understand your problem with trusting us. You trusted JD. Look where it got you. You aren't the first girl he schmoozed, gained their trust, then victimized. You know that, don't you? You have three friends he also victimized."

Amber stared long and hard at Pete.

"Our goal is to get you back on your feet. If you don't want to be reunited with your family, we'll help you make other arrangements—safe and comfortable arrangements. If you want to be with your family, I need your help. If I call your dad and tell him you're here with me, Amber, I bet he'll be the happiest man on earth. The one thing keeping that from happening is your unwillingness or inability to trust us. Am I right?"

After staring at her hands for several seconds, Amber nodded. Mascara-dyed tears streamed down her cheeks.

"What can we do to fix that?"

"I don't think you can," Amber moaned.

"Because you're protecting your family?"

Amber's lower lip quivered.

Pete tried another angle. "JD was into human trafficking, not murder. Succeeding at murder requires a whole different set of skills. I can introduce you to a hundred girls who were told the same lies JD told you. Girls who escaped or were freed and whose families are safe—were never touched by the JDs in their lives or the thugs they claimed would take care of the families of girls who refused to cooperate. They too were trapped. You've been protecting the people you love. You're paying a high price to avoid chancing it. Had you ignored the threats, you'd have discovered they were baseless."

Amber's eyebrows rose as her eyes widened. She wanted to believe him. She wanted to be convinced. "The thing is, why would I trust anyone who said they heard the same lies from someone like JD? They might say that just because you asked them to. They could be the liars."

"Would they know enough about your life to stand up to your questioning? If they were lying, wouldn't you be able to trip them up?"

Amber contemplated that, then whispered, "Maybe, maybe not."

"I'll contact the law enforcement officers where your family lives. I'll personally speak with them. I can guarantee they'll provide protection until we're certain your family is safe. Child trafficking is a national epidemic, Amber. Everyone in law enforcement is doing their best to eliminate it. With your help, we can make inroads. By cooperating, you'll be protecting other girls—girls like your sister Madison."

Amber winced. If only that was true. Could she ever again trust a guy? Not likely.

Unwilling to give up when it felt like he was so close, Pete tried another approach. Pulling his cell from his pocket, he placed it on the table. "Want to call your dad?"

Amber's face lit up, but only for a flash. Then the implications sank in, and she shook her head. "If I do, your phone will save the phone number." She lashed out, angry about the attempt to trick her. "You said JD made threats to hold us. Maybe you're making promises to get information, to solve a case, to get promoted. You said we couldn't trust JD. I say we can't trust you."

"I can't force you. I can only provide the opportunity." Pete sighed.

"So can we go?"

"I can't permit you to walk out the door. I wish it was that easy. I know you're not eighteen. Fifteen seems far more likely. In good conscience, we can't allow a fifteen-year-old to walk away. How would you get home? Do you have enough money to pay the rent and buy food? If JD has a group of friends watching his back, they might decide to pick up where he left off. We can't let that happen to you."

Tears flowed freely down Amber's pale cheeks.

"I'll call Child Protection," Martin said. "They'll take you home to get some of your things, then find a safe place for you to stay."

"You can't!" Amber pled. "If one of JD's friends sees us coming out of our apartment with stuff, they'll know something's going on. They may think we had him arrested. If what JD told us was true, they'll go after my family. I had it coming. My dad, mom, sister, and brother don't. I can't chance it. I won't chance it!"

The tears continued making tracks through her makeup.

"I want you to understand what you're up against," Pete said. "All of the TV and radio stations, and most newspapers had reporters and photographers at Crashed Ice. If they aren't out now, stories about tonight's murder will go out shortly. They'll be on all the major networks and in all the newspapers. What about Pearl and Opal? Tell us your address, so we can get them out of there, in case JD's friends pay a visit."

Amber's eyebrows flipped skyward and her hand shot up, covering her mouth. "I have to talk to Ruby. *Please*, let me talk to Ruby!"

EIGHT

"I have a few more questions, Amber. Then you can see Ruby," Pete said.

Martin stood and said, "Back shortly. I want to check on Marty."

Tonight isn't going well, Pete thought. He wondered what he should have done differently. He knew the chances of gaining the trust of either girl were slim. That didn't stop him from replaying the whole thing in his head, challenging each exchange. In the remaining minutes, he hoped to be more successful with a few additional topics.

"Does JD have any girls besides you, Ruby, Opal, and Pearl?" he asked.

"I don't know for sure, but don't see how he could." Amber rubbed her neck. "He takes us to every event that draws a crowd. Where would he take the others? To stand outside a church on Sunday mornings?" She smirked.

"I wonder if he's new to this business, since he's only been with you and Ruby for a few months. Have Opal and Pearl been with him longer?"

Amber responded with a hands-up shrug.

"Perhaps he found you after deciding he needed some new faces?"

Amber rolled her eyes. "It wasn't our faces that interested him."

"Did he ever threaten you by telling you if you didn't cooperate or bring in enough cash, you'd suffer the same fate as another girl who used to work for him?"

"I heard a lot of threats, but not that one."

"Any threats besides the ones we already covered?"

Martin returned during a protracted silence. Pete waited a minute, then told him, "Hang tough while I call the Child Protection Division."

"Wait!" Amber protested. "There's no need. I'm eighteen. I can prove it."

Before she could say more, Pete closed the door behind him.

Martin decided to fill the time discussing the weather, Crashed Ice, anything he could think of. A stony silence greeted his questions and comments. He smiled when Pete opened the door.

If looks could kill, Pete thought, seeing Amber's expression when he returned. "It may be a half-hour or more before someone arrives. Please get Ruby," he told Martin. "She might be getting nervous after being alone so long. I hate to make things any harder than they already are."

Amber thanked him profusely.

A minute later, carrying another chair, Martin ushered Ruby into the first interview room.

When Ruby sat next to her, Amber reached over and grasped her hand. Silence enveloped the room and continued until Amber said, "I drank too much hot chocolate. I have to pee."

"Me too." Ruby nodded.

Pete led the girls to the restroom and camped outside the door until they finished. By the time they came out, he figured they'd had enough time to plan a mutiny ... or surrender. The girls waited in the interview room while Pete and Martin conferred outside the room.

"Marty and Katie are both home, safe and sound," Martin said. "Marty told Katie she had to call him when she got home, since you were tied up." Martin smiled proudly.

"He's terrific, Martin." Pete smiled.

Pete suspected the girls were up to something and hoped he wouldn't regret permitting them to continue conferring until Child Protection showed.

They arrived before he could reconsider.

"Peter Culnane?" the woman asked, looking at Martin.

Pete extended a hand and introduced Martin.

After introducing themselves to the girls, Cynthia Zumbrota and Alan Preston explained the steps they'd follow and the reasons for each. The girls looked nonplussed.

"Can you modify that plan a bit, at least for now?" Pete asked. "The girls are afraid going to their apartment could tip off JD's friends, resulting in retribution for their roommates and families. Am I right about that Amber? Ruby?"

46

"Thanks," Amber said. "For a minute, I thought you were going to ignore everything I told you."

"That will never happen. Right now, my top concern is the two of you, as well as Pearl and Opal. I'll do everything in my power, both Martin and I will, to protect you and respond to your needs and concerns. Unfortunately, until you trust us, we can't protect your families or the other two girls. I understand. If you change your mind, give Martin or me a call. Here's a business card for each of you. Call any time."

Martin too handed each a card.

"Guess it's that time," the woman from Child Protection said and stood.

"Ruby?" Amber said.

Wide-eyed, Ruby nodded vigorously, which sent her hoop earrings bouncing.

"We decided to tell you our real names," Amber said, looking first at Pete, then Martin.

NINE

"Let's start with your real names, first and last," Pete began, looking from one girl to the other.

After a long pause, Amber broke eye contact, looked down, took a deep breath, and said, "Alyssa Gilbert."

Ruby looked questioningly at Alyssa, swallowed hard, and said, "Ella. Ella Henderson. I hate the name Ruby. Glad to be rid of it!" She scowled.

"I too prefer your real names," Pete said. "They seem to fit both of you much better."

"I hated Amber ... the name and the person JD attached to it."

"That person wasn't you," the thirtyish female social worker from Child Protection said. "She was a person created by the guy who victimized you—both of you and the other two girls."

Her middle-aged male counterpart nodded. "We want you to understand our mission is to help you get your lives back on track."

"You have a difficult path ahead of you. I won't lie to you," the woman said.

"Care to share any other details?" Pete asked.

Both girls looked noncommittal, standing with their arms pulled in close, shoulders hunched. Obvious to both Pete and Martin was that they were scared to help ... and to discover and face what lay ahead.

After several seconds, Alyssa sat back down and asked, "Still want those addresses?"

You could have knocked Pete over with a feather. "If you share them," he said, "Martin and I will immediately get things moving to protect your families and the two other girls."

Once again, Alyssa took the lead. "I'm from Virginia." Responding to the questioning looks, she added, "As in Minnesota."

48

"Your family's address in Virginia?" Pete asked.

Alyssa complied.

In response to Martin's questions, she also provided her parents' names and phone numbers.

"I live in St. Paul, both now and before JD ruined my life," Ella Henderson said. "The south side of what survived of the Rondo neighborhood to be exact. I grew up hearing my grandma's stories about how, before the construction of I-94, the Rondo neighborhood gave her a deep sense of community, security, and protection. Her grandparents helped raise her. She said all of that was destroyed when the Rondo neighborhood was split in half by the freeway. They used eminent domain to force people, including my great grandparents, out of their homes. Great Grandma said they got a fair price ... if you considered only the wood, brick, and windows. She said the people forcing them out couldn't understand or didn't care that the homes and neighborhood were so much more than that. She said fear, anxiety, disappointment, and frustration filled the neighborhood as the residents realized they couldn't change or alter the path of the freeway. She never forgave the City of St. Paul or the Minnesota Department of Transportation."

"Wow! What's gotten into me? Sorry. Anyway, won't Grandma be proud when she finds out what a white guy did to me?" Ella covered her face with both hands.

After she provided her parents' names, address, and phone numbers, Pete asked, "Are you willing to tell us how JD trapped you? I know it's difficult to talk about, so it's up to you."

"I was so stupid. It's really embarrassing. I went to the mall to return some stuff for Mom. I decided to stop for a cup of coffee, since I was in the vicinity. I was waiting in line, and this guy came up and told me I was beautiful. I was so embarrassed. I couldn't look at him."

"He said he was looking for someone like me to be on the cover of a magazine. Said he'd been looking all over for a face like mine, and he was running out of time. He told me he'd give me five thousand dollars if I agreed to be photographed. He said otherwise he had to keep looking. He didn't have time to waste. I'd taken a bus to the mall. I went with him. I was an idiot."

Alyssa stared open-mouthed at Ella as she shared her story, wishing she was brave enough to do likewise.

Pete wanted to strangle each and every man ... and woman—anyone who preyed on the insecurities of these kids.

"That is one of the tricks men like JD are famous for," Alan Preston said. "People in child protection hear it over and over again. The hard part is getting the word out to girls like you. Here's how it goes: tell a young girl how pretty she is. If she tells you to get lost, move on. If her head drops, she looks at the floor, or looks embarrassed, move in. Guys like JD are masters. They finely tune their skills. This is about JD, not about you. You can't beat yourself up for what you did in the past. You must learn how to protect yourself in the future."

"There are a few more critical details," Pete said. "For example, your ages?"

Again the girls looked questioningly at each other. After a pregnant pause, Alyssa blushed and said, "Fifteen."

"Same," Ella sighed.

Barely older than Marty, Martin thought.

"There are two other people we're intent on protecting," Pete said. "To do that, we need the address where you've been living."

"Oh my gosh, Pearl and Opal!" Alyssa and Ella said together and simultaneously recited the address in the Crocus Hill neighborhood.

"We have to see them or at least talk to them," Alyssa said. "They must be worried sick ... or scared to death. Either Ella or I, if not both of us, should have been back a long time ago."

"As soon as you leave, Martin and I will find them and explain everything. First, since you're in such a magnanimous mood, what are their real names?" Pete asked.

The girls looked at each other. Then Alyssa said, "Opal is Megan Dawson, and Pearl is Jessie Acton."

"I'm sure you know, you just did them a big favor," Pete said.

Alyssa walked around the table, ready to relinquish Pete's jacket. "Thanks!" she said, holding it out to him, smiling sheepishly. "And thanks for trusting me enough to let me wear it into the restroom. Sorry I was such a jerk. Sorry I can't tell you all you want to know."

"I understand. You were far nicer than I'd be in your situation. I wish you well and hope to hear from you. We'd like to talk when you're able to share more."

She shrugged.

Ella kissed Martin on the cheek. "Thanks for being so kind."

The girls walked away, separated by the social workers.

Protocol? Pete wondered. If so, would the man, the woman, or both go after them if they took off? Perhaps he and Martin should help escort the girls to the car. The thing was, this was the first in a series of opportunities for the girls to run. And his and Martin's night had just begun.

TEN

As soon as the Child Protection social workers departed with the girls, Pete read the text message he'd received while the girls provided their real names and the other details. It said, "His name's Josiah Damian St. Peter. Have address on vehicle registration. Call for details."

First, Pete called Alyssa's family. Martin contacted Ella's family.

It was nearly midnight. A groggy voice answered the phone at Alyssa's home.

"Is this Ms. Gilbert?" Pete asked.

"Yes? This can't be a telephone solicitation. Not at this hour."

"No, ma'am. My name is Peter Culnane. I'm an investigator with the St. Paul Police Department. I'm calling about Alyssa."

"Oh God, no! Please, tell me she's okay. Tell me she's alive."

"She's definitely alive."

"Thank God!" Alyssa's mom sobbed.

Pete waited for her to regain her composure.

"Where has she been? What happened to her? Was she kidnapped? Where is she? When can we see her?"

"Physically, she's well. You can see her as soon as you can get to St. Paul, Ms. Gilbert."

"Getting to the Twin Cities is a problem. My husband and I had to sell our second car. He isn't home. Won't be back for a few days. I wish I could see Alyssa right now. Can't you bring her here? I know it's a distance, but under the circumstances?"

"When did your husband leave?" *And is he in St. Paul?* Pete wondered, hoping not to put the family through what it could mean.

"A few days ago."

Not exactly forthcoming, thought Pete, asking, "Where is he now?"

"I don't have an address."

"So just you, your son, and your second daughter are there now?"

"Uh huh."

"Your husband must have a cellphone. I'd like the number."

"He doesn't have unlimited minutes. We pay exorbitant rates when he goes over. It's almost the end of his billing cycle. Can you call after Friday?"

"Will he be home before then?"

"Hoping so, but don't know."

"Alyssa is concerned about your safety. We have no reason to believe you are in danger, but I told her I'd ask the St. Louis County Sheriff's Office and the Virginia Police Department to provide protection. As soon as I hang up, I'll contact them."

"Please ask to speak to Deputy Montgomery, if he still works there. He's my second cousin."

"Did he know Alyssa was missing?"

"I assume that information passed between the police department and the sheriff's office. He didn't hear it from me. We aren't that close. We rarely speak."

Pete provided Alyssa's contact number, then ended the call.

Martin's conversation with Ella's father was less puzzling and more satisfying.

Her father's anxiety level dropped several notches when Martin told him for the fourth time, "Yes, she's alive."

"Her emotional state is fragile," Martin said. "You should speak with Child Protection." He provided a phone number.

"Why? What happened?"

"Ella should tell you."

"I'm thrilled she's alive. My wife, kids, and I have been praying for her since the day she didn't come home from the mall."

"How long ago was that?"

"Last September ... on the third. It became the day from hell, and extended to the week from hell, and the month from hell. We filed reports with the St. Paul Police Department. Not a single lead. We printed flyers and posted them on all the lamp posts and telephone poles. We stuck them on the bulletin boards of every grocery store in St. Paul and Minneapolis, and all the churches in both cities and the burbs. My son posted on social media. That's way out of my league. Was she kidnapped?"

"You need to talk to Ella."

"It's the middle of the night, but I don't want to wait another minute. Is there any way we can see her right now?"

"Call Child Protection and see what you can arrange. By the way, Ella requested police protection for your family. It begins tonight."

"That puts an ominous spin on it, doesn't it, officer?"

"Based on my experience, I think she's wrong about the need, but my partner and I respect her wishes."

"She's the one who disappeared. Why would we need protection?"

"I'd prefer you ask Ella."

"Thank you so much for calling! You're a godsend. God bless you, Officer! God bless you!"

"Aren't you the chatty one?" Pete smiled when Martin hung up.

"Not surprising. You'd think I just told him he won the mega lottery."

"I bet he wouldn't exchange this news for winning the lottery."

"So true. He wants to see Ella right now. That's easier for someone who lives in St. Paul than someone who lives in Virginia, huh?"

"Someone who lives in Virginia and might not have access to a car for several days. Hoping Alyssa's mom contacts her dad, and they find a way." He also told Martin how tight-lipped Alyssa's mom was about her husband's location and expected return.

Next Pete called the watch commander to fulfill their promise to the girls. He gave her the address for Alyssa's family and asked her to contact the police and county sheriff to request protection. He also gave Samantha the name of Alyssa's cousin, the deputy, and asked her to speak with him. He did the same for Ella's family.

In turn, Samantha told him they'd stationed squads in front of and behind JD's home to keep an eye out for any activity.

"I'll use his initials," Samantha said. "It takes too long to say Josiah. The only other time I heard that name was Colonel Josiah Snelling, the first commander of Fort Snelling."

"I'm impressed, Samantha. The name rang a bell, but I didn't know why."

"Lest you give me too much credit, I Googled it." She chuckled. "Anyway, last I heard, Lincoln is working on the search warrant. Are you ready? I'll give you St. Peter's home address."

Turned out Pete didn't need to write it down. He had a thing for numbers, and the progression made this house number easy to remember. The street was also easy to remember. St. Peter lived on St. Clair.

"Forensic Services will arrive shortly, so they're ready to go as soon as we have the warrant," Samantha continued. "They may have left it until tomorrow, but I told them you're anxious to get moving on this one. No activity around JD's home yet. Perhaps his friends don't watch the news, listen to the radio, or haven't pegged JD as the victim."

"Good news. Thanks for managing all of this for Martin and me, Samantha. You're irreplaceable."

"Quite the contrary. I'll be replaced as soon as my shift ends."

Pete shared the details with Martin and called Commander Lincoln for an update on the search warrant.

Lincoln anticipated a signature on the warrant within a half-hour. "Let's check on Megan and Jessie," Pete said. "I'm hoping they're at the apartment, so we won't have to break down the door."

"That's what I like about you. The eternal optimist." Martin laughed.

The good news was, Martin had parked his unmarked car at HQ before Crashed Ice. They abandoned the warmth of headquarters for the frigid parking lot and Martin's equally frigid car. The only difference between the two was that they didn't feel the wind while in the car. It was an appreciable differen

Sticking with their pattern, Martin drove.

Meanwhile, taking advantage of several free minutes, Pete contacted the St. Paul PD Vice Unit. Equipped with JD's full name and address, as well as the names of the four girls and where they lived, he hoped they could help each other.

ELEVEN

In less than a minute, Pete discovered he didn't benefit by waiting for additional details before contacting vice. They'd never heard of Josiah Damian St. Peter, AKA JD, but they started a file. He asked them to notify him or Martin if, going forward, they obtained anything.

When they reached the Crocus Hill apartment building where the girls lived, they pulled their stocking caps down over their ears and zipped their jackets to within an inch of their throats. They proceeded as quietly as snow in below zero temperatures permitted. In other words, each step elicited a squeak.

Pete pressed the security buzzer for the apartment occupied by the girls, hoping Jessie or Megan would assume it was Alyssa, Ella, or both.

"That you?" a voice answered.

Martin placed a gloved hand over his mouth and in his best soprano said, "Yes. Hurry. Freezing." When the buzzer sounded, he took his hand from his face and flashed Pete a smile.

Pete grabbed the door and held it for Martin, while taking advantage of the escaping warm air. Inside, he flashed Martin a thumbs-up and hurried silently to the third floor. Unlike the snow, the carpeting cooperated—until Pete reached the second to last step. It protested his passage by emitting a loud groan. Martin shook his head and succeeded in foregoing a repeat performance by stepping alongside the railing.

Reaching the girls' apartment, as a precaution, they planted themselves to the right and left of the door, weapons drawn, backs to the wall. They couldn't be too careful. There was no guarantee one of JD's buddies wasn't inside. Pete tapped on the door.

"Did you lose your keys again?" a voice said as the door opened a crack.

Pete shoved the door hard enough to send it flying open and the girl flying backward. He jumped through the doorway and glanced right and left, scouring the visible parts of the interior. "Police," he told the terrified, cowering girl. He kicked the door shut, then he and Martin searched all rooms for other occupants.

Finding no one, he returned to the girl and said, "Hope I didn't hurt you. I didn't want to scare you, but I also didn't want this to be my final hour. JD died tonight. We're here to help you. Are you Jessie or Megan?"

The tall, slim, dark-eyed, raven-haired beauty closed her gaping mouth and whispered, "Jessie. How do you know our names?"

Martin returned and stood at the door, looking out the peep hole, watching for the fourth girl.

"Alyssa and Ella told us."

Jessie stared wide-eyed at Pete.

"It took a long time, but they decided to trust my partner and me. We need to get you and Megan out of here, just in case."

"Just in case of what?"

"In case JD has a friend or two to step in and take his place. Or in case they decide you are responsible for his death."

"How did he die?"

"Let's take care of the critical issues first. Where is Megan?"

"I don't know. She left and hasn't returned. Are Alyssa and Ella okay? Were they hurt?"

"They're both fine. Is Megan often this late?" Pete sounded more like a worried father than a cop.

"We don't have regular hours. She was here earlier, now she's not."

"A girl's coming," Martin whispered and stepped back from the door.

Without the courtesy of a warning creak from the stairway, Pete heard a key in the lock. A girl with honey-gold skin and a healthy dose of oriental blood entered. She didn't quite reach his armpits and didn't look a day older than twelve.

Seeing Pete, she reached for the doorknob, ready to flee.

"Hold on," Pete said. "I'm a police officer." He put a hand on the door so Megan couldn't run. Then he shared the facts he'd already provided to Jessie.

"Where are Amber and Ruby ... I mean Alyssa and Ella?" Jessie demanded as soon as Pete finished. "I was so worried. At least one of them should've been back by now."

"They're safe. Grab a few things, and let's go. Hate to be an alarmist, but this probably isn't the best place to talk."

"Why should we trust you?" Jessie asked. "What if you're my worst nightmare? What if you're JD's friends?"

Pete extracted his badge. "I understand a couple of cops probably aren't the escape you were hoping for, but we can promise you a considerable improvement over what you've endured."

"How do you know what we've endured?" Jessie asked.

"Alyssa and Ella," Pete said. "Get ready. You may want to put on a few layers, so you have a change of clothes. For safety's sake, bring only what you can wear or stuff in a purse or backpack. Not sure when you can come for additional things. We may send someone to get things for you in a few days."

The two investigators followed the girls into their bedrooms. Pete stood facing the door in Jessie's room. Martin did likewise in Megan's room, giving the girls some privacy while they dressed.

Mission accomplished, the four of them moved as silently as possible down the stairs and out the door. Rather than wasting time trying to move silently over the protesting hard-packed snow, they dashed for the unmarked car. As soon as all four were buckled in, Martin took off.

"First time I was in a cop car," Megan chirped.

Jessie rolled her eyes, wishing the kid would shut up. "Okay, we're out of there," she said. "Tell us what happened and where we can find Alyssa and Ella."

"First, I need to make a phone call." Pete wanted to separate the girls before telling them anything else or asking any questions. He figured Megan was more likely to share the facts if Jessie wasn't in her face, so he called the watch commander. It was strictly a delay tactic.

"How about the other guy? Can't he tell us?" Jessie protested.

"The problem is, my hearing isn't that good. Based on past experience, if he's talking, I won't be able to understand what's being said on the other end of the line."

A deep sigh came from Jessie's side of the back seat.

Martin knew what Pete was doing. They'd worked together so long, he could read Pete's mind even before the thoughts appeared there. Pete flashed a smile when Martin sped up.

"Still on?" Pete asked when Samantha answered.

"Turns out you're right. I am irreplaceable," she laughed.

"Thought so. I need an update on the items you're working on for us."

"Also known as, you don't want to talk and need an excuse?"

"Afraid so."

"Want me to tell you a bedtime story?"

"On a scale of one to ten, that's a negative five. What else do you have?"

"Commander Lincoln got the search warrant. The Forensic Services Unit is working on the cellphone information, and they have staff on their way to JD's home."

"Great. Planning to act on that next."

"Maybe you should do something different, like go home and get some sleep first."

"It'll be a cold day."

"Then there's hope for you. The wind chill is currently thirty-five below."

"Anything else that can't wait? Martin's pulling into HQ."

Jessie dragged her feet every inch from the unmarked car into headquarters.

Megan skipped.

TWELVE

Pete led Jessie to interview room one, and Martin escorted Megan to room two.

"First, can I get you something to eat or drink, Jessie?" Pete began.

"All I want is answers." Jessie glared at him. "What happened to JD? And where are Alyssa and Ella?"

"I understand you went to the Red Bull Crashed Ice competition with Alyssa and Ella."

"So?" Jessie spit out the word.

It was obvious Pete wouldn't accomplish anything by pulling punches with this girl. "I also know why you were there," he said.

"Meaning?" Jessie appeared intent on staring a hole through Pete.

"I know JD was involved in child trafficking, Jessie."

"I'm not a child, and you still haven't told me what happened to him." Jessie's stare didn't waver.

Pete understood this kid's belligerence and kept his tone calm and measured. "Someone murdered him at Crashed Ice—shot him in the back. Any idea who might want to hurt him?"

"Do you mean besides Alyssa, Ella, Megan, and me?"

"I'd be surprised if you didn't all hate him. Any other ideas? Because of the cold and the way the person who murdered JD was bundled up, getting identification is complicated."

"Probably almost anyone who got to know JD is a candidate. He's easy to hate."

Pete anticipated the next answer, having spoken with Alyssa and Ella, but asked anyway, "Have you met or seen him around any of his friends, acquaintances, or family?"

"No."

"Did he ever talk about friends or family?"

"Never."

"Did he talk about anyone in the same business or mention learning from them?"

"No, but JD would never have admitted he didn't know it all." Jessie's jaw relaxed a few degrees.

A foray into the questions about JD being more anxious or irritable than usual was no more productive than when he'd asked Alyssa and Ella.

Then he said, "I contacted Ella and Alyssa's families. They're ecstatic. Both worried they'd never see their daughters again. Ella might be back with her family right now."

Jessie's eyes narrowed. "I don't believe you. Why would Ella and Alyssa trust you enough to tell you about their families? Don't they care anymore? What did you do to them to make them talk?"

Pete looked her straight in the eye and patiently repeated the facts he'd shared with Alyssa, adding, "Following through on the threats JD recited is virtually unheard of, at least in the Midwest. Even so, if you permit me to contact your family, I'll ensure police protection."

Jessie put her hands on the table, leaned in toward Pete, and looked him in the eye. "For how long?"

Without breaking eye contact, Pete said, "Until it's proven unnecessary."

"And who determines that? I'm sure it will be you, *not* my family."

"It will be on my shoulders and my partner's shoulders, and we don't take it lightly."

"I have two little brothers. Why should I trust you?"

"Because every day I risk my life to protect people like you and your brothers. Jessie, how did you get mixed up with JD?"

Jessie stared at Pete.

His return gaze didn't waiver.

She took a deep breath and said, "Mom threw me out last fall, after I was expelled. Said she didn't want me ruining my brothers' lives. Said she never wanted to see me again. She threw all my stuff out the front door and said she was going to change the locks. She did too. I checked a few days later, while she and Dad were at work and my brothers were in school."

"You're obviously a smart kid, Jessie. How did you get expelled?"

Jessie responded with a cold stare.

Pete moved on, attempting to maximize Jessie's cooperation not her irritation. He'd return to that question later. "Where did you stay after your mom threw you out?"

"A friend let me stay at her house. But after a few days, her mom said I had to find another place. Said I was too much of a distraction. Said if I stayed her daughter would be expelled too. Don't even know how she found out I was expelled. And did she think it was contagious?" Jessie rolled her eyes. "I left every morning with my friend and walked several blocks with her. Guess my friend told her. They're pretty close. I wish Mom and I were that close. Now the only family I have are Ella, Alyssa, and Megan." Jessie sighed deeply and shook her head.

"What about your dad?"

"He'd never go against Mom. He'd never stand up to her. I thought he loved me, but learned the truth when Mom threw me out."

"Sometimes people go to great lengths and make great sacrifices to keep the peace. Don't be too quick to draw any conclusions about your dad. Have you tried to contact him or anyone? Have you been in touch with any friends?"

"No times three. Don't dare."

"How old are your brothers?"

"Seven and nine. I sure miss them. I used to babysit them a lot. Read to them every night before I put them to bed. They looked up to me. I guess Mom was right." Jessie brushed away a tear.

Venturing into riskier territory, Pete asked, "How did you connect with JD?"

"I kept my stuff in a rolling backpack I got from my friend. Spent several days hanging out at the Minneapolis Public Library. That's where I slept. Dozed in the stacks. Saw JD a few times, but never spoke to him. One evening they were closing the library, so I grabbed my stuff and walked out the door. JD held it for me and started walking with me. He was so nice, so interested."

"He asked if he could get me something to eat. I was starving. I jumped at the chance. We spent hours talking. I'm so dumb. I thought he actually cared about me—was attracted to me. He offered to let me stay at his house. I was scared, but he convinced me I would have my own room. He swore he wouldn't touch me. Said I'd have to beg him before he did. Like I said, I'm an idiot."

"For a week he did as promised. Then things changed." Her lower lip quivered. "I tried to stop him by telling him I was a virgin. It was true. It was also the wrong thing to say. Once I told him, there was no stopping him. Several days later, once he'd had his fill of me, he moved me to the apartment he'd rented for Ella. Then he put me to work. He said I had to earn my keep. I told him I'd find a new place to live, and he said that would never happen. He said I was now his. He told me exactly what would happen to me and my family if I *ever* left."

"Knowing those things kept me from taking off. I told JD I didn't care what he did to my parents. Even though I initially trusted him, I never told him their names, where they live, or anything about them. I don't know why, but I was so relieved I hadn't. I told him they no longer meant anything to me. It isn't true. I still love them even though they want nothing to do with me. JD must have believed me. He didn't pressure me to find out about them."

"I bet your mom regrets what she said and did in a moment of anger. Would you like me to call her?"

"No." Jessie shook her head frantically. "She'd be furious and ashamed of what I've become. It's much worse than being expelled, and she hated me for that." Jessie brushed away a tear.

"The things that happened because of JD aren't your fault, Jessie."

"Of course they are. By believing him, I made it happen."

"JD raped you, Jessie, and forced you to work for him, correct?"

Jessie nodded, eyes closed.

"Then you didn't let it happen. You couldn't stop him, just like Ella, Alyssa, and Megan. Do you blame any of them?"

"No." She bit her lip and shook her head. She looked so forlorn, it tore at Pete's heart.

"When did all this start, Jessie? When did you go home with JD?"

"Last September. The sixteenth to be exact. It was the worst day of my life, and there's no close second."

"How old are you? Don't tell me eighteen. I know you aren't eighteen."

"Seventeen and a half?" There was a twinkle in her eye.

"How does fifteen sound?" Pete smiled.

"Way too young for all I've done."

"But accurate?"

Jessie nodded. "Afraid so."

"You're in the driver's seat, Jessie. We won't contact your parents without your permission."

"I know." She smiled. "You don't know their names, address, or phone numbers."

Pete returned the smile. "Correct, but even if I did, I wouldn't contact them without your permission. Do you want us to look out for them in case JD somehow got their information?"

Wanting this but knowing it required revealing her parents' location, Jessie looked deep into Pete's eyes. "Alyssa and Ella trusted you. Did you sell them with kindness? What if they made a mistake? What if their families are paying for their trust?"

"Remember what I said about guys like JD going after the families of their girls, that it doesn't happen in the Midwest? If you like, I'll show you the basis for that statement. You can read it for yourself. Do you want to do that?"

Another nod.

Pete stood. "Give me a little time to pull it together."

As he turned and reached for the door, Jessie said, "Okay, I believe you. And I know how protective Alyssa and Ella are of their families." She rattled off an address in south Minneapolis.

"Since I won't contact them without your permission," Pete said, "will you give me their names?"

"Promise you won't call them until I say it's okay?"

"I promise."

"Cornelia and Ted Acton."

Wanting to end on a positive note, Pete said, "Tell me about your brothers."

He watched a smile spread across Jessie's face. "They're both going to be professional basketball players. Teddy is nine, and he's already five feet five. Earl is seven and five feet tall. I'm not surprised. Mom's brother is six foot seven. They spend hours each day shooting baskets and scrimmaging. Both are on their school's basketball teams. I used to go to all the games and practices. They both played virtually every minute. They're each the best player in their grade. I miss them so much." Her smile faded.

"Let me check on my partner. It won't take long. Before I go, can I get you anything?"

"How about a Coke?"

"I'll find one." Pete smiled.

"Wait. What about Alyssa and Ella? Is Ella with her family or not?"

"I'll find out."

THIRTEEN

Meanwhile, Martin sought to learn anything Megan would share. Her smile and bubbly ride to HQ colored his expectations. He started by asking if she'd like anything to eat or drink.

"Whatcha got?"

He gave her a rundown, and she said, "Anything chocolate and a Coke."

"Sit tight." Martin smiled. "I'll be back before you can say 'supercalifragilisticexpialidocious.'"

Megan giggled.

Now all I have to do is keep things this cordial, Martin thought. He returned, handed her a Coke, peanut butter cups, and a Hershey bar. Plopping down on the chair across the table from her he said, "I have your first name, Megan. How about sharing your last name?" They had gotten it from Alyssa and Ella, but this provided a chance to test her veracity.

"I don't think I should tell you." She frowned and concentrated on unwrapping a peanut butter cup. After freeing it from the packaging, she smiled and took a bite.

"My partner and I spent a lot of time with Alyssa and Ella. They're great kids. Before long they shared their last names. Gilbert and Henderson, right?"

Wide-eyed, Megan nodded. "Are you sure they told you?"

"Sure as I'm sitting here, Megan. In fact, it took a while longer, but they also told us where their families live and the names of their parents, brothers, and sisters."

"No way!" Megan shook her head emphatically.

"Alyssa's family is up north in Virginia, and Ella's family is right here in St. Paul, aren't they?"

66

Megan sat wide-mouthed.

"I spoke to Ella right here in this room. She sat where you're sitting. If you answer a few questions, you might be able to see them tonight. I can't guarantee it, but I'll do my best. Will you help me?"

Megan shrugged.

"Will you tell me your last name, Megan?"

Megan looked at the table, rubbed her cheek, and ran her fingers through her long black hair. Then she said, "Dawson ... and my family's in Stewartville."

The last part came out so fast, Martin had to play it back in his head to decipher it. Double checking his interpretation, he asked, "By Rochester?"

"Uh huh."

Martin tested her level of trust with the next question. "Where do you go to school?"

"I graduated from John Marshall last spring."

Martin recognized the name. It was a Rochester high school, either supporting what she said about her family's location or indicating she was familiar with southeastern Minnesota.

"So you're a prodigy."

"Huh?"

"What's your favorite subject?"

"Math."

"I'm jealous. I never got math. I had really thick hair until I pulled most of it out doing math homework."

Megan giggled.

"You think I'm kidding? Okay, that's a slight exaggeration. Are Alyssa, Ella, and Jessie your friends?"

"Yes, best friends. They do their best to protect me," Megan sighed.

"That's good. Do they succeed?"

Megan frowned. "Only once in a while. It's not easy."

"What makes it so difficult?"

"I better not say." Megan shook her head. "And I don't like to talk about it."

"Alyssa and Ella already told us all about JD and what he's done to the four of you, so it's okay to talk. He died tonight, Megan. He'll never hurt you again or force you to do anything. You can go home to your family. I know they'll be thrilled to see and hear from you. If you give me their phone number, you could be with them in the time it takes them to get here."

Megan shook her head as tears streamed down her cheeks. "I can't go home. They won't want to see me. When they find out what I've done, they'll hate me. They won't be able to forgive me."

"I have kids, Megan, and I know they could never hate you, no matter what."

"You're wrong. You don't even know what I did."

"You mean what JD forced you to do?"

"No, what I did so JD could force me to do things."

"No matter what you did, you didn't deserve what JD did to you."

"You're wrong. It's my fault."

"Do you want to talk about it?"

"Can't." *Sob*.

"Would you like to talk to your parents?"

Megan shook her head vehemently.

"Because you're afraid what they'll say?"

Nod.

"Do you have any brothers or sisters, Megan?"

"One brother, one sister."

"How old are they?"

"My sister is sixteen. My brother is fourteen."

"How old are you, Megan?"

"I know I look young, but I'm eighteen. I'm the oldest kid in my family."

"You're also a lot older than Alyssa and Ella. I guess they take care of you because you're smaller and look more like twelve than eighteen, huh? What year were you born?"

"*Umm*," Megan stared at the ceiling and appeared to be counting backward.

"If you're eighteen, Megan, you must have had a facelift."

Megan giggled. "No way."

"My son is fourteen. You look about the same age as some of his classmates ... and a lot younger than a few."

Megan looked down and scratched the back of her neck.

"You're eleven aren't you."

"I am not!" Megan shot back. "I'm twelve." Realizing Martin tricked her, wide-eyed, she covered her mouth.

"It's okay, Megan. The other girls told us their ages after a while. When did you hook up with JD?"

Megan's head dropped. "Last year. September thirtieth."

"Where did you meet?"

Megan bit her lip, and clenched and unclenched her fists.

After several seconds of silence, Martin continued, "Was it at a pool hall?"

"No." Megan slowly shook her head.

"I know. He saw you sitting in a bar, drinking martinis. After you downed your fifth, he sat next to you, amazed you were still conscious."

"No." She chuckled.

"Okay, I give up."

"I met him one day after school."

"Did he come to your school, Megan?" Martin feared the possibility.

"No. He met me when I got off the bus .... Actually, I think it was when I was shopping at the mall."

"Alyssa, Ella, and Jessie already lived in the apartment when you moved in?"

"Ella and Jessie, but not Alyssa. I was there for a few weeks before she moved in."

"Did JD have any other girls?"

Megan responded with a hands-up shrug.

"I'd love to help your parents, Megan. I'd love to take a huge weight off their shoulders by calling them and telling them we found you. Can I do that?"

Megan shook her head feverishly.

"Because you're afraid they can no longer love you?"

"Yes," she moaned.

"Megan, do you think it would be right for the parents of Alyssa, Ella, and Jessie to stop loving them for what they've done?"

"No, but they didn't do what I did. Please, don't ask me what. I can't tell you. I'm too ashamed."

After observing Martin and Megan through the one-way glass for a few minutes, Pete tapped on the glass.

"I know you're wrong, Megan, and I have kids. If you're willing, I can find someone for you to talk to. Think about it. You don't have to decide right now. Sit tight. I'll be right back."

Martin exited the room and spoke with Pete. "I think I need to let her be. A counselor will need to help her work through this. Child Protection must have someone—or at least access to someone."

"I agree. Let me contact them. Neither Megan nor Jessie is ready to face their parents. Child protection will take it from here. Back in a few minutes."

Pete left, and Martin returned to Megan. "I want you to know something, Megan. I think you're a terrific kid. There is nothing in the world you could do to change that, no matter how horrible you think it is. Please remember that. Will you do that for me?"

Eyes closed, Megan said, "I'll try."

"Good. Now for the time being you need a place to stay. A safe place. My partner's calling a place that will make arrangements for you. Here's my business card. You're good with math. Are you also good at remembering numbers?"

Nod.

"How about memorizing my number in case you misplace the card? I want to hear from you if there is *anything* I can do to help. Got it?"

"Yes, sir. Thanks." Megan crossed her arms on the table and rested her head on them.

"I'll check on my partner and be right back."

Martin saw Pete and Jessie as he closed the door behind him.

"I have great news," Pete said.

Martin surmised that, based on the expression on Pete's face.

"Let's join Megan, so I don't have to repeat it."

Megan beamed when she saw Jessie, and Jessie flashed her a smile.

"Here's the deal," Pete told the group. "I spoke today with Child Protection. Both Ella and Alyssa are with Ella's family. Ella's mom has been calling Child Protection every fifteen minutes to find out if they had Jessie and Megan. They want to take all four girls until the girls are back with their families. Child Protection was hesitant, but Ella's mom convinced them. She said the girls are like sisters. They banded together to survive the ordeal and shouldn't be separated at a time like this. Child Protection's on the way. They'll take the two of you and speak with you, jump through the necessary hoops, then take you to Ella's. It'll take a little time, so be patient. Okay?" He looked from Jessie to Megan.

Smiles filled two young faces. Each girl nodded when Pete looked at her.

Child Protection arrived almost before Pete finished sharing the news. They introduced themselves to the girls and escorted them to their car.

This time neither Pete nor Martin thought there was any danger of one or both girls taking off.

"Next?" Martin asked.

FOURTEEN

"Got a text, Martin. Commander Lincoln got the search warrant. Let's go to JD's and see how Forensics is doing. While you drive, I'll contact their on-call person to see if they've gleaned anything from JD's cellphone contacts, texts, and emails."

As he and Martin made their way to Martin's unmarked car for the umpteenth time tonight, Pete was convinced the temperature had dropped another few degrees. That made him smile. Seriously, without a thermometer, can anyone tell the difference between ten below zero and twenty below?

The coldest temperature he'd ever experienced was a wind chill of seventy-five below. Thinking back on that day, he knew there was definitely a difference between thirty below and seventy-five below. That day he'd parked his car and walked a few blocks before resorting to the skyways. On days like that, thank God for the skyways. After just a few blocks, his jaw had frozen to the point he could barely talk. That's when Katie gave him the red and gray wool scarf he kept handy for days like today.

En route to JD's, Pete learned no luck yet, when it came to JD's cellphone. "Hope things are going better at his home, Martin. Not particularly optimistic. These days most if not all his records could be electronic. Let's discuss likely suspects."

"The families of the four girls head my list, Pete. If anyone did what JD did to a member of my family, I'd want to murder them."

"Or perhaps someone figured out what JD was doing and had a friend or family member who was victimized by someone like him. Perhaps they decided to act on behalf of the person they knew. There are enough conceal and carry permits out there to equip an army."

"Could also be a competitor or a dissatisfied customer," Martin suggested.

"True. Murder seems like an overreaction to the latter, but we've seen stranger things."

Just before reaching JD St. Peter's street, they passed an alley providing access to detached garages on JD's block. Turning the corner onto his street, the first thing they saw was the Forensic Services van.

The homes on St. Clair Avenue were tucked onto narrow lots. Many were either a century old or on the verge thereof. Most were two stories and continued sporting what appeared to be the original wood siding. Even so, paint jobs looked current and the houses looked well-maintained. The colors ran the gamut, but tended toward subdued. JD's home was a soft gray Cape Cod style with dark gray peaks and white trim.

"Attractive, isn't it?" Pete said. "I wonder if it was his doing or the previous owner's."

Pete and Martin stepped over to the patrol officer limiting entry to JD's house and signed in. They ducked under the crime scene tape, ascended the front steps, passed through a three-season porch that sheltered only two wooden rocking chairs, and stepped into the house. Once inside, they scanned the environs, while looking for the crime scene supervisor.

They knew JD had been trafficking for at least four months. Based on what they saw, business was a booming failure, or he spent the proceeds on something other than household furnishings. The living room contained one chair, an end table with a lamp, and a love seat. Pete thought that last item was in poor taste. All of those furnishings looked like thrift store merchandise. No plants or knickknacks and nothing hanging on the walls. *Did he just move in?* Pete wondered.

"Been wondering how long it would take you to finish your nap and get here," a voice greeted them from the back of the house. "A blast of air conditioning alerts us each time someone opens a door. Wish I could can some of this and save it for August."

Martin and Pete passed the kitchen and bathroom on their way to that voice. It came from a bedroom. Both investigators noted an IKEA-style wooden table and two chairs in the kitchen. Pete wondered which came first, the kitchen furniture or the stuff in the living room. A single bath-size towel hung on the rod in the bathroom. The counters stood bare.

"Either he's really neat or has little," Martin whispered as they passed the bathroom.

"The latter seems more likely," Pete whispered back. "Doesn't look like the counter or mirror have been cleaned during my lifetime."

"How's it going?" Pete asked Pat, the Forensic Services lead investigator.

"So far, it appears he lives alone. No sign of another occupant, male or female. All the mail has his name. Only one toothbrush. One dirty coffee mug on the counter. One size clothing, et cetera, et cetera. Found a laptop and an iPad. They won't be of any assistance unless we crack the passwords."

"Find any notes on a desk, refrigerator, anywhere?" Martin asked.

"A few scribbles. Difficult to decipher. They'll require some translation. That's above my pay grade. Answering your next question, no word from the squads parked outside when it comes to anyone taking an interest in the proceedings here. It's possible however, he has a friend or three in a neighboring house, watching the proceedings from the security and comfort of their home. Haven't seen any lights go on, but no surprise there. They wouldn't want to tip us off."

"Mind if we take a look around?" Pete asked.

"Have at it."

Pete and Martin moved carefully through the house, touching nothing, and speaking with the investigators and the sergeant in charge as they went. A half-hour later, knowing little more than they did when they arrived, Pete and Martin left.

"Next?" Martin asked, pulling his stocking cap down lower and the collar of his jacket up over his ears.

Ducking out of the cold and into the unmarked car, Pete said, "I want to speak with Ella's family, but it has to wait. It's two in the morning, and we were instrumental in keeping them up until a short time ago. I'm anxious to track down Alyssa's dad. The secrecy surrounding his whereabouts is highly suspicious. I know many people living up on the range are experiencing financial hardships. I don't know if that includes Alyssa's family or if her mom was handing me a line about cellphone minutes."

FIFTEEN

Sunday morning at 6:45, after half-enough sleep, Pete pulled out of his driveway on the way to headquarters. While waiting for Martin, he contacted Commander Lincoln. Since the commander had his hands full, he asked Pete to call the St. Paul PD's representative on the FBI Anti-Trafficking Coordination Team.

Pete told that representative about the case he and Martin were working, including JD's full name and home address. After a bit of a search, the rep found they didn't have a file on JD. The rep said he'd start one and requested that Pete provide all the pertinent information about JD and the four girls, as well as any updates.

Anxious for a status report on the girls, next he called Child Protection. He learned all four girls were interviewed and examined at Children's Hospital before Ella was reunited with her family. Because Alyssa's family reported her missing and a warrant had been issued, initially she was taken to the Arlington Shelter. Tears were plentiful when Ella and her mom arrived at the shelter to get Alyssa. This recurred when they returned for Jessie and Megan.

The only other relevant development at Child Protection was a call from Alyssa's dad. "The long and short of it," according to the case worker, "he was thrilled she'd been found and regretted he wouldn't be able to see or speak with her until the end of the week at the earliest." *Ouch!* Pete thought, amazed the guy didn't drop everything to rush to his daughter. He wondered what could possibly prohibit it.

"Did you tell Ella's family the facts about her last few months?"

"Her mother and father, yes; but it was too late to go into detail. We'll do that later. I mentioned what we can do for Ella and the family."

After disconnecting, Pete worked on the stack of reports required by last night's efforts. He was plowing through the forms when Martin dragged himself in at 7:30.

Martin took one look at Pete and said, "How can you be so wide awake? How many pots of coffee have you consumed?"

"Four. I'll require a lot of pit stops. Hope you're not planning a stakeout."

"Actually, I was. But out of deference ...."

Pete shared details of his conversations with the FBI and Child Protection. "I'd like to start with Ella's family," he added. "I'm hesitant to call this early, but .... And at least one of us should be at the ME Office for the autopsy."

Setting aside his reservations, Pete used the phone number obtained from Child Protection to call Ella's home. When a very chipper voice answered, he said, "My name is Peter Culnane. I'm ..."

"I know who you are. I heard all about you. The good and the bad." The woman laughed.

"You sound mighty wide awake for someone who couldn't have gotten much sleep last night."

"I got *no* sleep. I was too excited to sleep. I still am."

She spoke so fast, Pete figured she must have consumed at least a gallon of coffee. "Are the girls awake?" he asked.

"All but Megan. Ella, Jessie, and Alyssa are in the living room. I've spent hours trying to convince Jessie and Megan that their parents would give the world to know they're okay, no matter what. Best I can tell, I accomplished absolutely nothing. I can't seem to get through to them."

"They've been through so much, it may take a lot of counseling."

"I'm sure you're right ... for all four of them. Poor girls. It's a crying shame. I'm trying not to hate the man who did this to them."

"Would it be okay if my partner and I stop by? We wouldn't stay long. Maybe forty-five minutes."

"I could ask the girls. No, second thought, just come. I'm so grateful for what you've done for me and my family."

Hope you still feel that way when we begin looking at you as suspects, Pete thought.

Traffic was light when Martin pulled out of the headquarters parking lot. Ella's family lived nearby, so Martin didn't venture onto I-94. Instead, he stuck with city streets.

On the way, Pete shared what he'd verified while going back over his notes. "Ella came under JD's control thirteen days before Jessie, and he added Megan fourteen days later ... another twenty days before he pulled in Alyssa. He may have had a pattern that was disrupted, or those variations might be coincidental. It's also possible he'd planned on three girls and decided to add a fourth," Pete continued. "I'm looking at the things that might disrupt a pattern or cause him to add a girl. Potential reasons for adding a girl are the need or desire for more income, or the need for a girl to manage the others or serve as his go-between. Based on what I saw with Ella and Alyssa, that's Alyssa's role, despite the fact she's the newest of the four girls. We didn't see Alyssa with Jessie, so it's also possible Jessie's the overall leader. It's been a little more than three months since he added Alyssa. Does that mean, monetarily speaking, four was the magic number? Or didn't he think he could handle more than four?"

"Maybe he needed twenty days to learn how to deal with a twelve-year-old," Martin said. "Or he had to determine if the apartment was big enough for a fourth girl. With Alyssa he reverted to girls who looked more like sixteen than twelve. Maybe things started getting away from him with a twelve-year-old, and he had to regain control. But the only reason that seems to provide a motive is the monetary one. Maybe he was in financial straits. Maybe someone was breathing down his neck, and he couldn't come up with the bucks."

"It's feasible. There might be something in his emails or texts, but if it deteriorated into threats, most people wouldn't text or email anything like that. The delivery's far more effective face to face. The browsing history on his search engine could be eye-opening."

Ella opened the door before they knocked.

Both investigators looked at her. *Wow*, Pete thought. *With her face washed clean, jeans and a sweatshirt in place of work clothes, and without the large hoop earrings, she's much prettier.*

"Come in, I guess."

"We'd like to talk to your parents first," Pete said. "And are your brother and sister home?"

"Mom, Dad, and Percy are here. Darcy's away at college."

Pete nodded. "Then we'd like to meet with them. After that, if there's time, we'd like to speak with you and your friends."

"About?"

"A few more questions."

Ella sighed and escorted Pete and Martin to the living room, then found her parents and brother.

She wasn't with them when they joined Pete and Martin.

Both Pete and Martin identified themselves, and Pete said, "We have a few questions. We'll try to keep this brief."

"I'm Larson," the older man said and nodded. When he spoke, his ebony skin accentuated his ultra-white teeth. He was just under six feet and sported signs of a sedentary life. He stood with feet spread, arms crossed, lips pursed.

"I'm Lucy. We spoke on the phone." Lucy smiled, extending a hand to both men—perhaps trying to compensate for her husband.

Pete saw where Ella got her looks. Lucy resembled a thin Oprah. The one startling difference between mother and daughter was the hair. Ella's was cut within a half-inch of her scalp.

"And I'm Percy." Ella's brother, a trimmer model of his dad, solemnly extended a hand.

"The sooner we begin, the sooner we finish," Ella's dad said.

"I understand you had no idea what had happened to Ella. Is that correct?" Pete asked.

"Yes," Lucy said. "After all those months without a word, we didn't think we'd ever see her again."

"The Red Bull Crashed Ice is quite a spectacle. Both Martin and I were there last night. Did any of you make it?"

"Thought about it. In fact, Percy and I talked about it," Larson said, "but the temperatures changed our minds. We're not that crazy."

"I had to work," Lucy said. "Never would have considered it anyway. I think it's crazy speeding down that track. You have to have a few screws loose."

"Where do you work, Lucy?" Martin asked.

"Regions. I'm a nurse in the ICU."

"Noble profession," Martin said. "How about you, Larson?"

"I manage the Midway Cub Foods."

"I don't envy you," Pete said. "Lots of weekends and holidays, huh?"

"You know it." Larson nodded.

Martin found Pete's comment amusing. When working a case, they worked days, nights, weekends, and holidays.

"When we spoke last night," Martin said, "you mentioned posting flyers with Ella's picture all around the Twin Cities. I'm amazed she went unrecognized."

"It's her hair," Lucy said. "She had such beautiful long hair and cut it all off. I'm her mother, and I might not have recognized her."

"Since you scrapped your plans to attend Crashed Ice, how did you spend the evening?" Pete asked.

"Percy and I went to The Crooked Pint and watched the races on the big screen."

"Sounds like a warmer spot than where Martin and I spent the evening. How long were you there?"

"From the first race through the last one," Larson said. He'd relaxed an iota, while talking about his job, but now crossed his arms again.

"Go with friends or just the two of you?" Pete continued.

Larson's eyes narrowed. "Just the two of us. Why all the questions?"

"Just a few more," Pete said. "Trying to get as complete a picture as possible. Can anyone vouch for you being there the whole time?"

"Probably not," Larson said. "Do you think we murdered this guy— this person who called himself JD? Until today, we'd never heard of him, much less what he'd done to Ella."

Percy looked questioningly at his dad.

"How about showing me your winter jackets," Pete said.

Percy stood, jammed his hands in the front pockets of his jeans, and walked toward the entryway closet.

"Hold on, son," Larson said. Turning to Pete he said, "Do you have a search warrant?"

"No sir."

"Then I guess you'd better leave."

"We'd like to speak briefly with the girls before we go," Pete said.

Larson scowled, yelled, "Ella!" then marched from the room.

Percy was right on his heels. He looked back over his shoulder and frowned at Pete and Martin before disappearing around the corner.

Lucy shrugged and followed her husband and son.

The two investigators weren't alone long before Ella appeared.

Pete decided to meet as a group, rather than separating the girls. "Is Megan awake?" he asked Ella.

Ella didn't know, but offered to check.

Pete asked her to get Megan, if she was awake, and the other two girls. "We have just a few questions for now."

When Ella returned, all three girls were close on her heels. The difference in appearance was marked. All three were prettier in a simple sort of way. Gone was the makeup, their hair was clean and in ponytails, and all wore jeans and sweatshirts.

After the girls found chairs, Pete and Martin pulled chairs close to theirs, making a tight circle. "Everyone feel comfortable talking here?" Pete asked. Four quick nods.

"If you answer a few more questions, we'll be able to proceed more effectively. Willing?"

Four shrugs.

"Did JD get stingier over the last month or so? Did it seem like he had money problems?" Pete asked.

"He stopped buying clothes for us, and we got fewer groceries. No more ice cream or candy bars," Alyssa said. "I figured it was because he decided we had enough clothes and didn't want us to get fat."

"When did he stop buying those things?" Pete asked.

The girls looked at each other. "Mid-November?" Alyssa asked.

"I guess," Ella said. "It's hard to say."

"Before Thanksgiving," Jessie said. "He bought us bags of candy and decorations for Halloween. He didn't do anything special for us for Thanksgiving or Christmas. No turkey or dressing, no pumpkin pie, no Christmas cookies. Not a single gift for any of us. You saw the winter outfits he bought for us. When it comes to winter clothes, other than the things you saw, we have some sweats and jeans. That's about it."

"He didn't use to be so stingy," Megan said. "After he brought me to St. Paul, he bought me four or five outfits."

"Oh, one other thing," Alyssa said. "I told him three weeks ago Megan's feet have grown, and her shoes and boots are too tight. I said she needs a size six. He still hadn't gotten her new ones."

"Did JD like to bet? Did he bet on the Crashed Ice races?" Martin asked.

"If you saw the way he screamed when his person didn't win a race, you'd think he bet every dollar he had on every race," Ella said.

"Did he ever mention his bookie?" Martin asked.

All four girls shook their heads.

"Did he talk about online betting?" Martin asked.

Again all four girls shook their heads.

"Megan, you've seen how thrilled Ella's family is to have her back, right?" Pete asked.

Megan hesitated, then nodded.

Pete figured the hesitation indicated she'd anticipated his next question, but continued anyway, "I'm positive your mom and dad will be just as thrilled to learn you're okay. Will you give us permission to call them? Will you tell us their names and phone number?"

Megan clenched her fists in her lap and looked at the other girls.

"It's okay, Megan," Alyssa said. "You told us all about your mom and dad. I know it'll be fine."

"For sure," Jessie said.

"Go ahead," Ella added.

Megan teared up and shook her head. "Sorry, not yet. Maybe tomorrow? Are you mad at me?"

"We understand." Pete nodded.

Alyssa reached for and held one of Megan's hands and said. "If you don't want to go home with your dad and mom, Megan, you won't have to. That's what the people from Child Protection told Ella and me last night."

Megan covered her small tear-stained face with her hands.

"Okay girls, almost finished," Pete said. "Jessie, last night you didn't want us to contact your family. Are you okay with it now? Have you thought about it?"

"Want my mom to call your mom, Jessie?" Ella offered. "A mom talking to another mom might help."

"Can I have until tomorrow to decide?"

"Absolutely," Pete said. "No pressure. We can talk tomorrow."

"Thanks. It's so hard to decide." Jessie frowned.

"I understand. It's complicated, and you need some time."

"Do you have any questions for us?" Martin asked.

"Neither Dad nor Mom contacted me," Alyssa said.

"Don't worry. They contacted Child Protection. They only have one car and can't make it quite yet," Pete said. "They were so relieved to learn you're safe. They plan to arrange a meeting ASAP."

Alyssa's head dropped. Her shoulders drooped.

"I understand you're disappointed," Pete said. "Your dad is disappointed too. He wants nothing more than to see you. He wishes he could drop everything and come right this minute." Pete hoped he was right.

"Did any of the people you met while working for JD suggest they wanted to hurt him?" Pete asked.

All four girls shook their heads.

"Did any of them offer to help you escape?" Martin asked.

Three girls shook their heads, and Jessie said, "Just once, but I don't remember who. Never got their real names anyway."

Sixteen

"What's your preference, Martin?" Pete asked as they trudged through a fresh layer of snow on their way to the car. "Too early to go to The Crooked Pint, but one of us could go to Forensics to check on their progress with the laptop, tablet, and cell, as well as check the crime scene photos for Ella's dad and brother. Both are about the right height, and they weren't anxious to disqualify themselves. One of us should attend the autopsy."

"If you don't have a preference, my nose prefers going to Forensics."

Pete arrived at the Ramsey County ME Office a minute to the good and joined the team assembled for the autopsy. The group included a forensic pathologist, forensic technician, and a scientist from St. Paul's Forensic Services Unit.

The room was designed for functionality with a drop ceiling, terra cotta floors, tile walls, and stainless-steel sinks along one wall.

Pete watched the forensic technician remove St. Peter's body from the cooler, roll the stainless-steel cart across the room, and connect it to a sink. Body fluids would drain from the cart into the sink. It was simple and efficient. The pathologist took photos of the clothed victim from every angle, both face up and face down and repeated the process after the victim's clothes were removed.

JD was a trim, five-foot-ten forty-three-year-old with broad shoulders and large feet and hands. His fiery red hair was in need of a cut. Giving him the benefit of the doubt, Pete thought its appearance might be due to the stocking cap that had all night to pack his hair down and make it look greasy. *Not bad looking*, Pete thought. *Wonder why he didn't succeed in connecting with an adult, why he preyed on young girls. Or didn't that have anything to do with it?*

Photos documented the condition of the body and included pictures of JD's face, hands, and arms. A series of close-ups captured the bullet wound in his back.

Each item of clothing was placed in an individual paper bag. Then all of those bags were placed in another paper bag, along with the victim's personal effects. The scientist from the Forensic Services Unit left, taking the clothes back to the lab, where they would be examined for trace evidence.

Next the technician weighed and measured the body and took x-rays, including a whole-body x-ray. The x-rays would show the location or locations of any slugs lodged in JD's body.

The pathologist conducted an external exam of every inch of the victim's body, looking for wounds, including defensive wounds and trace evidence. Bruising on JD's chest drew immediate attention. "See this small lump below his left nipple?" he said, looking up at Pete. "I think it's a projectile. Feels like one. We'll find out as soon as I finish here and we check the x-rays."

He examined and measured the entry wound in JD's back.

The external examination took an hour. In the process, the pathologist found no defensive wounds. This was anticipated, due to the jacket and gloves the victim wore at the time of the attack, as well as the fact he was attacked from behind.

After the external exam was completed, the technician drew vials of blood for all the necessary tests, including toxicology, DNA, and tests for diseases. Then the pathologist reviewed x-rays.

"This lateral shot shows the projectile by his left nipple," the pathologist said. "Before I do anything else, I'm going to extract it." Using a scalpel, he made a small incision and used a forceps to remove the bullet.

The technician held out a small manila envelope.

The pathologist held the projectile up for Pete to see. "It looks pretty good," he noted. "It should be useful to you." He placed the bullet in the envelope and signed it over to Pete to deliver it to the Forensic Services Unit.

A running commentary filled the autopsy room but did little to mask the sounds that followed. With the preliminaries completed, less pleasant sounds took over. First came the high-pitched whine of the autopsy saw. It filled the room as the technician, under the supervision of the pathologist, cut the sternum and ribs, making a Y from the shoulders to the pubic bone. "Can't see much, due to the amount of blood," the pathologist noted. He suctioned the blood out to see the damage made by the bullet and found the damage done to the heart. The odors in the room deteriorated markedly when the stench of the open body cavity and the bowel overpowered the smell of tissue and blood. This was a team effort. While all of this was happening, Pete did his part, telling about the progress thus far with the investigation. He mentioned the information gathered from the two girls who were with the victim at the time it happened, and the details gleaned from spectators. He explained why the victim was at Red Bull with the girls, that Child Protection came for the girls, where they spent the night, and his and Martin's visit to the home where the girls stayed.

"The bullet pierced the victim's back approximately 2.7 centimeters to the right of the left shoulder blade," the pathologist said. "The cause of death was damage to the heart and bleeding out. There was so much damage to the heart, he couldn't have lived even if they got him to the hospital immediately."

Pete was friends with the folks at the ME Office, but this remained an unpleasant way to spend a Sunday morning. *Apparently, Martin feels that way too*, he thought. When the autopsy was complete, he texted Martin to determine his whereabouts.

Martin was en route and would arrive in a minute or two.

Couldn't have planned it any better, Pete thought. After thanking everyone, he walked to the door and saw Martin pull into the lot. "Kind of you to warm up the car for me," he said as he slid in.

"Yeah, had to drive around for thirty minutes to accomplish that."

"I have the projectile, Martin. We need to get it to Forensics like yesterday."

"I'll come as close as I can to achieving that. What was the cause of death?"

"Massive injury to the heart, and he bled out. It was either a very lucky shot or the person who did it had a pretty good idea of the lay of the land."

"Hey, Pete, perhaps the bullet was fired by a weapon involved in a case that was solved, so we can go home, kick off our shoes, and take a nap."

"And kill all of our fun? Heaven forbid! We have a few minutes, Martin. What did you learn at Forensics?"

"The good news is, at the crime scene either the ME or Forensics discovered JD had an iPhone 7. Did you know after a while the fingers of a dead person won't unlock a device requiring fingerprint identification? I don't really understand it, but I think it has something to do with the electrical conductance of the fingers. Anyway, rather than risking it, Forensics used his finger to unlock and download his phone at the crime scene."

"I have the list of contacts. There are surprisingly few. If I didn't know better, I'd think he was a hermit. They checked his browser. It appears he was into online gambling. When I left, they were working to glean anything useful from the emails and text messages. He didn't have a single contact with the last name St. Peter or listed as "Mom" or "Dad." That may or may not be relevant."

"Too bad we can't use JD's phone to reach out to his contacts. No doubt our success rate would be significantly better. You look a bit more relaxed these days, Martin. Does that have anything to do with Michelle?"

"Actually, things are looking up. I told you one of her friends recommended she try alternative medicine. I was highly suspect, but by then we had nothing to lose. We'd spent months trying to determine what was wrong and gotten nowhere. We were so discouraged. We did a little research and made an appointment with a naturopath. Michelle met with him a couple of times, and I think we're finally getting somewhere."

"That's great news. What does he think is going on?"

"Remember she caught Marty's strep last spring and couldn't seem to shake it?"

"I remember she went back to the doctor a couple of times before it cleared up."

"Yes. She had to take three different antibiotics. Her naturopath said her condition stems from all those antibiotics. He said they threw her digestive system out of whack." Martin sighed and shook his head. "To make a long story a little shorter, apparently bacteria, yeast, and some other kinds of fungus live in your intestines. They're all supposed to work together to keep things running smoothly. In Michelle's case, the antibiotics killed all those bacteria, along with the strep, and left the yeast and fungus to grow unchecked. That's causing all her symptoms—the extreme fatigue, weight loss, and constant nausea."

"Ouch."

"As foreign as all of this is to me, Pete, the doctor says it's more common than you'd think. He's treated quite a few patients with similar conditions. He said it will take at least six months to get everything back under control and some balance restored."

"So how do you proceed?"

"Well, Michelle has quite the regimen of supplements she's taking right now, including antifungals and probiotics, but the biggest challenge is her new diet. Our new diet." Martin rolled his eyes. "No gluten, no sugar, no processed foods."

Pete raised his eyebrows, knowing how that would sit with his partner.

"Yeah," Martin shook his head. "I barely recognize much of what Michelle cooks these days. The good news is she usually feels up to cooking. Marty and I have committed to eating the same things she does, at least when we're eating together. We don't want her to feel like she's facing this alone."

"That's noble, but it must be hard."

"For sure. I know it's selfish, but Marty and I sure miss pizza!" Martin groaned, and Pete smiled.

"For the last few days, she's been pretty good. Even so," Martin shrugged, "anything unanticipated throws her for a loop. If one of Marty's teachers wants to meet with her about the most innocuous thing, a one-hour meeting puts her in bed for the rest of the day."

Martin took a deep breath. "The thing is, at least now we know what's causing it and how to move forward. We know that sticking with this diet, keeping up on her meds, and not pushing too hard will eventually get her back to her old self. That's a huge relief for both of us. For all three of us actually. Olivia is too young, but Marty's been so worried."

"The scariest part for me was not knowing. It was easily the worst five months of my life. But you knew that didn't you, Pete."

"Sure did. All I had to do was look at you to know what kind of day Michelle was having. It couldn't have been clearer if you'd written it on your forehead with a Sharpie."

"And I'd have had to try to erase it each time her situation got better or worse. Until recently, there was so little of the former and an overabundance of the latter."

Remember, Martin, any time you need some time off, all you have to do is ask."

"Thanks, I know. That's why I can continue doing this job."

Pete delivered the projectile, and he and Martin left Forensics with at least as much as they'd provided.

SEVENTEEN

Forensics had completed the review of JD's text messages. The technician reported they "found nothing recent indicating a single friendship or romantic interest with two possible exceptions. One was a series of six-month-old cryptic messages to and from someone not in his contacts. The second was a message sent two years ago on Christmas Day, begging him to call. There was only a phone number for that sender as well. The phone number has a 715 area code. That's western Wisconsin."

The technician handed a piece of paper to Martin and said, "Taking the mystery out of it, here are those two numbers."

"In this day of spam, wonder if those senders will answer an unrecognized number," Martin said.

"I think we'll have a better chance by texting, rather than calling," Pete said. "Hope they still have those phone numbers. Still going through the email?" he asked the technician.

"Yes. This guy appears to have deleted very little. There are almost four thousand messages in his inbox. If I was him, I'd rate most of these emails as spam. I started by examining his sent mail. So far nothing of value. I mean nothing of a social nature. He used Safari as his search engine. His history indicated he spent time in several chat rooms. Without his username and password, his activity there is inaccessible. Some people have websites save their username. Not surprising, he didn't do that for any of those of interest. Depending on how he linked up with the girls, one of them may at least know his username."

"If so, she's probably done her best to forget it," Pete said.

"As I told Martin earlier, this guy also visited several online gambling sites. There too, unable to access any details."

"How does someone like JD become so hardened, bitter, angry, mercenary, or whatever drove him to do this to young girls?" Martin asked.

"Solving this case may be contingent on discovering that," Pete said.

Martin nodded. He was thinking about Megan. Did she know one of JD's usernames? He suspected the answer was yes. He suspected he knew what she was so ashamed of, so unwilling to share. Her situation, the situations of all four girls, was heartbreaking.

"I'm not optimistic, but let's text all the people JD communicated with that way," Pete said on their way to headquarters. "People run the gamut when it comes to responding. Some respond ASAP. Others take days if they respond at all—even to senders they know. Let's start that way and not with phone calls. After a day or so, we'll try calling."

"What shall we say in the text?"

"I think something like, 'Need to reach you for JD. Please call ASAP!!' What do you think, Martin?"

"What if they know he's dead?"

"Since the family has yet to be identified and notified, his name hasn't been released. If they know, the question is how. Depending on the answer, they could be more or less likely to respond. It may depend on their relationship to JD."

"Sounds reasonable."

"JD never responded to the text that held the most promise, unless they changed their phone number. Hoping they haven't written him off. This person could be our best source for learning his story. I'm anxious to get moving. How about you, Martin?"

"Me too. It feels like we're handcuffed. Thus far, no known family, friends, or enemies. No eyewitnesses who can point us in the right direction. We usually have something to go on."

"Martin, what's up? You're not usually this impatient."

"The girls JD victimized are so young. I can't help thinking about Olivia. Granted she's still a baby, but Megan's only twelve. Can't help worrying about the world that will be my little girl's."

"I understand, Martin. The good news is, you know better than most the threats out there. She's lucky to have you as her dad. She'll be far better equipped than most to survive the challenges life throws her way and come through it unscathed."

"Doesn't that depress you, Pete? Are you sure you want to have kids?"

"Positive. I know it's a huge responsibility. I know despite a parent's best efforts, some kids go wrong or get victimized. I also know Katie will be a wonderful, loving mother. God willing, I long for a chance to share my life and my experiences with a couple of kids. I long to love and counsel them. I long to learn from them."

Back at headquarters, Martin followed Pete into Pete's office and pulled a chair up so they faced each other across his desk. They split the workload and sent text messages to JD's contacts and the list of phone numbers not connected to contacts gleaned from his texts. Copy and paste reduced the steps and made it more expeditious. In about twenty minutes, they'd completed the job.

One person responded before they'd finished. That phone number wasn't in the list of contacts.

"Okay, Martin, let's do this. Either you or I will call that number and identify ourselves as JD's friend. We'll tell them JD was hurt last night and say we're trying to contact all of his friends. Then ask if they can provide names and phone numbers."

Pete got the vote. As he entered the number, a call from an unrecognized number interrupted him.

EIGHTEEN

Due to the case he and Martin were working, the first thought crossing Pete's mind was the caller was one of the girls or someone from Child Protection. "Culnane," he answered.

"Sir, this is Jessie Acton. I want to talk. Can we meet today? Can we meet right now?"

"Have you told Child Protection you want to do this?"

"No. Can you tell them for me?"

"How about if we work it from both ends, Jessie? Are you at Ella's house?"

"Yes. I think Child Protection is coming for us."

"Did someone tell you that?"

"No, but ..." Jessie trailed off.

"Do you think Child Protection's preparing to move you? You have a voice in what happens. They won't just place you in a foster home. You know that, don't you?"

"They told me that, but I'm afraid what will happen if you don't help me talk to my mom. Will you take me to see her? If you're there, maybe she'll listen to me."

"Child Protection will have to come along, Jessie. Is that okay?"

"Only if there's no other way."

"Is it okay if I also bring my partner, Martin?"

"That's fine. Then it will be three against one," she chuckled.

"Child Protection wants only one thing, Jessie. That's to take care of you and protect you."

"But only to a point. Sooner or later I'm just a number, just another case. If I don't fit neatly into one of their boxes, I'll get shoved into the closest fit. I'm afraid of what that'll look like and how it'll feel."

"Do you have a basis for saying that? A friend or family member?"

"No. I just know. It's intuition. Don't you sometimes rely on intuition to do your job?"

More than I'm sometimes willing to admit. "Jessie, call Child Protection, and I'll do likewise. See how soon someone is available to meet you, Martin, and me at Ella's house. While you're doing that, I too will call them. Call back as soon as you arrange something. Meanwhile, please cut Child Protection some slack. You could be pleasantly surprised."

Pete hung up and called Child Protection. He was still on hold when his phone rang. A little checking indicated the call came from the same number Jessie used a few minutes ago. Pete let it ring three times then, before it was too late, added Jessie to the call, making it a conference call. He hoped Jessie would disconnect before Child Protection picked up.

"Culnane," he answered.

"It's Jessie. They can't do it until tomorrow. Do we have to wait?"

"Stay right by that phone, Jessie. I'll call back in a few minutes." Pete disconnected with Jessie, returning to the Muzak. He ran into mild resistance when his call was answered. Turned out the timing was less than optimal. A little pressure changed priorities.

"Be there in ten to fifteen minutes," Pete told Jessie. "Do the other girls and Ella's mom know with whom you were speaking?"

"Yes. Tried to come up with a good story, but decided they'd figure it out if you showed up. Decided I'd better tell the truth."

Pete and Martin picked up Alan Preston, the Child Protection staff member who came to headquarters last night, on their way to Ella's.

"If her mom won't take her back or if Jessie decides against returning home, Brittany's Place is there for girls like her," Alan said. "It's an emergency shelter in St. Paul for homeless and trafficked youth."

"Plan B," Pete said. "Hope Jessie won't need it."

"The three men conferred the remainder of the distance, agreeing on how to proceed as Martin parked the car. Pete got out and walked to the front door, while Preston moved to the front seat.

Pete returned to the unmarked and opened the back door for Jessie. Then he walked around the car and got in back with her. "Ready to face your mom?" he asked.

"Can we talk first?"

"Sure. Any place special you'd like to go to do that, Jessie?"

"Have you ever heard of Keys Restaurant? I guess that's a stupid question, huh? Anyplace is fine. I just think Keys has really good bakery stuff."

"Downtown?" Martin glanced at Pete in the mirror.

"Perfect."

Out of the corner of his eye, Pete caught Jessie's smile. He wondered how much she'd share.

Pete and Jessie followed Martin and Alan into the restaurant. They were ahead of the lunch rush, so had no problem getting seated.

Pete orchestrated things so Martin and Alan sat across the table from Jessie and him. She'd called him, so he did this in case he'd become her security blanket.

The four of them made small talk until their order was taken. Then Pete turned to Jessie and said, "How can we help?"

Jessie fidgeted with her silverware, while looking closely at each man.

Noticing this, Pete said, "Would you be more comfortable if we had a woman here with us?"

"No." The response came without pause.

"Are you sure? I can certainly change the composition of this group."

"No. It's just hard to get started. I already told you, Mom threw me out. It's complicated."

"We want to help you. The more information we have, the better we'll be able to help you work things out with your mom. That's very important to us."

Jessie took a deep breath and began, looking deep into Pete's eyes, seemingly oblivious to the other two men. "I told you I was expelled. I want you to know why. I want you to know it wasn't just me. I'm hoping you can help me get my mom to understand and take me back. I really miss her, my dad, and my brothers. It all happened because I took a knife to school."

NINETEEN

"I know taking a knife to school was stupid," Jessie continued, "but my school didn't have a metal detector. I didn't want to hurt ... or kill anyone. I just wanted these four girls to leave me alone. I don't know why they hated me, but they did. Maybe it was because my hair was dyed pink, orange, purple, and green. I didn't fit in anyway, so I did it to show the other kids I didn't care."

"Anyway, these four girls always hassled me. I hated it, but I couldn't change it. That's just the way it was ... until the day they followed me into the girl's bathroom. They pushed me into one of the stalls and grabbed my hair. They shoved my face into the toilet and flushed it. I got water up my nose and down my throat. I thought I was going to drown. It took me forever to stop coughing and get cleaned up. I was written up for not having a hall pass and being late for my next class, but that was nothing. As the girls left, they said, 'See you tomorrow. Same time, same place. Make sure you're here, or else. Tell anyone and we'll make it ten times worse.'"

"The next day, I took the knife to school. I hid it in my backpack. Got to the lavatory first, backed up against the wall, and waited for them with the knife in my boot. I stood there hoping they wouldn't show. I wasn't that lucky. I pulled the knife and said, 'Come any closer and I'll slice you.'"

"That's when things fell apart."

Pete cringed, wondering how many of the girls were injured and how badly.

"That's when Ms. Sunburg, my Language Arts teacher, walked in. She saw the knife and told me to accompany her to the principal's office. She told Mara she'd get her side later."

"Why would a teacher go in the girl's bathroom, rather than using a faculty bathroom?" Pete asked. "Did she suspect something was going on?" *If so, how did it end up this way?* he wondered.

"Teachers often use our bathroom, supposedly to save time. I think they're actually trying to catch girls smoking."

"Please continue," Pete said.

"Well, when the principal, Ms. Brooks, heard about the knife, she blew up. 'As you know, Jessica,' she said, 'we have zero tolerance for weapons on the grounds or in the buildings.' She suspended me until the school board made a final decision. A little background information might help. Ms. Brooks considered me a troublemaker, a rabble-rouser. I've been vehement in my opposition to the Enbridge pipeline. Portions go through treaty territory. The pipeline will contribute to climate change. If you care about the land and the people, it's bad. We need to get away from oil and begin concentrating on green energy. All these pipelines are threatening some of the most pristine wetlands for wild rice. That wild rice is harvested by my people. I'm Ojibwa. I imagine you understand all this activism did anything but endear me to Ms. Brooks. I think she was happy to have me out of her hair."

Pete smiled. "I admire you for standing up for your beliefs. What kind of knife did you have?"

"A paring knife. I didn't want to go to school, but Mom would have blown up if she found out I skipped. I saw it on the kitchen counter as I was walking out the door to wait for the bus. As Gibbs says on *NCIS*, 'Rule nine: always carry a knife.' I decided it was a good time to start. I couldn't think of a better solution."

"And?" Pete said.

"The school board went along with the principal. They decided they'd be setting a dangerous precedent if they didn't expel me, so they did. I could have registered in another high school, but would have needed Mom's help, and she'd already written me off."

"Didn't anyone bother to get the facts that led up to you bringing a knife?" Martin asked.

"First, Ms. Sunburg said she'd talk to Mara and her friends. She's a good person. I actually think she liked me, so I'm sure she did. I'm also sure all four said I was crazy, and they did nothing. It would have been one against four. No one would have believed me. Besides, can you imagine what my life would have been like if I told Ms. Sunburg, the principal, or the school board why I brought a knife? Having my face shoved in a toilet would have been a picnic compared to what I'd have been up against after that. No thanks! Do you believe me?"

Pete observed her facial expressions and the way she relayed the details without breaking eye contact with him. She was telling the truth, an outstanding actress, or a sociopath. "Yes," he told her, "I believe you. How about your mom? Did you tell her about this?"

"No, we'd been fighting a lot. She got angry when I was suspended and blew up when I was expelled. She said I brought shame on the family. She said I was out of control, a loose cannon. Like I told you, she told me to get out and never come back."

"We hear a lot about mother-daughter stress from adolescent girls," Alan said. "Mother-daughter relationships are often difficult at your age."

"Will your mom be home now?" Pete asked.

"She should either be home or on her way home from church."

"What would you like to do now, Jessie? Should we go talk to her?" Pete asked.

"I hope you'll help me figure that out. I want to, but I just don't know. If Mom thought I was a disgrace and a bad influence on my brothers before, what will she think when she finds out what I've been doing? This was a stupid idea, wasn't it?" Jessie shook her head, eyes moist. She looked lost.

"I disagree, Jessie," Pete said. "What have you got to lose? Worst case, you'll be where you are right now. Don't you agree, Alan?"

"Yes, I do. I've seen it time and again. A parent reacts and spends months regretting it. Your mother is probably praying you return. We can help her understand you are the victim, not the villain."

"I agree, Jessie," Martin said. "Before we go, is there anything else you can tell us about JD? Were there places you went regularly? Parties or certain bars? We know sporting events are a big draw. Can you name any other regular spots?"

"First," Pete said, "What's your home address? We can talk about those things on the way."

Jessie rattled off the address. "It's only about a mile from the Minneapolis American Indian Center. Do you know where that is? It's by Bloomington Avenue and Franklin."

"I know exactly where it is," Martin said. "It'll take maybe fifteen minutes to get there."

"Jessie, in an effort to ease the way, I'd like to talk to your mom before she sees you," Pete said. "It's probably not necessary, but just in case. Is that okay with you?"

Jessie nodded emphatically.

"Okay, let's continue this conversation on the way. If needed, you'll have extra time with Martin, while I speak with your mom."

En route to south Minneapolis Jessie told the three men JD took her and the other girls to sporting events. Otherwise, the men usually came to their apartment. "JD must have a website or something to connect with these men. We worked a few private parties, but they were rare."

Pete asked the locations for the private parties.

"They were never at someone's home. I think people were too careful for that."

"Can you remember the dates for any of those events?" Pete asked, hoping to get the name of at least one person who'd arranged an event.

"No. Sometimes I don't even know the day of the week. Dates mean nothing anymore. There's nothing to look forward to."

Pete winced, but only internally. He didn't want Jessie to see his reaction.

Looking again for a motive, Martin asked, "Did you ever see anyone light into JD, grab him by the shirt or jacket, punch him, or scream at him?"

"Once or twice. I don't know for sure, but it may have been over price. I'm sure you know what I mean."

"Could you identify any of those people?" Martin asked.

"No," Jessie frowned and shook her head. "I stayed as far away as possible. They weren't in my face, and I figured it was JD's problem, not mine."

"Did you have any regulars?" Martin continued.

"A few."

"How did you address them? Did you call them by their first names?" Martin asked.

"Only a few of them, and they might not use their real names."

"What were their names, Jessie?" Martin asked.

"Those were the few good guys. I don't want to get them in trouble."

"You don't know their last names, correct?" Martin asked.

"Correct."

"In that case, providing first names won't get them in trouble ... unless their first names are something peculiar like, well, Astroturf. Was that one of the names?" Martin was thinking about JD's list of contacts.

"What mother would name her son Astroturf?"

"Someone who loved professional baseball or football? So if none of the names are that peculiar, how about sharing them?"

"There were just two, but like I said, I'm not positive they used their real names."

"What names did they use?" Martin asked.

Jessie looked out the window and waited almost a minute before saying, "Eddie and Ken."

"When I asked you at Ella's, you said one person offered to help you escape," Pete said. "You couldn't remember whom. Was it Eddie or Ken?"

Jessie shook her head.

"Willing to do me a favor?"

Jessie nodded.

"Do you still have my business card?"

Another nod.

"If you remember that name, nickname, first name only, whatever, will you call? It could be a critical piece of information."

Jessie shrugged noncommittally and said, "Take a right at the next corner. Then go two blocks and turn left. Our house is on the second block and on the left."

Pete caught her reference to "our house" and read it as a good sign. Jessie's family lived in the Powderhorn neighborhood, just south of Lake Street. Many Minneapolitans appreciated the small-town feel these neighborhoods provided.

Jessie's street was lined with saltbox style, two-story homes circa the 1930s. Either the residents were benefiting from the upswing in the economy or investors were buying up some of these homes. Several displayed add-ons. Residents accessed their detached garages via the alley that ran north south. The yards were compact, but a respectable distance separated the homes.

The second story porch on Jessie's home provided the opportunity to take advantage of warm summer nights. The third-story attic sported natural shaker trim that complimented the natural wood fence surrounding the home.

"That's Mom's car parked in front." Jessie pointed, craning her neck to see out the windshield. "She must be home. I'm scared. Should we wait a few days ... or weeks?"

"Hold tight, Jessie. Let's give it a try," Pete said. "First, I have another question. Did you see Eddie or Ken last night? Did one of them find you at Crashed Ice and take you home?"

"I wish! No. That was the first time I saw the guy who took me home last night."

Still sitting in the back seat, Jessie did her best to hide behind the scant camouflage provided by the car. She wanted to see her mom's face. She wanted to see her reaction to this cop. She was glad they weren't in a car with St. Paul PD plastered on the doors.

Martin noticed the sidewalks at Jessie's former home, unlike most in the neighborhood, were clear down to the cement. While awaiting the next development, he contemplated the course of this investigation. Pete was good. Good enough to get through to Jessie's mother?

He noticed Pete speaking more than usual with his hands. The woman who answered the door didn't invite him in. *Bad sign?* Martin wondered. He continued observing the interaction as surreptitiously as possible, thankful the house was ahead of them, so nothing blocked his view. Then his heart sank. He saw Pete shrug, turn, and head back to the car. The look on Pete's face said it all. "No go."

Much as he wanted to slam the steering wheel, Martin didn't. He wanted Jessie to experience a few more seconds of optimism.

Pete was halfway down the stairs when he stopped, turned back to the house, and paused for several seconds. Then he ascended the four steps back to the door.

TWENTY

This time the woman opened the door, and Pete entered.

Martin said a silent prayer. Please Lord, have this mother welcome this poor girl home.

In less time than it takes to microwave a Jimmy Dean breakfast sandwich, Pete headed back in their direction. This time he wore a controlled smile. He was barely down the steps when two boys dashed down the steps and passed him. One of them must have asked which car, because Pete pointed to the unmarked.

Martin got out of the car, walked around to the back door, and opened it. He saw no reason to stall the boys. Jessie jumped out and both boys grabbed her in a group hug. It was still in progress when Pete reached the group. He no longer hid his smile.

"Her mom will meet with the four of us," he told Martin as he motioned to Alan to come.

All three men noted the failure of Jessie's mom to join her sons in welcoming Jessie. All three followed the tight little group up the steps and into the house. Jessie's mom moved to the side, permitting all three of her kids to enter. The two cops and social worker followed them in.

"Teddy, get a chair from the kitchen, then you and Earl go clean your room."

"But, Mom," Teddy moaned, "we want to stay with Jess. We ..."

"Do as I say, now." Her tone left no room for discussion.

Grumbling and dragging their feet, both boys headed toward the back of the house. When they returned, Teddy carried a wooden chair. He deposited it in front of his mother, then he and Earl turned and charged up the stairs two at a time.

"All legs, aren't they?" Pete said. "Jessie told me they're seven and nine. NBA look out." He smiled and saw the grimace on Jessie's mother's face relax for the first time since his arrival. He hoped it was a harbinger of good things to come.

Jessie's mom rearranged the wooden chair, sat on it, and motioned the others to occupy the more comfortable options. The room was modestly decorated, but neat and clean.

"Ms. Dawson," Pete said, "I'd like to introduce my partner, Martin Tierney, and Alan Preston from Child Protection. This is Alan's department. He'll tell you what the last several months have been like for Jessie and what lies ahead."

Jessie had her mom's dark hair and eyes. In both cases, her mom's showed the age difference. Mother and daughter were approximately the same height—five nine or ten.

"Do you want to be here for this part?" Alan asked Jessie.

"Yes, please."

Alan spent about fifteen minutes explaining how girls are recruited, coerced, and victimized by child traffickers.

Jessie squirmed throughout that dissertation. She wasn't the only one. Her mother repeatedly shifted position, crossing and uncrossing her legs and arms, rubbing her neck, scratching her chin.

Alan wrapped it up by explaining the options open to Jessie and her family and encouraging counseling. "Doesn't matter how tough or resilient you are," he said. "I'm sure you've both heard of post-traumatic stress disorder. Counseling can help you derail it or give you tools and resources to get through it. I have a list of resources for you," he said, retrieving a folded sheet of paper from his suit coat and handing it to Jessie's mom. "My phone number is at the bottom. I'm happy to help any way I can. Speaking of that," he continued, "should I arrange for a place where Jessie can stay?"

"Over my dead body!" Jessie's mom shot back. "She's home now. You do want to stay, don't you, Jessie?"

"I sure do, Mom!" Jessie jumped up, hurried to her mother, dropped to her knees alongside her mom's chair, and gave her a protracted hug. That hug went both ways.

Her mom took Jessie's face in her hands and asked, "But Jessie, why did you take a knife to school? I've tried and tried to understand."

Tears flowed down her mom's cheeks, while Jessie shared the details. When she finished, her mom sobbed, "I'm so sorry, Jessie. I should have known. I should have asked. Can you ever forgive me?"

"I understand, Mom. I love you. I never stopped."

Their embrace tightened.

"I have another question," Alan said. "Will you be registering with a new high school?"

Jessie looked at her mom.

"Of course. You do want that, don't you, Jessie?"

"I sure do." Jessie's smile continued lighting the room.

Pete would have liked to take Jessie back to Ella's, giving her a chance to share her success story with Megan and Alyssa. But he didn't want to provide an opportunity for a change of heart ... unlikely as it seemed. "You don't need to do it right now," he told Jessie, "but you should call your friends. Do you have Ella's phone number? I don't think they would, but I'd hate to have them decide we took you some place other than home. After all, might that cross your mind if Alyssa or Megan left with us and didn't return?"

"Well, yes." Jessie nodded.

"Here's the number, just in case," Alan said, taking out a business card and writing Ella's number on the back.

"Thanks." Jessie smiled broadly. "I'll call. I promise. I owe you. Thanks for everything!"

"One more question, Ms. Dawson," Pete said. "Where were you last night between seven and eleven?"

"What does that have to do with anything?"

"It's something I'm asking everyone we meet with."

Wearing a bewildered look, Jessie's mom said, "I was here with the boys. Ted was at work."

Pete got Ms. Dawson's home and cellphone numbers, and the three men got up to leave.

Jessie and her mom walked arm in arm to the door.

"Wait until your dad gets home, Jessie. He isn't going to believe his eyes. He'll be ecstatic."

Happy for the segue, Pete asked, "Where is your husband now?"

"He's at work, again."

"Where does he work?" Martin asked.

"At the State Capitol. He's a Capitol Security guard."

"That's where he was last night?" Martin asked.

"Yes, they increased the number of guards on duty, because the Crashed Ice competition was just down the road. They weren't taking any chances."

"Capitol Security guards aren't armed, are they," Pete said.

"No. Can you believe it in this day and age?"

A fifteen-minute break could get you to Crashed Ice and back to the Capitol, Pete knew.

TWENTY-ONE

"How did you break down the wall, Pete?" Martin asked as soon as the men were back in the unmarked. "How did you get through to Jessie's mom?"

"There were already major cracks in the wall. I told her Jessie is a strong, brave girl who since she last saw her did her best to protect a younger girl. I said right now she really needs her mom. Drop you off at your office, Alan?"

"Just a minute. Let me make a call."

While Alan did that, Pete and Martin checked for additional responses to the texts sent before Jessie called.

Both completed the process before Alan hung up. Martin had none. Pete had one. The one received just before Jessie called. It said, "Identify yourself!!"

Unwilling to discuss the investigation in front of Alan, Pete and Martin used the trip to St. Paul to gain information on child trafficking from the perspective of child protection.

"Runaways are the number-one targets for these guys. They're often pulled in during their first day of homelessness. It's pretty scary for these young kids who find themselves without a safe place to sleep. Malls are also common hunting grounds. They approach girls who are alone, check their reactions to a few standard lines that distinguish the most vulnerable from the rest, and play up to the vulnerable. They've made it into a science."

After dropping off Alan, Pete called the phone number connected to the one response to their text messages. His call wasn't answered. He didn't leave a message.

They spent the rest of the trip to HQ discussing their game plan. "Let's wait a few more hours, then call the person who seemed to have a personal connection to JD, as well as the one who may have," Pete said. "Neither responded to our texts. Feels strange thinking of JD as the victim, doesn't it?"

"Sure does. We have a job to do. Otherwise it would be hard to care who took him out, especially if it was a friend or family member of one of the girls."

"Maybe it was another trafficker. That would make catching the person satisfying. Two birds with one stone."

Pete pulled the list of JD's contacts from a suit coat pocket and looked for the two names Jessie mentioned—the repeat customers who treated her unusually well—Eddie and Ken.

"Struck out," he said. "Not a single Ed, Eddie, Edward, Edwin, or any other name beginning with an E in JD's contacts. Likewise, for Ken, Kenneth, or any name beginning with K."

"You didn't really think you'd find either, did you?" Martin asked.

"No, I didn't think any of JD's patrons would be that careless or foolish, but ever the optimist."

"We still need to review the video at The Crooked Pint, assuming it exists, to see if it proves or challenges the presence of Ella's brother and father," Martin said.

"And I'm anxious to speak with the other parents. In fact, let's stop at the Capitol on the way to HQ to see if Jessie's dad is still there."

Martin took the Marion Street exit off I-94 and drove past the Sears store—a St. Paul landmark—on the way to the Capitol. He skirted the cement barriers and parked in front of the main stairway.

The two investigators walked up to the Capitol Security checkpoint and held out their badges. "We're looking for Ted Acton," Martin told the guard.

"I don't think he's working this shift, but I'll check."

The guard made a channel-wide announcement, asking if Ted was on duty.

"I'm in the SOB. What's up? Ten Four."

"He's in the State Office Building," the guard translated for Pete and Martin.

"Yes, I recognized the acronym." Pete nodded. "Should we head that way?"

"Why don't you meet with him at our office? Know where it is?"

Both investigators nodded, and Pete bypassed the elevators on his way to the closest stairway.

Martin shook his head and followed.

They did a 180 at the bottom of the stairs and headed toward the Capitol Security offices and the tunnel connecting the Capitol with the

SOB. About halfway there, both men saw a guard approaching the offices, gripping a black down jacket in his left hand.

"Ted Acton?" Pete asked just loud enough to be heard across the remaining distance.

"Yes, and you are?"

Pete and Martin identified themselves, and Pete asked if there was a private place where they could talk.

"There should be lots of options on a Sunday. Follow me. Let's see what we can find."

Pete and Martin followed him through the door alongside the "Capitol Security" plaque and down the hall. They passed one vacant office and entered the second. Three chairs sat on the doorway side of the office, backs to the door and facing the desk. Ted turned one of the chairs so it faced the door and said, "Make yourselves comfortable. Wasn't expecting a visit from the St. Paul PD. What can I do for you?"

Martin took the lead, asking, "Where were you last night between seven and ten thirty, Ted?"

"At the Red Bull Crashed Ice."

"So you're a Crashed Ice fan?"

"Not really, especially in those temps."

"What time did you arrive?"

"A little after seven. Planned on getting there earlier, but the crowd was worse than I'd anticipated."

"And what time did you leave?"

"Right after the last race."

"Where did you spend your time?"

"Didn't stay in any one place. I moved around the whole time."

"Made it hard to see the races, didn't it?" Martin asked.

"Nigh on impossible."

"If you weren't there for the races," Pete said, "why did you subject your body to those temperatures for that long?"

"I was looking for someone."

"Does that someone have a name?" Pete asked.

"Yes."

"And it is?"

"Let it suffice to say I didn't find the person. I understand someone was murdered up by the Cathedral last night. Is that why you're here?"

"What did you wear last night?" Pete asked.

"The jacket I threw on the desk," Ted pointed a thumb back over his shoulder, "a stocking cap, a wool sweater and turtleneck, insulated pants, and gloves. I think that covers it, unless you want a complete list down to my skivvies."

"Does your stocking cap double as a ski mask?" Pete asked.

"There were times last night I wished it did, but no. I wanted the person I was looking for to get a good look at my face."

"Did you get your wish?" Pete asked.

"Unfortunately, no." Ted sighed and shook his head.

"Did you go with anyone?" Martin asked, moving back into the driver's seat.

"Yes, I went with my brother."

"What's his name?"

"Leroy."

"So you went to the races because your brother wanted to go?"

"No, he went because I wanted him to go with me."

"And the only reason you were there was to connect with someone. There had to be an easier way to do that."

"You aren't going to let it rest until I tell you, are you?"

"How long have you been with Capitol Security?" Pete asked.

"Twelve years."

"In other words," Pete said, "you've been around long enough to know we can't let it rest until we get what we need."

"If you're here about the murder, my brother and I were working our way up the hill after scouring downtown for the person I was looking for. We were still more than a block away when the commotion began. I knew the person we were looking for would not hang around and get caught up in a ruckus. So, me and my brother headed back downtown, doing one last sweep, checking over the people in the vicinity."

"Who were you looking for, Ted?"

"My daughter, okay? I haven't seen her in months. I'm worried sick about her and thought she might be at the races."

"Why would you think that?"

Ted crossed his arms and said, "I told you who I was looking for. You're going to have to be satisfied with that."

"We need your brother's phone number, Ted."

"Knowing Leroy the way I do, he won't answer a call from an unfamiliar number."

"Call him, Ted," Pete said.

Ted called his brother's home and cell numbers. Each time he dialed, he held his phone out so Pete could see Leroy's name on the screen. He shrugged when there was no answer either time. "Want me to have him call you?"

"Please," Pete said and gave him a business card, knowing it was likely a waste of time. If Ted was lying, he'd have time to get his brother on board. The thing was, it was just as likely if he called Leroy. He got the number anyway.

As Ted escorted him and Martin to the door, Pete said, "Call your wife. She has news for you."

"About Jessie?" Ted's face lit up. Then he sighed and shook his head. "No, Ted. Get real," he muttered.

TWENTY-TWO

While Martin drove the several remaining blocks to headquarters, Pete called Ted's brother. No luck. He left a message saying he got the phone number from Ted and asking for a return call ASAP.

At headquarters, Pete and Martin parked themselves in Pete's office and downloaded Larson and Percy Henderson's driver's license photos. Then they drove to The Crooked Pint. The location was north of downtown, and the city didn't have street cameras in this area. With any luck, the owner took the precaution of installing at least one security camera.

They walked up to the counter, identified themselves, and asked the hostess if she worked last night.

"*Everyone* has to work Saturday nights," she frowned.

"Did you spend the night hostessing?" Pete asked.

"No, I also waitressed."

"Do you have security cameras?" Martin asked.

Placing her hands on her hips and looking sideways at Martin she said, "I don't think so, but I'm not sure. Never heard any mention of them."

Pete showed her the photos of Larson and Percy.

"Have you ever seen these two guys in here?"

"Yes. They're regulars." She smiled and nodded.

"Did you see them last night?"

"Sure did. They were here rooting for their picks in the Crashed Ice races."

"Any idea what time they arrived?" Martin asked.

"A while before the races began, I think. I can't be more specific."

"Do you remember where they sat?" Martin searched for details.

"See the TV over there, to your right?" She tilted her head in that direction. "They planted themselves in front of it. They carried on so, it gave me a headache."

"Any idea who waited on them?" Martin asked.

"That's usually Bev's station, and I think it was last night."

"Is Bev here now?" Martin asked.

"Yes. Want to talk to her?"

"Please."

A woman with a nametag asserting she was Bev wound her way from the back of the restaurant and approached Martin and Pete. Pete showed Bev the photos and asked if she'd ever seen the two men.

"Yes. I understand you're wondering about last night."

"That's right," Pete said. "Did you wait on them last night?"

"Sure did. They were enthralled by the races. They must have been happy with the outcome. They left me a great tip!" She grinned.

"Any chance one or both left for a time during the races?" Pete asked.

"Both? Definitely not. They'd have lost their spot. One of them? Maybe. I spent the night concentrating on who needed to place an order or get a refill. Do you have any idea how busy we were last night? I spent the whole night running."

"Do security cameras monitor the exits?" Martin asked.

"Not that I know of. You have to ask the manager."

"Is the manager here now?"

"Not for at least another hour."

Walking back to the car, Pete said, "Let's return to JD's neighborhood and talk to his neighbors. There was a time when everyone knew their neighbors. Unfortunately, that's no longer the case. Even so, let's give it a try."

"Tell me what's happening with your wedding plans," Martin said on the way. "Did you decide on a destination wedding? It's the rage."

"I'm grateful Katie doesn't feel compelled to have the wedding of the century."

"Come on, Pete. It's no longer such a big deal. We're well into the twenty-first century. Anyway, if she wants a destination wedding, she may be sacrificing her dreams to avoid driving you away."

"You're right, Martin, that would send me running. She might relish a destination wedding, but it's impractical for our families. And my grandma might not be up to it. I won't consider anything that makes it difficult or impossible for her to attend."

"Your relationship with your grandmother is wonderful. Do you ever think about life without her?"

"It sometimes crosses my mind after we've had an especially nice day together, like when she shares family stories with me. I think about a time when that won't be possible and have to stop myself before it drags me down. I tell myself to enjoy what I have for as long as I have it and not let the inevitable depress me. There will be plenty of time for that after she's gone."

"If you're like me, Pete, that's not always easy to do."

"True. We have that in common. Who do you worry about?"

"Michelle, especially after she got so ill and our efforts to find a cure seemed so futile. I'm more optimistic now, but since a cure is still a ways down the road, it's difficult to be confident she'll ever again be the person I married. I also worry about my parents and the kids. Every time Marty or Olivia is ill, I'm totally stressed, because usually I can do little but let it run its course. Back to your wedding plans, so far all you've told me is what it won't be."

"It will be a church wedding. The wedding and reception will be in the Twin Cities and accessible via bus or light rail and a reasonable walk. I believe Katie finalized the location, but that's not my department. The registries were finalized. That, at least in part, is my responsibility. And I'm invited. I think that's about the extent of it."

"Accessible via bus or light rail, huh? Is the reason for that spelled D-o-c?"

Martin referred to a homeless man who had helped them solve a case a few years back. The victim had been homeless. Pete had befriended Doc and maintained sporadic contact.

"I'm impressed, Martin, and yes."

"Do you think he'll come?"

"I hope so. He'll definitely be invited."

"He might not come if he doesn't have the right clothes."

"I plan to offer to take him shopping. If he comes, I'd love to introduce him to Grandma."

"Surely you're not talking about turning into a matchmaker?"

"That wouldn't be the goal, but if they hit it off, I'd be happy for both of them. She could be just what he needs to move beyond whatever it is that drove him to homelessness."

"He still hasn't told you?"

"No. I've given him the opportunity, but I'll never push."

"Back to your wedding. There's at least one other thing that is either your department or a joint decision. Where are you going on your honeymoon?"

"Either her house or mine. I haven't finalized that yet, since we won't need to book it very far in advance."

"I hope you're kidding, Pete."

"I am. I want to surprise Katie. I've been thinking about my conversations with her. About the places she's been and loved and the places she'd like to go. If we were getting married between December and March, I'd book it out west at a ski resort. Probably Jackson Hole in Wyoming or Winter Park in Colorado. We could go to either location in May and go hiking, but I'd spend the time wishing there was snow. I'm thinking maybe Costa Rica or Hawaii."

"Both sound great, but Hawaii's a mighty long flight. Are you and Katie both able to sleep on an airplane?"

"I am. Not sure about Katie. I've never flown with her. Perhaps I should find a surreptitious way to get the answer."

"Unless you want her to spend the first whole day in bed .... Never mind." Martin chuckled as the red worked its way from Pete's neck to his face. "Why Katie, Pete? What drew you to her?"

"Her brain," he told Martin. "She's so intelligent, so knowledgeable. And her heart. The heart beating inside her slender, athletic frame is so kind, generous, forgiving, and loving. I'm so lucky I met her, so lucky she puts up with my schedule and all that being engaged to me entails."

Pulling onto JD's street, both investigators noted the Forensic Services van still parked in front of his house. In the daylight, they got a better look at JD's neighborhood. Before canvassing the neighborhood, they signed in and ducked under the crime scene tape for the second time that day. Entering the home, they located the sergeant. He had good news. "We found a Christmas card and a birthday card. Both were signed 'Mom.'"

"Tell me they were in the envelopes and there was a return address on the envelopes."

"They were in the envelopes and there was a return address on the envelopes."

"Really?"

"No, but that's what you instructed me to say."

Pete's smile faded.

"However," the sergeant continued, "the Christmas card was in an envelope with the return address. The envelope is over on the desk. I have a photo of it, but you might as well take your own, saving me having to forward mine."

"Was there a message or just the signature?" Martin asked.

"There was a message. It said something like, 'Miss you, son. Please call! Better yet, come for a visit.'"

The name on the return address label was not the name of the person they suspected had a personal relationship with JD..

TWENTY-THREE

Pete and Martin exited JD's house. Martin pulled his stocking cap down over his ears. "Do you want this side of the street or the other side?" he asked. "The Vikings aren't in town, so if any of JD's neighbors have the same livelihood, at least a game won't have them out and about."

"You take this side. Let's do this block and the one on either side of it. We can meet inside JD's once we finish. No sense waiting in a frigid car. Good luck."

Pete walked to the corner, crossed the street, and went right another block to start at the beginning of his tour. He hoped the people who came to the door invited him in, rather than talking through the storm door. That was not an option at the first two homes. No one came to the door. Pete wondered if people were out getting groceries in preparation for the Vikings-Eagles playoff game later today. Thankfully, the pattern didn't persist.

At the next home, a girl who stood waist high answered the door. In response to Pete's request to speak to her mom or dad, she stood in place and yelled, "Daddy! Mommy!"

Her voice was so shrill, Pete wished he was wearing a stocking cap.

Seconds later, a petite woman wearing oversized sweats and a headband over short, curly brown hair approached. The first thing she did was invite Pete in. "You should be wearing a stocking cap ..., or better yet a facemask," she told him. Then she squatted down face to face with the child and said, "Amy, how many times have I told you *not* to use your outside voice in the house?"

"Sorry she subjected you to that," she said, standing and looking up at Pete. Smiling, she added, "What can I do for you?"

Pete pulled out his badge and ID and showed them to her. "You may have noticed department vehicles parked on the next block. We're investigating a murder."

"Are you talking about the one at Crashed Ice? I heard about it."

"Do you know most of your neighbors?"

"Most, but not all."

"Going east, on the next block, other side of the street, do you know the man in the second house from the corner?"

The woman concentrated on the ceiling for a few moments. "Sorry, just picturing the house. You said east of us, one block and two houses, right? The gray Cape Cod with dark gray peaks and white trim?"

Pete nodded.

"Sorry, I know he moved in last August, but I haven't met him."

Doing his best to find a politically correct way to ask the next question, Pete said, "I don't know your marital status or if you have a significant other. If so, might he or she have known this neighbor?"

The woman smiled. "I have a husband, and I know he's far less likely to know any of our neighbors than I. He's always working."

With three exceptions, Pete got a comparable reception at all the homes where someone answered the door.

The man who lived directly across the street from JD was unhappy about the lack of street parking, due to the "ruckus" across the street. "Are they leaving soon?" he asked. "I have friends coming over to watch the Vikes."

"All I can tell you is they're doing their best to wrap it up. Did you know the guy who lived there?"

"Not well. I invited him over a few times to watch Vikings games, Wolves games, and Wild games. He must have season tickets for every Minnesota team. He was only available for away games. I think he attended every home game for every team."

"Did he ever have friends over?"

"I don't spend a lot of time looking out the front window, but I never saw anyone go to his house or come home with him. That's why I invited him over."

"What kind of guy was he?"

"Quiet. Very quiet. Strangely enough, he never seemed that interested in the few games he watched with me. It seemed a little crazy for a guy with season tickets. He was always polite, respectful to my wife, stuff like that. He never invited me to his house. That struck me as odd. I don't know what he did for a living. He usually left in the late afternoon, and I have no idea when he returned. I base all of this on when I saw the lights off and on over there. From that perspective and only that perspective, it helps that the sun sets so early during the winter. I can't wait for daylight savings. Joe didn't seem to work the same days each week. I never saw any pattern ... but I didn't really try.

If the elderly woman next door had a porch with a rocking chair, and if Joe had lived there all summer, she could probably be more helpful." He smiled and shrugged.

A short, stocky, elderly woman wearing an emerald-green, velour running suit and a white turtleneck answered the next door, but added nothing of value to the picture under development. She told Pete she used to know all her neighbors. Not now. "No one talks to anyone," she complained. "On two different occasions I took fresh-baked cookies over to that man. He said thanks and that was it. He didn't invite me in, and he didn't write a thank-you note. The only activity I see over there is the turning off and on of lights."

Pete wondered if she was lonely. It seemed likely. He hated to see it, especially in the elderly.

The next neighbor had a slightly different angle. "I didn't know him from Adam, but I was out front on the street one afternoon, stuck in the snow, and spinning my tires. I got out of my car a half-dozen times to spread dirt and shovel. He must have heard me, because he came over and told me I had to rock the car. He said as soon as the tires started spinning to stop and go from forward to reverse and vice versa. Each time I put it in forward, he pushed from behind."

The neighbor shook his head. "I'd probably still be stuck there if it wasn't for him. I asked him in for a beer. He's really shy. If he wasn't answering one of my questions, he had nothing to say. When he answered a question, it was usually 'yes' or 'no.' I asked what he did for a living, and he said, 'A little of this and a little of that.' I told him if he was looking for a change, I might be able to help. Figured I owed him. He said he was set for now but would let me know if that changed. After that, he always waved and said 'hi' when I saw him, but we never got together, again. I think he was a real loner. Why are the cops at his house?"

"Sorry, no comment."

Pete now had a sketchy picture of JD. He wondered if it was skewed. Would they succeed in meeting with the guy's mom? If so, what would they learn? Would it affirm or conflict with this information?

Walking back to join Martin, he again wondered about the person who appeared to have a connection with the victim. Was it another family member? An ex-girlfriend? Did he ever date? If so, did it have anything to do with the path his life took?

His cellphone vibrated, interrupting his thoughts. He waited until he reached JD's to determine why. It was Forensics, just not the people working JD's house. A text informed him a person they'd suspected had a personal connection with JD called every hour for the past four hours. Prior to the first call, someone texted him with the same frequency. Since they no longer had access to his phone, they couldn't determine the name or number for that person. Obviously, the texts he and Martin sent got someone's attention. Pete was reading that message when Martin arrived.

After they'd settled in the unmarked car and he'd started the engine, Martin shared his findings. His canvassing benefited from dealing with neighbors living on the same side of the street as JD. Those nearby could see JD's garage and any traffic between the garage and the house—which didn't necessarily mean they would. The only helpful information came from the woman whose house sat on JD's east side.

"Here's what she said. JD moved in around the middle of August. He hadn't been there long before he brought a girl home. She'd thought about calling the police but thought it might be perfectly innocent. The girl seemed to willingly accompany him. She was there for barely more than a week, then she didn't see that girl again. Before long there was a new girl. She again saw them coming and going for about a week, then she didn't see that girl again either. It was more than a month before it happened a third time. She decided the next time it happened she'd call the police. Well, as you and I know, JD took the third girl, Megan, right to the apartment, and by all indications stopped after Alyssa ... or at least had yet to expand beyond four girls."

"Too bad she didn't follow her instincts and call the police when she saw him with Ella," Pete said. "Let's go talk to JD's mother."

TWENTY-FOUR

"I'm dreading this next interview," Pete said. "Sharing the news about a deceased family member is hard."

"I agree. It's one of the hardest things about this job."

"I wonder if she knows what he's been doing," Pete said.

"Or why he was doing it."

"Hope she can tell us about his friends and how to reach them."

The good news is the unmarked was warming up, so the trip via I-35E was comfortable.

Some Minnesotans claim the state has two seasons—winter and the Fourth of July. Others judge it by the months with a possibility of snow. In that case, it includes every month but July. Measurable snow has been recorded as late as June 4 and as early as August 31st.

Martin was thinking winter—and longing for spring—on the way. "Did you see we're supposed to get dumped on again tonight? They're predicting another six to nine inches."

"I haven't seen the news, much less the weather, or checked the app. Since there's nothing we can do about it, like stay home, it's rarely a priority. Sometimes it's better not to know."

JD's mom, Sylvia Brooten, lived in a villa home in Vadnais Heights, a suburb north of St. Paul. There were four attractive groupings of brick with vinyl siding linked homes. The unit of interest was beige with chocolate-brown shutters and white trim. Brick ran under the windows and surrounded the front door and double garage.

It took two attempts with a lengthy interlude for the late middle-aged woman wearing a USC sweatshirt, tight-fitting jeans, and slippers to answer the door. Reading glasses clung to the end of her nose, and the slightly askew placement revealed she wore a wig. She kept the storm door closed and locked while learning the identity of the two strangers. Thankfully, once that was accomplished, she unlocked the door and invited them in.

They followed her into the family room. An area rug in shades of green and brown ran almost baseboard to baseboard, protecting the hardwood floors. Two groupings of upholstered chairs and a couch, covered in flowered and plaid fabrics, filled the room.

Sylvia led them to one of the groupings and asked the reason for their visit.

"I regret to inform you, Ms. Brooten," Pete said, "your son Josiah was murdered last night."

"Oh my God, no! Are you sure? Who identified him?"

"We used his driver's license and car registration," Pete said. "We know its Josiah."

Sylvia covered her face with shaking hands.

Pete and Martin gave her time to deal with the news. They sat patiently until she looked up.

"Who would do such a thing? Who could possibly hate Josiah that much?"

"That's what we're trying to determine," Martin said. "We hope you'll help by providing information about your son."

"What would you like to know?" she said with a shaky voice.

"When was the last time you saw him?"

"It's been a little over two years. I've tried and tried to reach him. He refused to answer or respond to my calls or texts. I got his address through a Google search. Went to his place twice. If he was home, he didn't answer the door." She used a sweatshirt sleeve to dry her eyes.

"Do you have any other children?" Pete asked.

"No," she moaned. "We tried for years, but I guess it wasn't meant to be. Now I have none," she sobbed.

"What was he like as a child?" Pete asked.

"Josiah was a strong introvert. His dad died when he was nine. When that happened, for a couple of years he shut himself off. Then Danny moved in a couple of houses away. They were in the same grade and same class. Somehow Danny penetrated the shell that had separated Josiah from everyone but me." Sylvia shook her head. "They became best friends. Josiah started doing things again. I was so grateful." Sylvia sighed. "In the end, I wasn't sure if Danny was a good thing or a bad thing."

"Why is that?" Martin asked.

"Josiah never dated in high school or college. Thanks to Danny, in his mid-thirties he met a woman ten years younger than him and fell in love. I didn't like her. She treated Josiah like a trained puppy. She said jump, and he asked how high. I tried introducing him to other women, but it was like he was attached to Tiffany at the hip. Things moved too fast. They dated for about nine months and got engaged, spent months planning their wedding, and she left him at the altar. Literally. It destroyed him. I couldn't get him out of bed. He lost the job he'd had for fifteen years."

"After several months of that," she continued, "I told him he had to pull himself together and get a job. I thought I was doing the right thing. Tough love, you know." She again blotted her tears with her sweatshirt. "Unfortunately, I harped on it until he packed his stuff and left. I wasn't here when he took off. Not sure I could have or would have stopped him. I was pretty exasperated, and I did a poor job of hiding it. I blame Tiffany, and I blame myself. I should have handled it better. It's curious how much clearer things are in retrospect. After he moved out, and when I could no longer reach him, I started beating myself up for being so impatient."

"You can't blame yourself," Pete said. "It sounds like you were doing your best to help him put his life back together."

Sylvia sniffed. "That's what I thought at the time, but I was obviously wrong." She excused herself and returned with a handful of tissues.

"What's Tiffany's last name?" Pete asked.

"Rice. Who would think something as seemingly innocuous as rice could cause such trouble, huh?"

"Do you have Tiffany's phone number?" Pete asked.

"Actually, I do. It's been years, but I never take the time to update my contacts. There was a time when my chances of reaching Josiah were much better if I went through her." Sylvia retrieved her phone and gave them the number.

"What did your son do for a living?" Pete asked.

"I assume you mean before Tiffany destroyed him?"

Pete nodded.

"He was an accountant at Simpson Accounting. It's a small firm in White Bear Lake."

"Did he have any friends there?" Pete asked, planning to check for himself.

"I don't think so. There were only two other people. To the best of my knowledge, he never did anything with either of them. I know he didn't invite them to his wedding." Sylvia blotted the tears that continued welling up and running down her cheeks.

"Did he ever mention their names?" Pete asked.

"I don't think so. If he did, I don't remember them."

"Can you give us the names of any of your son's other friends?" Martin asked.

"I only knew about Danny. Like I said, Josiah was an introvert. A strong introvert. Maybe even an extreme introvert."

"What's Danny's last name?" Pete asked.

"Jackson."

"Do you know where Danny lives or works, or have a way to contact him?" Pete asked.

Sylvia shook her head.

"Josiah never added Danny to my contacts."

"Does his family still live in the neighborhood?" Pete asked.

"Josiah and I lived in a different neighborhood back then."

"Have you stayed in contact with his family or do you know where they now live?" Pete persisted.

"If they moved, I never heard about it. I'm still in touch with a few former neighbors, but not the Jacksons."

Pete and Martin got the address for the home in North Oaks.

"Losing a dad can be mighty tough on a kid," Pete said, walking back to the unmarked. "Danny could be instrumental in solving this case. But for now, Tiffany is our top priority."

TWENTY-FIVE

Pete scanned for the phone number Sylvia provided for Tiffany in the list of JD's contacts.

"I agree," Martin said. "Tiffany Rice now tops the list. What did you find, Pete? Is she one of JD's contacts? Is she the person who appeared to be close to him?"

"Yup, and by all indications she responded to my call by texting and calling JD. Danny Jackson is also one of his contacts."

"What makes you think Tiffany will answer if you call again?"

"I'll text first, saying, 'You've tried desperately to reach JD. Call for info.' I hope that does it."

Rather than sitting in front of Sylvia's home, Martin used GPS to get directions to what at least had been Danny Jackson's parents' home in North Oaks.

Before he could put the car in gear, Pete's cell vibrated.

"Culnane," Pete answered.

"Who are you and what's going on with Joe?" a female-sounding voice demanded.

"Before I answer your questions, I have a few of my own."

"And why would I answer your questions?"

"Because that's the only way I'll answer yours."

"First, at least tell me Joe is okay."

"When's the last time you saw him?" Pete asked.

"At our rehearsal dinner. He and I were supposed to get married."

"So it didn't happen?"

"Correct, and I haven't stopped regretting it."

Pete heard a deep sigh.

"Who opted out, you or Joe?" he asked.

"Me," she whined.

"Why?"

"Do we really need to go into all this? What purpose can it possibly serve?"

"It's helping me understand him."

"I could say cold feet, but that would be a lie. A couple of weeks before our wedding, I met a guy who swept me off my feet. It took months for me to discover how stupid I'd been. I went to see Joe's mom. She told me he'd been there but moved out. She said she didn't know where he was. I texted and called, and texted and called. I must have tried to reach him a hundred times. I mean literally, one hundred. I even called Danny. He refused to help me reach Joe. He said he wouldn't give me another opportunity to hurt Joe. Now please, tell me how to reach Joe."

"Do you know where Danny is living?"

"No. All I have is a phone number."

Pete wrote the number in the small spiral notebook in which he saved these details.

"What does Danny do for a living?"

"He manages a restaurant in downtown St. Paul."

"What's the name of the restaurant?"

"The Hub."

"Do you and Danny still have any friends in common?"

"Just one."

"And who is that?"

"Rob."

"Last name?"

"Foley."

"Do you have an address and phone number for Rob?"

Pete wrote down the address and phone number and asked what Rob did for a living.

"He works for his dad."

"Doing?"

"It's a heating and air conditioning business. I think he does it all. Answers the phone, makes service calls, whatever. I think he's in the process of buying the company from his dad. At least he was."

"Had you and Joe rented an apartment?"

"No, he bought a house for us in Stillwater. It would have been an easy commute for me. I went there several times, hoping to find him. After many months I finally got up the courage to knock. Found out he'd sold it, so I gave up."

Pete shared the scant details about Joe with Tiffany and told her he's investigating the case. He wasn't surprised by her reaction.

After disconnecting, he told Martin the other side of the conversation and said, "Let's stay put until I try to reach Danny." He entered the phone number.

TWENTY-SIX

It came as no surprise to either investigator when Danny didn't answer the phone. The same outcome met Pete's attempt to reach Rob. At least they had an address for Rob. However, since they were in the vicinity of Danny's parents' home—or former home—they started there. Martin followed city streets most of the way, and in about five minutes they reached their destination.

In 1883, Great Northern Railroad baron James J. Hill began developing North Oaks farm. It was an experimental farm and country estate on five thousand acres north of St. Paul. For the first ten years, this farm was Hill's base for his efforts to breed dual-purpose cows that provided beef and produced milk.

After his son Lewis died in 1950, Lewis's children converted the farm into a residential community focusing on preservation of the natural environment. North Oaks is privately owned. All services, including roads, are provided by the homeowner's association. Law enforcement is provided by contract with the Ramsey County Sheriff.

The sign at the entrance said, "Enter by Invitation Only." Most of the homes are wood and brick, single-story, ranch-style in natural browns, grays, and beiges so it helps them blend into the surroundings. Entering this neighborhood felt more like entering the woods.

Two-lane winding roads that don't include a center line connect the homes to each other and the outside world. An occasional "Turtle Crossing" sign, posted in all seriousness, often brings a smile to a first-time visitor.

Due to the curved roads, Martin was even more thankful than usual for GPS. He found the address provided by JD's mom and parked on the street. The driveway consisted of pavers that, unlike the driveways of some of the neighbors, had no trace of snow or ice. "Wonder if I can get whoever is responsible for this to clear my driveway each time it snows," Martin said.

"And miss out on all that exercise? You're kidding, right?"

"Wrong, but until I attain your rank, it won't fit in our budget."

The two investigators made it a quick trip up the driveway, hoping to find a warm place to ask a few questions. They did, but that didn't help their cause. Danny's parents no longer lived there. The current residents had been there almost two years and had no idea where the previous owners now lived. "If we were buying the place on a contract for deed, I might be able to help you," the man who answered the door said. "Unfortunately, that's not the case." But he furnished the name of his real estate agent and her work and cellphone numbers, in case follow-up paperwork had required the seller's address.

"Mighty accommodating," Pete told Martin on the way back to the unmarked car.

But searching for Rob became the next priority. Pete called the real estate agent, while Martin drove to Rob's home ... or at least the address that had been his. That took them south on I-35E, then west on I-694, the northern bypass for I-94.

The real estate agent answered her cell and was helpful.

Pete gave her the address for the house she'd sold and the name of the purchaser, and she checked her records. She didn't have an address for the Jacksons. "However, if you're interested, I have a couple of lovely homes that are priced to sell. Can I show you a few great deals?"

"Not at this time, but I have your number, in case I change my mind." If she was talking North Oaks, Pete would love to live there but that wasn't in the cards. Not even if the home was a steal.

Like the homes in North Oaks, the homes in Rob's neighborhood— or former neighborhood—were primarily ranch-style circa the 1970s, but that's where the similarities ended. The Shoreview lots were less than half the size, and the vegetation wasn't nearly as fetching. On the other hand, the lots and homes were significantly larger than JD's. The homes had been here long enough to have sizeable trees, most of which were deciduous, hence adding only shades of brown to the scenery for several more months. An occasional blue spruce broke the monotony. By all indications, the resident was home. Cars filled the driveway and were parked bumper-to-bumper on the street, extending past two neighboring homes in both directions and on both sides.

"Think they gathered for a playoff party?" Martin asked and parked a few additional doors down from the house of interest.

The two investigators made the trek back to that house, and Martin rang the doorbell. Based on the level of noise escaping the house and attacking the ears of the two investigators, whatever the occasion the party had already begun. When the doorbell failed to elicit a response, Martin pounded on the door and yelled, "Police. Open up." As he prepared to repeat the process, the door opened.

An average-height man with a receding hairline and jowls, who appeared to be JD's contemporary, looked questioningly at Martin and Pete. After looking at their badges and IDs, he said, "You've got to be kidding. We aren't that loud. Don't tell me a neighbor called the cops."

"That's not why we're here," Martin said. "Are you Rob Foley?"

"Yes, so?"

"We need a few minutes of your time ... and privacy. Our car might be the best location. Grab a jacket."

"This doesn't sound like an emergency. Can't it wait?"

"We'll wait only long enough for you to get a jacket," Martin said in his most officious voice.

Rob rolled his eyes and spun around. He returned a minute later, wearing a jacket, and exited a much quieter house. He followed the two investigators past a string of cars to the unmarked, grumbling all the way. Once Rob occupied the back seat, Pete took the first turn, asking, "What do you do for a living, Rob?"

"I work at my dad's heating and air conditioning business."

"How do you know Danny Jackson?"

"I did a job for him."

"How long ago was that?"

"About four years."

"Does he still live in that house?"

"Yes, so what?"

Martin took a turn. "What's the address?"

"I'm not sure I'm allowed to tell you. There might be privacy requirements or something."

Martin shrugged. "If you prefer, we'll continue the questioning at headquarters."

"Wait a minute. Let's not get crazy. He lives in Falcon Heights, a few blocks off Snelling." Rob rattled off the address.

"How often do you see him?"

"Not often," Rob said. "I work weekdays, and his hours are mostly nights and weekends."

"What does he do for a living?"

"He manages a restaurant."

"What restaurant?"

"The Hub."

"I understand you and Josiah St. Peter are also friends," Pete said.

"Who?"

"Josiah, JD, Joe. Different people refer to him by different names."

"Never heard of the guy."

"JD and Danny are good friends. I'm surprised Danny hasn't mentioned him."

Rob responded with a hands-up shrug.

"Ever hang out at The Hub?"

"Rarely."

"Ever see this guy there?" Martin asked, showing Rob JD's driver's license photo.

"If I did, I don't remember him."

"He might have been hanging around with several young girls."

"I may have seen someone like that. Can't be sure."

"Where were you last night between seven and eleven?" Pete asked.

"I was home the whole time."

"Can anyone vouch for that?"

"I need an alibi? My wife and my two kids. My son begged me to take him to Crashed Ice, but I'm not crazy enough to do anything outdoors in this weather."

"Is your wife home?" Pete asked.

"Yes."

"Okay, that's all for now, except we need to speak with your wife."

"You're going to drag her out here too?"

"Can't say for sure, but that may not be necessary. Got your cell?"

"Yeah."

"Call your wife. Tell her to meet us in the garage," Martin said.

Pete and Martin refused to give Rob an opportunity to confer with his wife in their absence, lest he be inclined to cement his alibi before she spoke with them.

Rob called his wife. The call went to voicemail. He rubbed his neck. "That was her cell. I'll try our home phone."

A smile told Pete and Martin this phone was answered. It was also obvious Rob's wife hadn't answered it. He asked for Julie and waited more than a minute before saying, "Honey, a couple of cops want to talk to you. Grab a jacket, hat, and mittens. We'll meet you in the garage."

A woman, bundled up well enough to withstand the temperatures at last night's races, stepped into the garage.

"We won't need you again, at least for now," Martin said, excusing Rob.

"I think I should stay. Julie, would you like me to stay?"

"If she needs you, you won't be far away. Thanks for your help," Martin said.

Rob grunted and left his wife to fend for herself.

As soon as he closed the door behind him, Martin asked, "Where were you last night between seven and eleven?"

"Why?"

"We're conducting an investigation. Asking these questions of a lot of people," Martin said.

"I was home until 7:30 or so. Then I went to a movie and a bar with friends. Girls night out."

"So you didn't go to Crashed Ice with Rob?" Martin continued.

"I'm quite sure Rob didn't go ... unless our son Hamilton talked him into it. No, he couldn't have. If he had, I'd have heard all about it when I got home."

"How old is Hamilton?"

"Fifteen."

"And you also have a daughter?" Martin asked.

"Yes, Lily."

"Age?"

"Seventeen."

"We'd like to talk to Hamilton," Pete said.

"He isn't here right now. Want him to call you?"

"Does he have a cell?"

"Perhaps next year, depending on his grades."

"Do you remember Rob's friend JD, who also goes by Joe St. Peter?" Pete asked.

"No, but that's not unusual. Rob has his friends. I have mine. I have a group of friends he doesn't do things with and vice versa."

Pete handed her a business card. "Please ask Hamilton to call first opportunity he gets. Meanwhile, is your daughter home?"

"No. The kids try to avoid their father's gatherings at all costs." She chuckled.

"Does she have a cell?" Pete asked.

"Yes."

"Since she isn't likely to answer if I call, please call her either from your cell or a cordless," Pete said.

Without a word, Julie walked to the door, opened it, and disappeared. Before Pete and Martin had time to worry about it, she returned with a cordless, used her teeth to pull off a glove, and dialed.

When her daughter answered, she said, "Lily, a couple of policemen are at the house. They have a few questions for you. Hold on." She handed the phone to Pete.

Like her mother, Lily asked why Pete was asking her questions. Like her mother, she settled for the vague answer. She told Pete she, her dad, and her brother were home last night during the hours in question.

Returning to the unmarked, Pete asked, "Getting hungry?"

"I can count on one hand the number of times you've asked. What's up?"

"I think we should check out the food at The Hub and hopefully bump into Danny. Rob said he works weekends. Convenient, huh?"

TWENTY-SEVEN

Thanks to it being winter, the swarms of locals returning from their cottages in northern Minnesota moved mostly faster than a crawl this Sunday afternoon. The season narrowed it down to those with year-round places, especially those into snowmobiling and cross-country skiing. That helped.

Before long, the two investigators sat in a booth with padded seats and a red-and-white checkered tablecloth that masked the composition of the tabletop. The light fixtures hung few and far between, but the windows provided ample lighting since the sun wouldn't set for another thirty minutes.

"Better check the menu before sundown," Martin suggested, "unless you're carrying a flashlight."

Pete snapped his fingers. "Left it in the car with my nightstick."

The menu offered a little something for everyone.

When their waitress showed, Martin ordered a cheeseburger, fries, and a Coke.

Pete ordered broiled salmon, a salad, and water.

Sure, rub it in, Martin thought.

"By the way," Pete asked their waitress, "is the manager in?"

"Last I knew." She smiled. "Let me check."

"Don't you think we should have eaten before you asked?" Martin said. "I'd hate to get thrown out before I eat."

"Then put on your best manners and try not to be your usual obnoxious self." Pete laughed.

They didn't see the waitress again until she delivered the food. When she didn't say anything, Pete said, "You were going to see if the manager's here?"

"Oh, that's right. We're short-staffed. I forgot all about it. I'll check right now."

The first mouthful sent Pete's taste buds dancing, and this persisted until he'd finished.

"How's the burger?" he asked Martin.

"One of the best I've ever eaten. I'm amazed we've never heard of this place."

"You know cops. We have our hangouts, and that's where everyone goes."

Pete had no more than uttered the words when a man headed their way. He was average height and trim, with thinning brown hair and a goatee, close-set brown eyes and horn-rimmed glasses.

Seeing him approach reminded Pete of his first reaction to The Hub. He'd wished they had tables as well as booths. A booth was harder to spring from. Just in case, he repositioned himself on the edge of the bench, then hid his intent by standing when the man arrived.

Martin followed suit.

Extending a hand, Pete said, "Are you the manager?"

"Yes. Is something wrong?"

"Nothing. The food is great." Pete introduced himself and Martin. "I'm glad we found you," he said. "We have a few questions, regarding a case we're working. I understand you and Josiah St. Peter were good friends."

"I'm glad you used the past tense. It's been a while."

"When's the last time you saw him?" Pete asked.

"Last summer. Definitely before Labor Day. Definitely before the State Fair. It might have been in July."

"You'd been good friends since you were kids. What changed?" Pete asked.

"Joe changed." Danny shook his head. "It got so I couldn't stand to be around him."

"How did he change?"

"It started two years earlier when his fiancée dumped him. Don't get me wrong. He was devastated, and I understood. It took months for him to haul his butt out of bed. He almost lost the house he'd bought for himself and Tiffany, his fiancée. He was always close with a buck. He used every penny he'd saved and paid cash. Sorry, I'm rambling ... wasting your time. The whole thing still bugs me." Danny scratched his goatee.

"Please continue," Pete said.

Danny shrugged and said, "I think the only reason he eventually got out of bed was the realization he was on the verge of losing that house, due to the second mortgage he got for the repairs. It was a fixer upper. He and Tiffany did a lot of remodeling. They both did the work, and she did the decorating. For that reason, he couldn't walk into that house again. Her name was written on the walls, floors, furnishings ... figuratively speaking, of course."

"Joe put the house on the market. Thanks to the work they'd done, he got back everything he'd paid and ended up another twenty grand to the good. Most people would rejoice. Joe became even more bitter. I thought maybe because he'd fallen in love with that house. I never found out. He refused to talk about it ... or anything else."

"Ultimately his anger and bitterness doomed our friendship." Danny shook his head. "He refused to move on. I was his only friend. We couldn't do anything with my other friends. Joe drove them away. One day I told him he needed to get laid. I actually thought it might help," Danny sighed. "After screaming every expletive in the book, he told me in revolting detail what he'd do the next time he was alone with a woman. He made me sick. I considered calling the police, but what would I report? I was afraid a friend was going to hurt a woman? No woman in particular, just some woman?"

"Joe became angry, bitter, cantankerous, vengeful, ruthless. I saw it in everything he said and did. With time, he got worse rather than better. He no longer bore any resemblance to the kid I befriended. The last time I was with him, if I had to describe him in one word it would be evil. I couldn't stand to be around him anymore. I told him I never wanted to see or talk to him again. I told him he better not come here looking for me. I said if he did, I'd call the cops."

"He lost his job after his fiancée walked, correct?" Martin asked. Danny nodded.

"Did he get a job once he got moving again?" Martin asked.

"He spent months trying to land a job as an accountant. He failed time and again. He had the credentials. The only thing I can think of is his personality shone through, and no employer wanted to deal with it. That of course fueled his anger and his hatred for Tiffany ... for all women. Suddenly everything was someone else's fault."

"Where did he live and what did he do for food, stuff like that?" Martin asked.

"I felt sorry for him, so I let him stay with me for almost a year. His car was paid off. During much of that time, he leeched off me. I don't know where he got the money to buy the few things he got. He may have been panhandling or shoplifting. By then, neither would have surprised me." Danny paused and scratched his chin.

"About a year ago, he got into sports betting, and he spent a lot of time at the casinos. Last I knew he was scraping by, but barely."

"Did he run through the money he got from the sale of the house he'd renovated?" Pete asked.

"I'd be shocked if he touched a penny of it. I know he didn't while he stayed with me."

"Why would you let him sponge off you when he had all that money?" Pete asked.

"It sounds crazy, but he was so screwed up. I wanted to help."

"Why would he shoplift or panhandle rather than spend some of that money?" Pete tried to understand.

"That became his 'house money.' He told me he was going to show Tiffany by buying a far better house than the last one. He refused to spend it on anything else. Once he got an idea like that in his head, there was no changing his mind. I'm no psychologist, but maybe he had obsessive compulsive disorder. Anyway, before we parted, he started looking for a house."

"He wouldn't even use that money if it meant not eating?" Pete asked.

"Absolutely not. If things got really tough, he could borrow money. The good news is, aside from gambling, he wasn't much of a spender."

"Did he borrow money from you, Danny?"

Danny sighed and bit his lip, "Yeah."

"A significant sum?"

"Yeah. That was before I kicked him out and before he became so bent on getting even with the world. It was back when I still believed he'd land a job."

"Did he repay you?"

Danny bit his lip and shook his head.

"And you wrote him off despite that unpaid debt?"

"Yeah. I had two choices. I could let him owe me money and drag me down, or I could cut my losses by getting him out of my life."

"Have you heard from Joe since you told him the two of you were finished?" Martin asked.

"No. In Joe's way of thinking, contacting me would mean he's weak. He wanted to be in control. He made an exception with Tiff. She was his first girlfriend, and he had no idea how to deal with a woman. She was happy to take the lead, and he was so enthralled with her he permitted it. When she walked, he went over the edge and became a total control freak. I think that's why he didn't date after Tiff. He wasn't confident enough around women to take the lead, and dating would mean putting himself out there."

"It also explains why he'd never again communicate with Tiff –no matter how much he wanted to get back together. He couldn't take the first step, and after what happened he could never again permit her to."

"Has he ever been in here?" Martin asked.

"After what I told him, I'd be amazed—unless he was out to prove something. If so, I didn't see him. I don't see everyone who walks in, you know."

"Where were you last night between seven and eleven?" Pete asked.

"Right here." Danny jabbed an index finger toward the floor. "The same place where I spend every Saturday night. Last night, due to Crashed Ice, we were even busier than usual. I loved the fact it was so cold. Things were jumping. People had to find a place to warm up. I heard a spectator was murdered. Is that why you're here? Was Joe that spectator?"

"With all the spectators at Crashed Ice, why would you think it was him?" Pete asked.

Danny shrugged. "I don't know. It just occurred to me that could be why you're asking all these questions."

"We can't release information about that person's identity before the family is notified," Pete said.

"Are you and Tiffany still friends?" Martin asked.

"No. I couldn't forgive her for destroying Joe."

"When's the last time you spoke with her?"

"Funny you should ask. Today. She called me because she got some strange message about Joe and couldn't reach him. I think she actually thought it might mean they could get together again."

"Would she like to?"

"She hasn't come right out and said it, but my money says yes."

"Did Joe like women?" Martin asked.

"As opposed to other men?"

"No, as opposed to disliking them," Martin clarified.

"He liked them from afar. Not very comfortable with them, but Tiff did a lot to change that ... at least temporarily. She taught him how to talk to a woman. She taught him what they want to hear."

Both investigators thanked Danny for his time, and waited for the bill. It appeared their waitress didn't want to interrupt Danny, because she arrived shortly after he left them and asked if they wanted dessert. Martin wanted to try the cheesecake but refrained.

When the waitress returned with the bill, Pete showed her a photo of JD and asked if she'd ever seen him at The Hub.

"The face is familiar, but I don't know if it's from here or not."

"If he came here, there might have been some young girls with him," Pete said.

"And he's an equal opportunity kind of guy? I mean every race is represented?"

"Did you work last night?" Martin asked, taking the reins.

"Yes, from six until closing."

"Was it busy?"

"And how!"

"Was the manager here last night?"

"Yes."

"Doing?"

"The usual, tending bar and intervening when a discussion got heated."

"Does the staff, including Danny, get regular breaks?"

"Yes."

"Do you know what Danny does on his breaks?"

"He usually goes back to his office or outside for a smoke."

"How often do you get breaks?" Pete moved into the driver's seat.

"One every four hours, but Danny isn't a stickler with us—or himself."

"I understand it wasn't a priority, but did you notice when he took breaks last night?"

"No. I had a job to do."

"What do you do on your breaks?"

"I go to the restroom and outside for a smoke."

"You go outside for a smoke on bitter cold nights like last night?"

"It's that or suffer from withdrawal."

"Do you remember when you took your breaks last night?"

"One break, around ten. That's about halfway through my shift."

"Did you grab a smoke?"

"Yeah. I really need to get back to work."

"Almost finished," Pete said. "Was Danny outside smoking when you were?"

"No. He came back in as I was going out."

"Do you take time to put on a jacket before going out for a smoke?"

"Not necessarily, but always in this weather."

"Last night, when you passed Danny on your way to take a break, was he wearing a jacket?"

"I'm not sure, but I assume so. Do you have any idea how cold it was last night?"

TWENTY-EIGHT

"Wow, if we can believe Danny, JD became a real piece of work," Martin said as he and Pete exited The Hub. "Murdering JD wouldn't get his money back. What would it do for Danny?"

"Consider this. Suppose JD didn't stay as distant as Danny demanded. Maybe that scared Danny or made him nervous. Danny said JD wanted to be in control. Sounds like JD was at The Hub with the girls. Did Danny lie? Did he see JD there? Was JD there taking charge or to prove something?"

"Another possibility," Pete continued. "Knowing he'd never see the money, he could have gotten a perverse pleasure from eliminating his former friend—a friend who had the money to reimburse him but didn't. A friend Danny went out of his way to help."

"Danny mentioned the text Tiffany received. We also texted him. Curious, or should I say suspicious he didn't mention that. He may have deleted the message without reading it. Or maybe he doesn't think we know he's on JD's contact list. Maybe he thinks we have numbers and no names. Maybe he thinks he can melt into the background."

Before returning to the unmarked car, Pete and Martin surveyed the street in front of The Hub and the two adjacent streets, looking skyward. They searched for city video cameras located on the street corners. Both investigators took note of the businesses with cameras visible on the outside of the buildings.

"What's next, Pete?" Martin asked as they slid over car seats that did a convincing imitation of blocks of ice.

"I assume you mean besides warming up the car." After determining they'd seen cameras on the same businesses, Pete contacted the watch commander and asked to have a patrol officer collect last night's footage from those businesses, as well as the footage from other businesses in the vicinity with cameras mounted inside the buildings. He also asked to post an officer in front of the apartment building wherethe girls lived. One or a few johns could drop by to see if the girls are still there. In the short term, at least until the victim's name is released, our person of interest might be the most likely to do that. I'm interested in the plate numbers of people who pull up, sit for a bit, and drive away without getting out or picking up anyone."

While Pete spoke to the watch commander, Martin contacted the Closed Circuit TV Unit (CCTV). He requested last night's street camera footage from nine until eleven for the cameras they'd identified. He and Pete hoped one or more of those cameras indicated if Danny settled for a smoke and stayed outside The Hub last night. It wouldn't have taken long for someone on a mission and knowing where to find JD to get to the Cathedral and back. Danny walked back in around ten o'clock. He'd definitely had time.

After hanging up, Pete said, "It will take some time to get the footage, so let's head to Crocus Hill."

"The girls no longer live there. What are you planning?"

"We might learn something useful from the girls' neighbors. Why don't you rate heated seats?" Pete asked as the chill of the car seats penetrated his trousers.

"You mean bun warmers?" Martin laughed. "How about you. Do you have them? If so, I'm happy switching to your car."

"Well no, but I don't think I'll ever buy another car without heated seats and a heated steering wheel. Both are great."

"And the winter lasts so long. But what if you have quintuplets next year and triplets a couple of years later?"

"I'd be thrilled. Katie probably less so. It would certainly alter our priorities." Pete smiled. "Did I tell you twins run in my family?"

Of the three residents who answered the doorbell, only one provided something useful. An elderly woman lived in the street-facing, ground-floor apartment two floors below the four girls. She came to the door in a bathrobe and slippers.

After learning they were police officers, she invited Pete and Martin in. "I'm Eleanor. Please excuse the way I'm dressed." Eleanor blushed and brushed the front of her bathrobe, trying to smooth any wrinkles. She didn't try that tactic with her face.

"I got up very early," she explained. "I had to prepare and deliver the readings at the 7:00 a.m. Mass. But don't worry. I wasn't going to bed. I just like to be ready, so I don't have to spend time when fatigue sets in." She offered them coffee and asked them to join her at the dining room table.

They followed her through the living room and into the dining room. By all appearances, Eleanor didn't have many more years under her belt than her furniture, but it appeared meticulously maintained.

Pete asked if she knew the four girls who lived above her.

"I rarely see them, but they're always polite when I do. They seem very young. It sounds unkind, but I wonder if they're prostitutes. Lots of men go up to the third floor. I know that's where they go. After the first week or so, I'd open my door and listen for the creaking step. I know the other people on that floor and everyone on the fourth floor. None of these men are visiting them. Besides, this didn't start until the girls moved in. First there was one girl. A few weeks later there were two, then three, then four."

"That would have been fine, but once the snowbanks appeared, these men regularly block the sidewalk connecting the main sidewalk to the street. When my daughter picks me up, I often have to walk way down the street to find a sidewalk that's open. When you're my age, you don't dare attempt to climb over the snowbanks. Thanks to the constant melting and refreezing, everything is coated with ice. I can't afford a broken hip. These bones aren't as strong as they once were."

Pete nodded. "I bet this isn't your favorite season."

"I'm counting the days until spring."

"Can you describe any of the men or their cars?" Martin asked.

"Yes, and I wrote down the license plate numbers, in case I get angry enough to call my council member ... or the police. My daughter said the police can't do anything about it. Is she right?"

"I'm afraid so," Martin said. "Even so, are you willing to share your list with us? We'd sure like to see it."

She walked to the desk that extended from her kitchen counter and opened the top drawer. Returning to the table, she handed a five by eight spiral notebook to Martin.

Pete stood, walked around the table, looking over Martin's shoulder. The first four pages contained neat columns that held the make, model, and license plate numbers for dozens of cars. Occasionally, a series of question marks filled the space otherwise occupied by the make and model. One space containing the license plate number had a small IL in parentheses.

"Does the IL stand for Illinois?" Martin asked.

"It sure does." Eleanor smiled. "I was surprised someone from Illinois drives here so often."

"How often do you notice that car?" Martin asked.

Eleanor paused and said, "At least every two or three weeks."

"Did you get this information only for the times someone was coming to pick you up?" Pete asked.

"Well, no. If I noticed someone blocking the sidewalk and the sidewalk was free of ice, making it a safe trip, I went out and got the information."

"Did any of these cars block your sidewalk last night?" Pete asked.

"Yes, and it was particularly upsetting last night. There was no excuse for it. Business at the local establishments was suffering. Apparently, everyone was downtown at the races that started at the Cathedral. There was plenty of parking, but a man parked right square in front of the sidewalk. Others must share my sentiments about this. Someone pulled up right behind him, parked, and accosted him when he returned to his car."

"How long did the man have to wait for him?" Pete asked.

"A half-hour or so? Maybe longer. I'm not sure."

"And someone sat in their car the whole time?" Pete asked.

"Yes, and he had to burn a lot of gas. He turned the car on long enough to warm it up, then turned it off. He kept doing that the whole time he sat there. I could tell he was doing that. I saw the exhaust each time he started it."

"You said he accosted the man who'd blocked the sidewalk?" Pete asked.

"Yes. As soon as the man blocking the sidewalk walked back to his car, the other man got out of his car, approached him, and grabbed his jacket. It only lasted a minute, then they both drove away."

"Are you sure the person who grabbed the offender's jacket was a man?" Pete asked.

"Well, I assumed it was. Used to be women never acted that way."

"What was the person who grabbed the guy blocking the sidewalk wearing?" Pete asked.

"I have no idea." Eleanor smiled. "Guess I'm more interested in license plate numbers than the way people dress."

In light of that revelation, Pete didn't ask what the other person wore. He did ask if she could identify the car driven by the man who was grabbed.

"Yes, that's my last entry."

"Any chance you got the make, model, and plate for the car driven by the person who grabbed him?" Pete asked.

"I know it was a Camry, but I didn't attempt to get the license plate information. No need. That person didn't block the sidewalk."

"Had you seen that Camry in the neighborhood before last night?"

"Never in front of the sidewalk. And barring that ..."

"I understand." Pete smiled.

"Do you mind if I use my phone to photograph these pages?" Martin asked. "Otherwise, I'll have to spend a lot of time copying it, then hope I didn't transpose any numbers or letters."

"Are you dyslexic?"

"Thankfully, no. I have enough trouble without the added challenges that would entail."

"For sure. I know. I'm dyslexic."

TWENTY-NINE

Great! Martin thought, wondering if they'd be able to make heads or tails of license plate numbers documented by someone who's dyslexic.

"Don't worry," she added. "I checked and double-checked all those entries. I didn't want to get the wrong person in trouble." Eleanor grinned.

"Too bad that apartment building doesn't have security cameras," Martin said as he and Pete descended the steps to the notorious sidewalk. He said nothing about the fact the unmarked blocked the sidewalk Eleanor monitored. He knew Pete too caught the faux pas. He'd never considered all the implications. The dearth of street parking often made it difficult and highly inconvenient to avoid doing this.

"I wonder if she added you to the list," Pete chuckled. "If so, she can share your plate number with the next cop who drops in."

"Keep it up wise guy, and you can do the driving." Martin had no more than said it before considering what a special relationship he and Pete had. He didn't know many cops who'd dare talk that way to a superior. "Want me to start the car to get some heat in here before you start searching for the owners of those vehicles?"

"Yes, I want you to start the car, but let's do this at HQ. If we print your photos of Eleanor's notes, we can make notes on the pages."

"So logical ... and organized."

"You don't think I attained this rank on looks alone, do you?" Pete smiled.

"It did occur to me. Are you suggesting you didn't?"

"I'll let you draw your own conclusions."

Both men nodded at the officer they passed as they drove away.

"Ask and you shall receive," Martin said, referring to the officer posted outside the apartment building.

Back at headquarters, Martin sent the four photos of Eleanor's notes to the printer and waited impatiently for the laser jet to upchuck the printouts.

As soon as he had the pages, he took two and gave two to Pete. Both men used the Driver and Vehicle Services portal on their desktop to look up the Minnesota license plates. By the luck of the draw ... or with a little shuffling ... Pete ended up with the page with the Illinois plate. He contacted the data operators in the Illinois PD communication center and obtained that owner's name and address.

"Find any Eds or Kens?" Pete asked when Martin rejoined him.

"An Edgar Kerrick in Bayport and an Edward Montgomery in St. Paul. No Kens. The last offender of record, the guy who was grabbed last night, is Samuel Ulen. He lives in Edina. How about you?"

"Remember the Illinois plate?"

"Sure do. What did you find?"

"That's my only match. The owner is Kenneth Lamberton. He lives in Rockford."

"Too bad we can't hang our hat on it being an Ed or a Ken," Martin said. "We could show the driver's license photos to Jessie and ask if any of them is the Ken or Ed she'd mentioned. But we don't know if either was JD's customer."

"Our chances of finding the people on Eleanor's list at home are far better on Sunday evening than during the day on a weekday. Let's start in Edina with Ulen, check on Edward in St. Paul, and head northeast to Edgar in Bayport. But first, I'm itching to talk to Alyssa's dad."

"Her mom was adamant about waiting until after Friday because he's almost out of minutes," Pete continued. "That's five days. I'm not willing to wait that long. His wife either didn't know or wouldn't share his whereabouts last night. And he's willing to put a daughter who's been missing for four months on the shelf that long?"

"Do you think they have financial issues? Or did she make it up to give him time to disappear?"

"The latter would be a bad idea. It would make her an accessory."

Pete called Child Protection, got the number, and told Martin to pull his chair in close enough to hear both sides of the conversation. Then he called.

After five rings, the call went to voicemail. Pete hit redial.

This time the phone was answered, but it took multiple rings and the threat of another transfer to voicemail.

"Yes?" an out-of-breath voice answered.

"Jonathan Gilbert?" Pete asked.

"Yes, sorry I'm so out of breath. I was in another room."

Pete identified himself and mentioned he was connected with Alyssa's case. "I understand you're short on minutes," he continued. "Is there another number I can call to save your minutes?"

"Well ... that's okay, I guess."

"It's your call, but if there's another number ..."

"Just a minute."

Pete heard a muffled conversation in the background. Jonathan returned and recited a number. Pete called the number. He smiled when the same voice answered. Cutting to the chase, he began with, "Where were you last night, Jonathan?"

"In Hibbing. Why?"

"How long have you been in Hibbing?"

"Since Friday afternoon."

"Why are you there?"

The question met with a protracted pause. Pete waited impatiently, strumming his fingers on his desk.

"I'm not supposed to say."

"Why is that?"

"I guess it doesn't matter if I tell you. I just can't tell my family or friends, or anyone who knows Hank. He's my friend Dave's dad." Jonathan's voice dropped to a whisper. "He can't take care of himself and shouldn't be left alone. I don't understand why. Guess it's just precautionary. Dave doesn't want anyone to know. He lives with his dad, but left town on business. That's why I can't pick up my wife and drive down to get Alyssa. He'd be furious if I told anyone or had someone stand in for me. Money is tight these days, ya know. I can't afford to give up what Dave pays me when he travels."

"When will he return?"

"Good question." Jonathan's voice returned to a normal volume. "My best guess is sometime between Wednesday and Friday, but it could be Saturday or Sunday."

"What kind of business is he in?"

"Developing computer games. How is Alyssa doing?"

"I understand you spoke with Child Protection. They're the experts in that area."

"Yeah, but they're paid to put a certain spin on it, ya know."

"Actually, Jonathan, I have yet to see anything like that."

"I guess. I just want to get her home. I didn't think I'd ever see her alive again. She didn't have enough money to take care of herself for more than a few days. I thought eventually someone would find her body. I didn't know what else to think. So glad I was wrong."

"Have you been speaking with any of Hank's neighbors?"

"Not really. Say 'hi' if I see them when I get the mail or shovel the sidewalk. That's about it."

"Where is your car parked?"

"Out front. Too much crap in the garage to fit a car in. I'm praying we don't have a snow emergency. I'd hate to try to find enough space for it out back, ya know."

"What's Hank's address, Jonathan?"

"Are you planning to come up?"

"No, just checking to see if your story holds water."

Jonathan provided the address.

"What kind of car do you drive?"

"A nine-year-old Escort. Nine years ago, the economy in Virginia was better, ya know."

Pete told Jonathan to let him know when he left for the Twin Cities and ended the call. Then he called a friend with the Hibbing Police Department and asked him for a favor. He gave the friend the address and asked him to check if there'd been an older Escort parked out front since Friday. Some of your folks may have noticed it. If not, I'd appreciate it if you ask a few neighbors.

Tommy agreed to take care of it.

Then Pete checked the internet for the distance from Virginia to Hibbing. Twenty-four miles. It was a reasonable commute, but that didn't matter if Hank couldn't or shouldn't be left alone. Pete knew there were lots of reasons that might be a bad idea. For starters, there was the danger of Hank starting a fire or falling.

Pete wondered if his grandma would one day be in that predicament. He hoped not. She was fiercely independent. She'd be miserable. He pushed the thought out of his head.

THIRTY

Martin headed west to Edina where the homes are inhabited primarily by the well-heeled. En route they benefited from excellent views of the St. Paul and Minneapolis skylines.

Martin parked a house away from their destination, a sprawling white-vinyl bungalow with white trim and an attached two-car garage.

The man who answered the door was of average height and in need of either a diet or some self-discipline. What was left of his hair was gray and curly. By all indications, he hadn't shaved today. Pete and Martin went through the drill and asked his name. It matched the one on the vehicle registration.

"We have some questions, Mr. Ulen," Martin said.

"About?" He glanced at his watch and added, "I have a conference call scheduled. I can give you fifteen minutes. That's it. Follow me."

He led them to the living room. An abstract patterned area rug in shades of blue and green, with an occasional splash of red, added a flash of color. Upholstered traditional furniture in white and shades of gray filled the room. A lighted painting that could pass for a Monet hung behind the sofa.

"I understand you know JD St. Peter," Pete started.

"I'm good with names, but I don't recognize that one."

"He sometimes goes by Joe or Josiah," Pete said.

Samuel held his hands palm side up.

"Where were you last night between seven and eleven?" Martin asked.

"I was right here."

"Can anyone vouch for that?" Martin asked.

"Only if a neighbor is keeping tabs on me." Ulen smirked.

"You drive a 2018 Lexus RX?" Pete asked.

"Yes," Samuel said. Raised eyebrows replaced his smirk.

Pete recited Eleanor's address and told him he was seen outside that apartment building last night.

"You've got the wrong guy," Ulen insisted, shaking his head.

"In that case, who borrowed your car?" Pete asked. Without waiting for an answer, he stood and said, "Come with us. We'll go talk to that person."

"*Umm, umm,*" Samuel bit his lip and transferred his attention to the picture window.

"We aren't here about what happened in that apartment building," Pete said. "That's not our department. We want to know what you did after you left."

"I walked out to my car and drove straight home." Samuel pulled out his handkerchief and wiped his face.

"What happened between the time you walked out of the apartment building and you got in your car?" Martin asked.

"Nothing."

"We know who you were with in the apartment building. We know she's a minor. She can identify you in a lineup," Pete said.

"Are you talking about the guy who came up, grabbed my jacket, and got in my face?"

"Yes," Pete said. "I'm giving you one chance to confirm what he said. If you lie, forget the conference call. We'll haul you in."

"He asked me where I hooked up with the girl," Samuel said, squirming in his chair.

"And?" Pete asked.

"I said I didn't know what he was talking about. He said he saw me go into the apartment building with a girl. I gave him the location. I wanted out of there." Samuel's face was now as scarlet as his area rug.

"What location did you give him?" Pete asked.

"The correct one. If this guy sat in his car the whole time I was in the apartment, he may have written down my plate number. I didn't want him to come looking for me."

"The location you gave him was?" Pete asked.

"At Crashed Ice ... by the jump ... by the Cathedral."

"What time did this guy confront you?" Martin asked.

"Around nine o'clock." Ulen mopped his face, again.

"How tall was he?" Martin asked.

"A little shorter than him." Samuel tilted his head toward Pete.

"What was he wearing?" Martin asked.

"Hell, I don't know. I just wanted to get away from him."

"Was he wearing a down-filled jacket?" Martin asked.

"All I remember is his leather gloves. One of the seams was ragged and scratched my jaw as he grabbed my jacket. It really hurt because it was so cold. I was surprised how much it hurt."

"Did you pay attention to the make and model of this guy's car or the plate number, just in case he came back?" Pete asked.

"He drove a black Toyota Camry. I didn't catch the plate number. I just wanted to get out of there."

Anxious to call the Closed Circuit TV Unit, Pete couldn't wait to get back in the car. He wanted to know if there was a camera on one of the four corners on the north or south side of the girls' block. He hoped so. It might be the only way to find the owner of the Camry.

Martin waited impatiently for Pete to hang up.

THIRTY-ONE

"There's a camera on the northeast corner of the girls' block," Pete said, putting his phone on mute. "We have a couple of options. I'm happy to do whichever you prefer, Martin. We can interview the guy who lives downtown and go from there to HQ to check the footage from that camera. Or we can ask CCTV to check the footage while we interview the two Eds and call it a day, picking up with the Camry tomorrow. Which do you prefer?"

"I'd like to drop everything and speak with the driver of the Camry, but there's no guarantee we'll find the Camry in the footage or be able to decipher the license plate. If we can, by then it'll be too late to call on the owner tonight since we have no proof what Ulen told us is true. He lied about other things. He could have been deflecting the guilt."

Pete nodded and took his phone off mute. He asked CCTV to check last night's footage from the camera they'd identified. He told them he was looking for a black Toyota Camry that was there between 7:30 and 11:00 p.m. He explained he wanted the license plate number. He also asked for a copy of the footage.

When Pete hung up, they were already on their way to downtown St. Paul. Martin took the Tenth Street exit off I-94. From there it was only a couple of minutes to their destination.

Edward Montgomery, the St. Paul resident on Eleanor's list, lived in the City Walk condominiums. The high-rise had a security system requiring visitors to call the resident they visited to get buzzed in. Thankfully, when they arrived the office was occupied. Pete explained who they were and convinced the employee to provide access to the lobby and elevators. Ed's apartment was on the twenty-fifth floor.

Luck was on their side. Edward answered the door when Martin knocked. According to his license, he was sixty-nine. He could have passed for that plus a decade. He styled his gray hair in a comb-over, wore reading glasses on the end of his nose, dress pants, and a pinstriped shirt rolled up to the elbows. The temperature in his condo explained the last item.

He greeted the two investigators asking, "How did you get in? No one's supposed to get in without calling."

After Pete and Martin introduced themselves, he calmed down and invited them into a compact unit with a small kitchen to the left and the living room straight ahead. Pete noticed the bedroom and bath off to the right on his way to the living room. Through the sliding-glass doors that formed one wall of the living room stood a great view of the St. Paul Cathedral. The living room had enough space for a loveseat, two chairs, a TV, and little else.

As soon as the three of them were seated, Pete asked, "How do you like living downtown?"

"I love it. Everything—the Ordway, the Fitzgerald Theater, and a variety of restaurants—is within walking distance. If I want to leave my car in the ramp, busses and the light rail are only a few blocks away. It was better before Macy's closed, but a short time later Byerly's opened a grocery store where the Police Department used to be."

"You have a spectacular view," Pete said. "Did you watch them construct the racecourse for Crashed Ice?"

"Yes. It was quite a process. I also watched the races from the comfort of my living room."

"It's quite a few blocks from here to the Cathedral and several to the end of the course. I'm amazed you could decipher anything," Martin said.

"I couldn't have without powerful binoculars." Edward smiled.

"Where were you Saturday night between seven and eleven?" Martin asked.

"Right here. I had a Crashed Ice party. Do I need an alibi?"

"Let's say you do," Pete said.

"I can give you the names of guests. One lives next door. If you don't believe me, let's see if she's home."

"First another question or two," Pete said. He recited Eleanor's address and said, "Your car's been parked there multiple times."

"Yes. So what?" Edward sounded like a petulant adolescent.

"Why do you park there?"

"To eat at restaurants I like. Finding parking is a problem."

"Out of deference to the people who live there," Pete said, "you should avoid blocking the sidewalk. What if an elderly person fell and was seriously injured climbing over a snowbank because you'd blocked the sidewalk, making that the only way to get to a car?"

"Never thought about it," Edward shrugged, "but I'm not sure it's even possible to park and avoid blocking all of the sidewalks."

They went next door, and the neighbor was home. She said she was at a Crashed Ice party next door from seven until midnight. "At his place," she said, nodding at Edward. "And I didn't see a single race." She smiled and rubbed Edward's back.

The wonders of Viagra, Martin thought.

"Two down but still under consideration," Pete said. "Let's try our luck in Bayport."

"I beg your pardon. Luck has nothing to do with it."

Martin caught I-35E, exited onto east Highway 36 to Stillwater, and followed the St. Croix Scenic Byway. According to the registration for this car on Eleanor's list, Edgar Kerrick lived in Bayport, situated along the St. Croix River. The address belonged to an attractive, three-story home with a porch and attached two-car garage. The houses on this street all appeared less than a decade old, and they varied widely in size and style, including a one-story next door.

The woman who answered the door had large blue eyes and shoulder-length brown hair. She wore jeans and a Notre Dame sweatshirt. Pete identified himself and Martin and said, "We'd like to speak with Edgar."

"Me too." Her eyes grew moist. "Sorry. Edgar died."

"I'm sorry. My condolences."

"And mine." Martin nodded.

"How long ago?" Pete asked.

"Last fall. I miss him so much." She swiped away a tear.

"We came about the Lincoln registered in his name," Pete said.

"Now it's my car. I never changed the registration. Garages and service centers are less likely to play games when they think there's a man in the picture." She smiled. "If I'm correct in assuming this will take more than thirty seconds, come in."

Martin inhaled deeply, relishing the smell of fresh-baked chocolate chip cookies as he followed her.

She led them through a spacious foyer with a vaulted ceiling, past the kitchen with painted cupboards and stainless-steel appliances, and into the great room. Print and striped recliners formed a semicircle in front of a brick fireplace. She motioned the two investigators to sit.

"You have a lovely home, Ms. Kerrick," Martin said.

"Please, call me Pat. Initially, I wanted to get out of here as soon as possible after Ed died, but the experts say not to rush into anything. I'm so glad I listened. Now I find comfort in being in a place my husband occupied. Sometimes it feels like he's here with me. That provides some consolation."

"Do you have other family?" Martin asked.

"Yes. A son in Maple Grove and a daughter in Phoenix. I wish she was closer. Even Kansas City, for example, would be an improvement."

Pete gave her the address for the apartment building where the girls lived and said he'd heard she sometimes parked there. "Is that true?"

"Yes." Pat nodded. "My sister lives in that apartment building. Is this about Eleanor?" She smiled. "Eleanor chastises me on a regular basis. I understand it's difficult for her if I block the access to the street. It's difficult for my sister to get in my car if I don't park there."

"We're not here to hassle you, Pat," Pete said. "We're looking up people on Eleanor's list, trying to locate people connected with a case we're working."

Sensitive to Pat's all-too-recent loss, the investigators spent several more minutes visiting with her about her life and pastimes. Then Pete thanked her for her time and assistance, and he and Martin said goodbye. Pete glanced at his watch. "It's been a fifteen-hour day, and we got little sleep last night, Martin. Let's hang it up."

While Martin drove Pete to HQ, Pete called the watch commander to learn if any cars were spotted lurking outside the girls' apartment building.

She said, "The officer saw the same silver Honda with an Illinois license plate pull up to the curb three times tonight. The times were about an hour apart. The driver parked and craned his neck to look through the windshield at an upper level of the building. He may have been looking for light in the girls' apartment, because all three times occurred after dark."

The plate number recited matched the Illinois plate on Eleanor's list. So Pete said, "Please tell the next officer who sees that car that the driver might have everything or nothing to do with this case. Ask them to find a reason to question the driver. I'd like their name and address since they may not be the owner."

The watch commander provided the plate number for another car of potential interest. This driver pulled up to the curb about a half-hour before sunrise and sat there until shortly after sunrise.

THIRTY-TWO

After checking in with Katie and completing a to-do list, Pete crawled into bed. Despite the season and a thermostat set at 66 degrees, he relished the crisp, cool feel of the sheets. He drifted off to sleep thinking about what the future might hold for the four girls.

Monday morning, he completed his run, itching with every footfall to reach headquarters. After completing the run, he hustled into headquarters at 7:00 a.m., anxious to see the results of the two requests to CCTV and the request to the watch commander for business footage in the vicinity of The Hub. With the help of CCTV, one question was answered. They provided the Camry's license plate number. He checked the DVS portal on his desktop, found the owner, and frowned.

He decided to wait for Martin before viewing the street camera and business footage in the vicinity of The Hub. Four eyes ....

Knowing Tommy was an early riser, he next called his friend with the Hibbing PD.

"You may have done an old guy a favor," Tommy said. "We spoke to neighbors to check on the whereabouts since last Friday of the man in question. As you know, neighbors are usually in the know—especially in a neighborhood of elderly people who've lived in the same houses for decades. The consensus among Hank's neighbors is that his son is using him. The kid had Hank declared incompetent and took over the management of all his accounts. The neighbors said Hank is totally competent. Said he probably wasn't eating right, but that's a far cry from incompetent."

"I stopped at the house and spoke with Hank and the guy you were checking on, Jonathan. I agree with the neighbors when it comes to Hank. I don't think Jonathan has any idea what's going on. I think he's just helping a friend and making a little money in the process."

"Anyway, according to the neighbors, Jonathan's been there since Friday afternoon. The only time his car isn't out front is when he and Hank go out to eat."

"I'm not sure what social services can do without risking making things worse for Hank. He seems resigned to the situation. He may even prefer having his son or a proxy staying with him compared to being alone. I have some friends in social services. I'll talk to them."

"I didn't realize what I was unleashing when I called you, Tommy. Thanks for your help. Give me a call next time you're down this way."

"I will. And I expect you to do the same the next time you have an overwhelming desire to visit the tundra. By the way, if you get tired of law enforcement, mining up here on the Iron Range might be an attractive alternative. Keep that in mind."

"Sounds great, but I can't be that selfish, Tommy. Too many people down here depend on me." Pete laughed.

"It's getting deep in here, Pete. Great hearing from you. Be well ... and safe."

Martin walked in as Pete looked up the not-Illinois license plate number the watch commander provided last night. "Happy Monday, Pete. You look like you made the most of hanging it up before dawn."

"I did, and I spoke with Katie. She's picked the color for your tux. I think you'll look dashing in chartreuse."

Martin rolled his eyes. "If I wear chartreuse, I'll be dashing for sure. I'll spend the whole day dashing away from women. They won't be able to resist me. Speaking of chartreuse, I know it's early, but have you heard from Megan?"

"I may be missing something, but what does Megan have to do with chartreuse?"

"To the best of my knowledge, nothing. That was my attempt to find a segue." Martin chuckled.

Pete shook his head. "I'd hoped Jessie would call her and encourage her to contact us. So far, no go. If we don't hear from her today, one of us should reach out to her."

"What's the game plan for today?"

"Get a few of the guys together for some poker, followed by lunch, then maybe a movie. How does that sound?"

"Disappointing. I'd hoped we got the license information for the Camry and could arrest JD's murderer before we did those things."

Pete slapped his forehead with the heel of his right hand. "Oh yeah, we did. I forgot to put that at the top of the list. I got so enthused about playing poker and seeing a movie. We also have the footage that could help us determine if Danny lied to us. Pull up a chair. We have our work cut out for us."

An hour later, after carefully reviewing all the footage, they still didn't know. The street cameras showed Danny exiting The Hub and moving away from the door. It didn't show whether he stayed alongside the building or walked away. The next time it showed him, he was entering The Hub. That was twenty minutes later. None of the footage from the businesses contained images of Danny ... or anyone wearing a black, down-filled jacket.

"Hell!" Pete said, snapping his fingers.

"What do you think, Pete? Is it possible he isn't in the footage from a single business because he knows their locations and their coverage?"

"A distinct possibility. Bottom line, the footage doesn't remove Danny from consideration. Twenty minutes was a long time to stand outside The Hub, considering the temperature. Let's check out the owner of the Camry."

Both men grabbed their jackets and gloves. It was a little warmer today, so Martin threw his stocking cap on the back seat.

Martin appreciated this opportunity to confer. He was anxious to talk to his partner and trusted friend. "Last night I discovered, much to my chagrin, that Michelle and I have reached a new benchmark with Marty," he began. "Friday, he asked to go to a movie with his friends. The names he provided were all boys. Yesterday one of Michelle's friends told Michelle she saw Marty leaving the theater with a girl. She said they weren't with a group. The problem is, we told Marty he isn't allowed to date 'til he's sixteen. I'd prefer twenty-five, but that'd never fly." Martin smiled and shrugged. "Raging hormones are already a concern. We hoped a few more years would bring additional wisdom."

"His date on Friday night became the point of contention, or should I say dissension, last night. It got so bad, I wanted to be back at work. Anyway, Michelle got hot and bothered about Marty's lack of contrition. She said he can only take his cell to school. For the next month, he has to put it on the kitchen counter when he walks in the door after school and leave it there until he goes out the door again to school. Marty, of course, thinks it's grossly unfair."

"I tried to explain that taking a girl to a movie wasn't what bothered us. It was the fact he disobeyed and then compounded things by lying about it. He told us the dating rule is totally unreasonable. He said maybe that rule could fly when Michelle and I were his age. Not now."

"Later, when he and I were alone, I told him you and Katie are waiting until you're married. Sorry I dragged you into the conversation, but he thinks the world of you. I told him his first time should be special, and he should save it for someone special. I said it would mean a lot more that way. In case none of that made an impression, I also told him a one-night stand can turn into an eighteen-year commitment. I even mentioned the example of someone he's met."

"Are you sure you want to have kids, Pete? At times like this, it seems I went from sleepless nights with a crying baby to worrying about becoming a grandfather."

"I'm not saying your concerns are ill-founded, but never lose sight of the fact Marty is a good kid. Don't forget the way he's stepped up to help with Olivia, the cooking, you name it, because Michelle's been so handicapped by this illness. Peer pressure can be unrelenting. How does a kid deal with restrictions his friends don't face? Most kids fight to be like everyone else ... just one of the gang. I think you did a great job last night. Keep talking to him, Martin."

"What are we going to do the next time, known to us only after the fact, he takes a girl out?"

"First, I think knowing how disappointed you and Michelle are might have the greatest impact. Second, if you were looking for a punishment that would have an impact, you may have come up with the best one of all. When I was a kid, I was grounded. With cellphones and computers, as best I can tell being grounded is no longer a big deal. Kids just go to their rooms and socialize via their cell. They also do that a lot each day, even when they aren't grounded. Do you think it would make a difference if you told Marty he can go places with groups of kids, just not a one-on-one with a girl?"

"There must be a better way of saying that." Martin shook his head. "I appreciate your thoughts on it. I have some thinking to do. Then Michelle and I need to talk. Time to change the subject. We're here. Ready to wrap up this case?"

"Don't hold your breath, Martin. The owner didn't accost Samuel Ulen when he was parked in front of the girls' apartment."

THIRTY-THREE

Martin knocked on the door of the house in the Macalester Groveland neighborhood. He and Pete were there looking for the Camry's owner of record. A man who could have passed for Methuselah in his later years answered. The guy may have been Martin's height, but due to the way he stood, he barely reached Martin's chin. Spindly wrists and hands clearly displaying every bone and knuckle protruded from his fisherman knit sweater.

After they identified themselves, Pete asked, "Donald Vining?"

"Yes, young man. What can I do for you?"

"Are you in the habit of loaning out your car?" Pete asked.

"No, my granddad always said, 'Never a lender nor a borrower be.'"

"Did you drive somewhere last Saturday night?" Pete asked, wondering where this was leading.

"No, son. I can't drive after dark anymore. My eyes aren't what they used to be. I had to give up night driving in 2005."

"Well, Donald, I have it on good authority that your Camry was seen in St. Paul last Saturday night between eight and nine. What time do you go to bed?" Pete asked.

"I'm usually tucked in by eight."

"I don't mean to get personal," Pete said, "but do you wear a hearing aid?"

"Two. One in each ear. They're supposed to be nearly invisible." He smiled. "I guess they are."

Pete liked this guy. "Do you have family in the vicinity?" he asked.

"Do you mind if we adjourn to the living room and sit down? I'd have asked earlier if I thought it would take this long. Don't get me wrong. I'm not complaining."

"Lead the way," Martin said.

He and Pete followed Donald into a lovely room decorated with traditional furniture. It included a bright pink loveseat, two upholstered sage-wood chairs, and a flowered platform rocker. The coffee table held a silk flower arrangement, and two end tables held carefully arranged knickknacks.

"Make yourselves comfortable," Donald said, settled in the rocker, and continued. "You were asking about my family. I have a son and two grandsons in the Twin Cities."

"Before we go on, I want to say you have a lovely home," Pete said.

"Thanks. It was my wife's doing. She's been gone for almost two years. She was the love of my life." Donald smiled.

"Do you see your family often?" Martin asked.

"From their perspective or mine?"

"We're interested in yours," Martin said. "In that case, nowhere near enough, but they all have lives." Donald sighed.

"Do you keep your car in the garage?" Pete asked.

"I sure do. I want it to last. I don't intend to buy another."

"Do you put many miles on it?" Pete asked.

"No. Pretty much just to church, grocery shopping, and to my doctor appointments."

"Mind if we look in your garage? Get a look at your Camry?" Pete asked.

"Be my guest. Do you want to go out the kitchen door? It's closer."

Pete and Martin followed Donald through an outdated kitchen with almond appliances and a linoleum floor. Donald took a key from a hook on the wall near the back door and unlocked the door. Handing the key ring to Pete, he said, "The triangular shaped one opens the garage door."

The two investigators trod the shoveled sidewalk to the garage. On the way, Pete looked back over his shoulder and said, "I sure hope his family takes care of the shoveling."

He unlocked the side door, opened it, and flipped on the overhead light. Aside from a lawn mower, a snow blower, and a variety of tools arranged meticulously on the walls, the garage was empty.

The investigators returned to the house, and Pete handed over the keys. "Thanks for your time and assistance, Donald. One last question. Does your family often take you to your appointments?"

"Only those with the eye doctor."

"But I imagine they're aware of your schedule," Martin said.

"Yes, it's not classified information." Donald smiled.

"Do you have a regular schedule for church and grocery shopping?" Martin asked.

"I'm definitely a creature of habit."

"When do you do your grocery shopping?"

"I always go on Monday mornings."

"Then you went this morning?" Martin asked.

"Yes. Are you hungry?"

"No, thanks." Martin smiled. "Do you go to church on Friday, Saturday, or Sunday?"

"I always go on Sunday morning."

"Planning any outings tomorrow?" Pete asked.

"Currently, nothing's on the schedule until next Sunday. Of course, that's always subject to change."

"It sounds like your car should last for many more years," Pete said.

"Glad you said that. I was starting to think it wasn't in my garage."

"It was pleasant speaking with you, Donald," Pete said. "Stay well."

"I enjoyed our visit. Stop in anytime." Donald smiled broadly.

"How do you feel about a stakeout?" Pete asked Martin as they walked away from Donald's house.

"Sounds inevitable, unless you have another plan. I'd sure like to know who has the Camry. The problem is, of course, we have no reason to expect it back before next Saturday night or early on Sunday."

"I wonder who has the best view of his garage. Who's most likely to see someone go in or come out? Let's drive down the alley, Martin."

The problem was, it looked like the only people with a good view were a next-door neighbor, someone across the alley and directly behind Donald, or someone who happened to be out in the alley. "Let's start with the people behind Donald, in case he suspects something and is watching out the window," Pete said.

"You know, Pete, Mom hates it when people drop in ... when they don't make arrangements ahead of time. Do you think we dare just drop in on whomever lives here?" Martin quipped as the two investigators approached the first door.

"Good point. Since we don't have a name or phone number, I suppose we could send a telegram."

"I'm just trying to educate you on current patterns of acceptable behavior ... and it's an uphill battle. Anyway, there must always be exceptions. This is one."

A woman with thin gray hair and a big smile, whom Pete estimated to be in her seventies or eighties, answered the door.

Martin and Pete introduced themselves, and Martin asked for her name. Then he asked if she knows Donald Vining.

"Of course. We've both lived here forever."

"Does he get out much, ma'am?" Martin asked.

"No, I stop by from time to time. I think he gets lonely."

"Does he still drive?" Martin asked. "Do you ever see him driving?"

"You're not planning to take away his car, are you?"

"No way!" Pete said. "That's not our department. My grandmother is at least as old as Donald. If anyone tried to take her car, they'd have to go through me." He smiled and continued, "We're wondering if anyone else drives his car."

"Oh, that's different. Yes, both his grandsons use his car. I know it and my friend next door knows it. I was torn over whether I should tell Donald. On the one hand, I thought he had a right to know. On the other hand, I feared it would be so hurtful. I didn't tell him."

"Tell us about his grandsons; start with their names," Martin said.

"Their names are Anderson Vining and Weston York."

"Different last names. They're not brothers?" Martin asked.

"They're half-brothers. Same father, different mothers. Weston's mother didn't marry his dad. He was still married to Anderson's mother. In fact, he still is."

"What's their dad's name?" Martin asked.

"Donald, Junior."

"How old are the grandsons?" Martin asked.

"Late twenties, maybe early thirties?" She pinched her lower lip. "I'm not good at judging ages."

"What kind of people are they? Have you met them?" he asked.

"Disrespectful, egotistical, entitled. Anderson more so than Weston. I hate to say those things about Donald's grandsons, but I assume you want the truth."

"Do you see them borrow Donald's car?" Pete asked.

"Sometimes. I have no way of knowing what percentage of the time they do it."

"When's the last time you saw one of them borrow it?" Pete asked.

"This noon. Donald hadn't been home that long. The car was probably still warm." She shook her head.

"Which one borrowed it?" Pete asked.

"Anderson."

"And the time before that?" Pete asked.

"Last Saturday."

"Which one borrowed it that time?" Pete asked.

"I don't know. The sun set a little before five. I knew it was being taken, because I was in my bedroom and saw the headlights light up the alley. It was too dark in the alley to see inside the car. All I know is, it wouldn't have been Donald. He won't drive after dark."

"Please describe Anderson's and Weston's builds," Martin said.

"They're both over six feet. Anderson looks athletic, Weston's a bit dumpy."

"Based on past experience, any idea when the person who took the car will bring it back?" Martin asked.

"Sorry, no. It would be nothing but a wild guess."

Pete and Martin thanked Millie, and each gave her a business card. "Please call if you think of anything else."

In lieu of knocking on more doors, with almost no chance of additional useful information, Pete and Martin walked out Millie's front door and took the long way around to the unmarked car. They didn't take a shortcut via Donald's sidewalk.

On the way, Martin pulled out his cell, anxious to know who was so adamant about reaching him. It had vibrated at least every ten minutes for the last half-hour.

THIRTY-FOUR

Martin looked at the phone number, put his cell on speaker, and played the voice messages. The first said, "This is Megan. I want to talk. Please call ASAP." All of the messages were from her, and each subsequent message sounded increasingly desperate. The fourth and last ended with, "Are you sorry you asked me to memorize your phone number? Do you hate me for all these calls?"

Martin didn't wait. He kept the phone on speaker and called the number Megan had recited. Ella answered on the first ring. Without being asked, she said any time they wanted to come would be fine. "Megan's so hyper, I don't think she slept at all last night. Here she is."

Megan answered, saying, "Thanks so much for calling. Are you mad at me?"

"Not a chance, Megan. It took me this long to wrap up a meeting."

"That's a relief. I talked to Jessie. She told me you and your partner convinced her mom to take her back. Do you think you might be able do that same thing for me? Soon Alyssa will be back with her family and I'll be the only one alone. I mean the only one not with her family. Can we talk ... today?"

Martin looked at Pete then said, "Of course we can. What time works for you?"

"Can you pick me up so we can go someplace and talk?" Megan whispered. Returning to normal volume she added, "Any time will work for me."

"I'll call Child Protection and get right back to you."

"I don't think this can wait," Martin said after disconnecting.

"I'm with you there. This kid is so insecure. She needs to know we're in her corner. Delaying our meetings with Donald Vining's grandsons isn't likely to have a significant impact on the outcome of this investigation."

"You'll be a good father, Pete."

Martin called Child Protection and connected with Alan Preston. Alan said they planned to meet with all four girls today and determine the options for each. He wanted to attend the meeting with Megan and said he'd be ready by the time they arrived.

Martin called Megan and asked if she could be ready in twenty minutes.

"Yes, sir! I'm ready right now. See you soon."

Pete saw Megan looking out the front window as they approached Ella's home. As Martin walked up the sidewalk, she opened the front door and ran toward him. "Can we meet in the car? I don't want anyone else to hear."

"We'll find a warmer place than that. Did you say anything to Ella's mom?"

Megan shook her head.

"Wait in the car. I'll be there in a minute."

Martin told Ella's mom Megan was going with them.

"I'm expecting Child Protection between 1:00 and 1:30. They want to speak with all the girls. They may be unhappy if Megan isn't here."

She looked so stern that Martin waited for her to start wagging a finger at him. "Alan Preston from Child Protection is with us," he said. "We should be back by 1:00 or 1:30—if not earlier. Please ask them to call me if there's a problem."

"Okay. It's your call," Lucy said. "I just don't want you doing anything that could harm Megan. She's a mixed-up kid."

"I know." Martin nodded.

He got in the car and said, "We have a few options, Megan. I think we should find a better place to talk. We can go to headquarters or a restaurant or the Rondo Library or the Central Library."

"I'd like to go to a restaurant, but I don't want to talk there."

"I take it you're hungry." Pete smiled.

"Yes sir."

"Let's stop at Keys and get her something to go on the way to headquarters," Pete said. "Does that sound okay, Megan?"

"Sounds great." Megan nodded.

Martin and Alan waited in the car, engine running, while Pete and Megan ran in. In no time flat, they headed back to the unmarked car. Megan was carrying a bag and wearing a smile.

At headquarters, Pete led the way to an interview room. It guaranteed privacy and barred unwanted interruptions. All four took off their jackets and got settled, and Megan pulled a mega frosted cinnamon roll out of the bag. Martin looked at it longingly, wishing Pete had also gotten one for him. Knowing Michelle's fixation on his diet didn't change that.

Alan listened intently as Pete started the discussion. "Megan, we're so glad to have an opportunity to speak with you. Anything you tell us could be instrumental in solving this case, and also in protecting other girls like you from people like JD. Where would you like to start?"

Megan's gaze dropped like a lead ball to the table. Reaching under her mane, she rubbed her neck. The three men waited patiently.

After a lengthy pause, she said, "I want to go home like Ella and Jessie. The thing is, I don't think my parents will let me. What happened is all my fault." Tears formed, overflowed, and streamed down Megan's cheeks. "You knew what to say to Jessie's mom. Can you think of something to tell Mom and Dad to fix things for me too?" she sobbed.

"Megan, you need to trust me when I say every girl I've spoken with who's been through this believed it was their fault," Alan said. "It's not."

"Do you think what happened to Jessie was her fault?" Pete asked.

Megan shook her head emphatically.

"How about Alyssa? Should she be blamed for what happened to her?"

More head shaking. "Ella?"

"No, but none of them did what I did," she moaned.

"Did each of them make a mistake that made it possible for JD to get control over them?" Pete asked.

Megan nodded.

"Do you know each of their stories?"

"Only parts," Megan shrugged.

"We can't share details, just like we'd never share details of your story. Have they said what happened was their fault?" Pete continued.

Megan nodded. She looked so forlorn.

"What do you think? Was it Jessie's fault?"

"No." Megan shook her head. "JD trapped her."

"How about Alyssa?"

"He trapped her too."

"And Ella?"

"Trapped."

"How about you, Megan? Were you trapped?"

Wide-eyed and frowning, Megan shook her head.

"So you saw JD at a mall, standing at a bus stop, some place like that, and said, "Hey buddy, I'd like to go to work for you if you set me up in an apartment. In return I'll give you all the money I make. Did it go something like that?""

"You know it didn't," she scolded Pete.

"You're right, Megan, but I know JD did something that caused you to do something you wouldn't have done otherwise. He found a way to talk you into doing something you didn't want to do, right?"

The tears continued as Megan nodded.

"Okay, this is the part I'm having trouble understanding, Megan. You agreed JD trapped you. You also agreed he trapped Jessie, Alyssa, and Ella, and it wasn't their fault. Why is it your fault that he trapped you?"

"The difference is the terrible thing I did so he could trap me." Megan's head hung so low her chin almost rested on her chest. "The others didn't do anything that terrible."

"Did he lie to you to get you to do it?"

Megan nodded. She continued fixating on the table.

"Sounds like the only thing you're guilty of is trusting someone who turned out to be a liar. Tell us about your first contact with JD."

"We met on social media. I started messaging this boy. I mean someone I thought was a boy. He was so nice. At first, we messaged a few minutes a week, then a few minutes a day. Then it was a half-hour and soon an hour. At the end it was hours every day. I had trouble getting my homework done on time. We messaged about everything. He sent me a selfie. At least he told me it was a selfie, and he asked for one of me. I took about a hundred selfies, trying to get one he'd like. He was so cute. I didn't want him to see my selfie and end it."

"After I sent it, he said I was beautiful. Mom and Dad always say that, but they're my parents. I don't feel beautiful. Not like some of the girls at school. I spent the time we weren't messaging looking forward to his messages. I thought about him all the time. The problem was when he said he wanted to see all of me. My first reaction was, no way! He kept telling me how special I was. Eventually I told him if he sent me a nude picture of him, I'd send him one of me. I never thought he'd do it. I thought he'd stop asking."

Megan twirled her long coal-black hair around and around her right index finger. "He sent the picture. What could I do? He begged. He said he'd never have sent the picture of him if he'd known I was going to cheat. He asked if it meant I no longer loved him and didn't trust him.

He said he still loved me. That was the first time he said he loved me. No boy had ever told me that."

"I had no idea I was messaging JD. I trusted him. I got up the courage, took a nude selfie, and sent it to him," Megan moaned.

"Dumb, huh?" she sobbed. "Right away he used that selfie against me. He threatened to post it all over social media and on my school's website if I didn't do what he said." Tears flowed freely.

Pete's heart broke for this kid—this child. He found a box of tissues and handed it to her.

The three men waited for her to find the courage—and the words—to continue. She sat, shoulders shaking, staring at her hands. She hadn't touched the sweet roll.

"Where did you meet with him, Megan?" Pete asked.

"At the Apache Mall in Rochester. I waited inside the main entrance, looking for the boy in the selfie. When JD walked up and told me his name, I didn't believe him. He told me some things that proved he was the person I'd been messaging. He said he knew of a good place to eat and said I should follow him. I told him I wasn't going anywhere. He said he was hungry, hated mall food, and I better follow him ... or else. I wanted to keep that picture from being posted. I did what he said."

"I followed him to his SUV and got in. He didn't stop until we got to St. Paul. The whole way, he told me where I would live, what I was going to do, and what would happen if I didn't do as he said or tried to run away. I couldn't let that happen to my family. At least I wasn't alone. Jessie and Ella, and later Alyssa, were very nice to me. They did their best to protect me, but no one could protect me from JD." Megan sobbed.

"Now he's dead, and I don't know what to do. I know people are saying they can help me, and I can go back to my family. I wish it was true. I don't believe it. If my family finds out what I did, they'll hate me. They won't want anything to do with me ever again."

"I understand why you're scared to see your family, but I think you're wrong about their reaction to what happened," Martin said. "I have a daughter. If all of this happened to her, I'd hug her and tell her I was sorry I was unable to protect her. I'd blame myself, not her. None of it could affect my love for her. Every minute she was missing would feel like an eternity. A lot of my friends have daughters. I guarantee they all feel that way ... both them and their wives."

Megan stared into Martin's eyes . "Would you feel that way if you were my dad?" she asked, looking at Pete.

"If I was fortunate enough to have a daughter, you'd better believe it. All I'd want would be to get her back and help her get past every bad thing that happened. Like Martin said, I'd blame myself for failing to do a better job of protecting her. I wouldn't blame her."

"You can't protect me from me, you know."

"You weren't the one who made all this happen, Megan. JD was," Alan said. "Guys like him are pros at manipulation. We need to do a much better job of making kids like you pros at seeing through their masks."

"Mom and Dad always say I can't blame others for my mistakes. I have to take ownership."

"Do you know much about baseball?" Pete asked.

Megan nodded. "My brother plays. I used to go to some of his games."

"Pretend I told you to do your best to hit the pitches of a major league pitcher. If you strike out, is it your fault or mine?"

Megan shrugged.

"Most people would say it's mine because it wasn't fair. In fact, they'd probably think I was a jerk for doing that to you. JD had all the tools and pretended he was a kid. Your only mistake was believing him. He spent a lot of time and energy making sure you did. I know I've made bigger mistakes. Thankfully, I never had to pay such a high price."

Megan sat for a minute, staring fixedly at the ceiling, then said, "Can we call my mom? She probably won't answer, but she might." She recited the number, then cocked her head to the right and frowned.

THIRTY-FIVE

"You know your mom," Pete said. "Is she more likely to look at a text or answer a call from an unknown number?"

"Maybe a text?" Megan looked wide-eyed at Pete.

Pete's text said, "Megan wants to talk. Please call ASAP." He thought about ending there, but considered all the things that might go through the mind of the recipient and added, "I'm a police officer. She's NOT in trouble."

Filling the time while waiting and hoping for a call, Pete said, "If you're up to it, Megan, Martin and I have a few questions about Saturday night."

"I'll try."

"You and Jessie left before JD was shot. Was there anything unusual about that night or the man you left with?"

"The guys we hook up with at sports events are pretty much like the others. They come for one reason, do it, and leave. A few ask questions. Some are careful. Some are not. Some are okay. Some are not."

"How about the guy you left with on Saturday night?" Martin asked.

"He was so so. I don't remember anything special about him. When he left, the guy with Jessie was still there. I walked a couple blocks and got a Coke. I didn't want to be there in case Jessie's guy decided he'd go for a two-for-one." Megan rolled her eyes.

"The guy last Saturday, was it the first time you saw him?" Martin asked.

"Yes." Megan nodded.

"Did he say or do anything that made him stand out?" Martin asked.

Megan bit her lip and stared at the ceiling, then said, "Nothing I can think of."

"So Saturday night was pretty much like any other?" Martin asked.

"No, lucky thing is, it isn't usually that cold."

"Did anything unusual happen before you left Crashed Ice? Did JD seem to know any of the people or get into any arguments? Anything like that?" Pete asked.

167

Megan again examined the ceiling for a minute, then said, "I don't think so."

"Megan, it's very important ...," Pete's vibrating cell interrupted.

Megan's eyebrows shot up. "Do you think?"

"Culnane," Pete said.

"Is this the police?"

"Yes, ma'am. And you are?" He recognized the number.

"I'm Megan Dawson's mother. Didn't you text me a few minutes ago?"

"Yes, but before I give her the phone, please give me her birthdate."

She rattled off a date, and Pete repeated it, and hearing it, Megan's head bounced up and down.

"Okay, I'll let you talk to Megan. First you need to understand that you, my partner, and I need to talk. The sooner the better. This is the best number to call."

Pete, Martin, and Alan exited the interview room.

They heard sobs as Pete closed the door behind them.

Alan monitored Megan's side of the call from outside the room, and Pete and Martin waited in Pete's office. While there, Pete accessed the DVS portal and looked for every Donald Vining, Jr., Anderson Vining, and Weston York living in the metro area. Thankfully, he found just one of each.

Meanwhile, Martin contacted Forensics to learn if they found anything potentially useful on the victim's clothing. It turned out trace evidence was gathered off the back of the jacket. They were waiting for those DNA tests as well as the victim's. The trace evidence could be valuable if it wasn't JD's and matched the DNA of a suspect.

The two men talked about the JD they'd uncovered thus far. "He went from discovering he couldn't control his fiancée to totally controlling four girls, and it took about two years," Pete said.

"How does a guy who has potentially no contact with another trafficker get set up and learn how to operate as one?" Martin asked.

"He may have learned it all on the internet and the dark web. The good news and the bad news is you can find anything and everything on the internet. You don't even need to be tech savvy. A little tenacity goes a long way."

"Of course. I knew that. That's why Michelle and I are so vigilant about Marty's internet activity. It amazes me that some parents are so hands-off about and oblivious to what their kids are doing."

They spent the rest of the time strategizing about the next best steps. A call from Megan put that effort on hold.

Pete noticed two things as he and Martin passed the one-way glass of the interview room that held Megan. The first was her smile. It stretched from ear to ear. The second was she'd finished the cinnamon roll. Both made him happy, and he too smiled.

"Mom wants to see me!" Megan announced, bouncing up and down as Alan and the two investigators entered the room. "She said she and Dad will reach St. Paul by 6:30 at the latest! She asked for an address. I told her I didn't know it, but she could call the number she'd just called. Is that okay?"

"Absolutely," Pete said, nodding.

"She's calling Dad. If they can both get off, they'll be here a lot earlier. She started crying when she heard my voice. She said she and Dad were so worried and afraid for me. They went to the police and kept checking every few days. They spent a lot of nights crying. She said my brother and sister did too. She said they tried and tried to figure out what happened. They didn't think I'd run away. They thought I was happy. I told her I didn't run away. She said the only thing they knew to do was pray, so that's what they did. I told her I did something very, very bad, but want to be with her and Dad when I tell them what. I said if they decide they don't want anything to do with me after I tell them, I understand. And you were right. Mom said there's nothing I could do that would keep her from loving me. She said we'll work through it together. When I said 'goodbye,' do you know what she said? She said, 'I love you, Megan.'"

Pete smiled and asked, "What do your parents do, Megan?"

"Mom's an ophthalmologist at Mayo. Dad's a physician's assistant in gerontology."

"Megan, we should take you back to Ella's," Alan said. "My people will be there soon, and they want to talk to you."

En route to Ella's, Pete revisited the question about last Saturday night and whether there was anything unusual about it.

Megan was unable to provide any leads.

Martin and Pete both recognized the car parked in front of Ella's home. It was the car that came to HQ to pick up Alyssa and Ella on Saturday night. It seemed a lot longer than a day and a half ago. Martin parked behind that car, and the three men walked Megan to the door.

THIRTY-SIX

Alyssa answered the door. "They're talking to Ella. They have been for a long time. I hope they don't want to talk to me that long." She frowned and rolled her eyes.

"Do you think they have her tied to a chair?" Pete asked. "If not, she's probably been with them this long because she wants to be. Sound reasonable, Alyssa?"

"I suppose," she shrugged.

"I spoke with your dad. Have you talked to him yet?"

"No." Her head dropped.

"He wants to talk to you, but he can't right now. He's anxious to see you, but he's helping a friend and can't leave. I'll let him tell you about it. Trust me, he'll be here as soon as he can."

Alyssa looked sideways at Pete. "You're not just saying that, are you?"

"Cross my heart," Pete said, complete with gesture. "Do kids still say that?"

"None of my friends do," she said and laughed.

"You have a great laugh. I hope you start laughing more often." Alyssa blushed.

Ella, followed by a woman from Child Protection, came out the kitchen door and approached them. "Ready, Alyssa?" the woman asked.

Alyssa answered with a hands-up shrug. "Do you want to come?" she asked, looking at Pete, then Martin.

"If we do, could that keep you from opening up, from being honest and sharing your story and feelings?" Pete asked.

"I don't know. I suppose."

"In that case, it would be better if we didn't. Do me a favor, okay?"

"What?"

"Tell them the truth. Help them to help you."

Alyssa shrugged and followed the woman from Child Protection.

"Are you glad you spoke with her?" Pete asked Ella. "No need to answer, if you prefer not to."

"Yes. She said a lot of things that got me thinking. How are you doing?" Ella asked, turning to Megan.

"I talked to my mom. She and Dad are coming today. Your mom and dad are great. I'm so glad they let us stay here. You feel like a sister, Ella. What if I never see you again?" She blinked a tear away.

Ella put her arms around Megan, who stood shoulder-high next to her, and said, "That will never happen, girlfriend."

"Time to get back to Donald's family," Pete said as he and Martin returned to the unmarked. "With any luck, some of them will be home. What if we find one of them with their grandfather's car? It could provide a great opening."

"And it would be grand theft auto."

Anderson lived in Eagan. When Pete looked up his dad's address, it was the same. Weston lived in West St. Paul. They began with Eagan, wondering what it would mean if Donald Junior knew his kids were stealing his father's car.

The Vining house, whether it belonged to Donald or Anderson, qualified as a McMansion, and their street was lined with more of the same. A covered portico sheltered the front door of the craftsman-style home with beige Shaker siding, brown shutters, beige trim, and a cream-color front door and garage doors. Supplementing the attached double garage, a single-stall garage laid claim to a spot to the right of the house. A wooden fence, separating this lot from the neighbors, but providing no privacy or security, grew out of the snow drifts.

Pulling up to the house, the first thing the two investigators saw was the black Camry with a familiar license plate number in the driveway. A man who would pass for a millennial answered the door. He stood six two—midway between Pete and Martin's heights. His chestnut-colored hair was tousled and in need of a trim, at least by Pete's standards. After they identified themselves, the man invited them in, but took them no further than the foyer.

Pete took the first turn and started by asking his name.

"Anderson Vining."

"Is that your Camry?" Pete directed a thumb toward the car.

"No, it's my grandpa's. I just had it serviced for him."

"Where were you last Saturday night between seven and eleven?"

"At my girlfriend's."

"What's her name?"

"Heather."

After writing down Heather's full name, address, and phone number, Pete asked if Anderson's dad was there.

"Hell no," Anderson grinned. "He hates winter."

"Where's your dad?" Pete asked.

"Gainesville, Florida. He has a house there in the Hale Plantation golf course development. He had aspirations of being a pro golfer."

Martin took over the questioning while Pete stepped outside to call Heather. Much to his chagrin, he reached her voicemail. So much for eliminating the possibility of Anderson helping her match his story. The chances just dropped dramatically. He didn't leave a message.

When Pete returned, Martin was asking, "When did your dad leave for Florida?"

"He left in early October. I don't remember the exact date. He does his best to get out before the first snowfall."

"Does he return for the holidays?" Martin continued questioning.

"Not a chance. I usually go down there."

"When does he return to Minnesota?"

"Mid-April. He always stays long enough to qualify for Florida residency. No Florida state income taxes, you know." Anderson smirked, apparently impressed with his father's machinations.

"I understand you have a half-brother," Pete stepped back up for the next few rounds. "Are the two of you close?"

"We're friends, but not best friends."

"What does he do for a living?"

"He's a troubleshooter for a Wi-Fi company."

"What are his hours?"

"The usual, eight to five."

"What's his phone number?"

Anderson checked the contacts on his cellphone and recited it.

"How about you, Anderson?" Martin took over. "What do you do for a living?"

"I manage Dad's properties."

"Does anyone besides you and your grandfather drive your grandfather's Camry?"

"Not that I know of."

"Are you sure?"

Anderson hesitated and examined the floor before saying, "To the best of my knowledge, no."

THIRTY-SEVEN

Pulling his cell from his pocket, Pete listened to two voice messages he'd noticed when calling Heather. Both from Alyssa. He told Martin who he was calling, while touching the numbers to connect with her.

Ella's mom answered and handed the phone to Alyssa.

Alyssa answered, saying, "Mom got a ride with a neighbor. I've been trying and trying to reach you. She'll be here by ten o'clock tomorrow. Can you be here before her? I want you to be with me when she arrives and while I talk to her. Please. Is there any way?"

Pete figured she was nervous and wanted reinforcements. "That shouldn't be a problem. Martin and I will do our best."

"Oh, thank you, thank you. See you tomorrow. If possible, please be here by 9:30, just in case they leave earlier than planned."

"You need to do the talking tomorrow, Alyssa. Martin and I will be there to support you if that's what you're looking for."

"Yes, please."

"Okay, see you tomorrow, barring anything critical requiring our attention." He hoped that wouldn't happen, but the demands of their job were often unpredictable.

"Thanks, again! See you tomorrow."

"Alyssa seems to trust you," Martin said as Pete tucked his phone in a pocket. "She may want you there to do the same with her mom."

"She doesn't understand that parents really love their kids no matter what." Changing the subject, Pete asked, "In the mood for lunch? I'd hate to cheat you out of an opportunity to eat some comfort food."

Martin jumped at the chance. His stomach was growling. He wondered if Pete heard it, prompting the question.

While they were eating, Pete's phone vibrated. He found two text messages. The first came from the watch commander. When he called, she said, "The guy who showed up around sunrise came back. This time he walked up to the building and rang a doorbell. Turned out to be for the girls' apartment. He stood there for about ten minutes, left after no one responded, returned to his car and drove away."

Megan's mom left the second message. She and her husband were on their way. She needed an address and asked Pete to call ASAP.

She answered Pete's return call, saying, "My husband and I just left Rochester. I need the address where Megan's staying."

Pete explained he and his partner needed to meet with them before they met with Megan. He provided the headquarters address and arranged to meet her and her husband there in ninety minutes.

Ms. Dawson asked, "What's going on with Megan? Why are the police involved? Can she come home with us?"

Pete gave her the number for Child Protection and asked her to speak with them before they arrived in St. Paul.

The man who'd checked out the girl's apartment twice today became the next priority. Thanks to the license information provided by the officer stationed there, Pete already had the name and Burnsville address of the vehicle owner.

The trip to Burnsville took thirty minutes, give or take a few traffic lights and stop signs. When the two investigators reached the address on Gordon Orrock's vehicle registration, single-story homes, each attached to another, surrounded them. The homes were so similar, it looked like they could have been cut out with a cookie cutter. The siding was beige or light blue, and all had identical beige brick, trim, shutters, and shingles.

Martin parked the usual few homes down the street. Had his gloves been flexible enough, he'd have crossed his fingers that Orrock was home. When he and Pete reached the front door, Martin knocked firmly.

A portly, middle-aged man of average height with a receding hairline and red nose answered the door.

"Gordon Orrock?" Pete asked.

"Yeah, who's asking?" Orrock scrutinized the two investigators.

Pete and Martin displayed their badges and IDs.

"We have some questions," Martin said, beginning the preliminaries.

Orrock stood there, looking dumbfounded.

"May we come in or would you rather come out to our car?"

"Oh, sorry. Please, come in."

"Are you alone?"

"No. My wife's here."

"Is there a place where we can get some privacy?"

"Let's meet in the den. Irene is watching TV. She won't bother us, and the volume is loud enough, she won't hear us."

Seeing the off-white, low-pile, plush carpet, Pete removed his boots before stepping out of the tile foyer.

Observing him, Martin did likewise.

Gordon led them through a beautifully decorated living room, furnished with off-white and wood French provincial, and navy and kale-green accents. His wife sat fixated on the TV and didn't acknowledge their passage.

The den appeared to be a man cave. An oversized leather recliner faced a big-screen TV on the wall. An impressionistic painting of a flock of mallards hung over the recliner. A desk, complete with a high-backed leather chair, stood against the far wall. Two wooden, IKEA-style chairs with red padded backs and seats skirted the recliner.

Gordon went straight to the recliner, sat down, and motioned Pete and Martin toward the IKEA-style chairs.

Pete took over the questioning. "Gordon, where were you Saturday night between 7:00 and 11:00?"

"Right here." Gordon pointed at the floor.

"Can anyone vouch for that?"

"Yes, my wife. What's this about?"

"Who lives here besides you and your wife?"

"No one."

"Does the name JD ring a bell?"

"No." Gordon scratched his neck.

"How about Pearl, Ruby, Amber, or Opal? Do you know them?"

"No." Orrock shook his head, accentuating his answer.

"I understand wanting to get rid of JD, because of what he was doing, Mr. Orrock."

"Who is JD?"

"He's a pimp."

"I don't know any pimps!"

"Okay, does child trafficker sound more familiar?"

Gordon shook his head.

"Look, Gordon," Martin said, taking a turn, "today you went to the apartment building where the girls my partner mentioned live. Why did you do that?"

"In Crocus Hill? I went there to visit a friend. He should've been home. I don't know why he didn't answer the doorbell."

"You went there three times in two days."

"You're telling me. We keep getting our signals crossed. Pretty soon I'm going to give up on him."

"Give up on whom? Who were you looking for?"

"Andy Truman. He moved there this month. He insists the apartments in that neighborhood are hard to beat. Bad time to be moving. Any winter month is a bad time to move in Minnesota."

"There's no Andy Truman living in the apartment where you rang the bell." Martin said.

"All I know is, Andy said it's the first apartment building north of Grand and on the right."

"Is his building on the east or west side of the street?" Pete took another turn.

"*Umm* ...." Gordon looked at his hands, contemplating this for several seconds, while pointing his fingers up, down, and sideways before smiling and saying, "East."

"Well, Mr. Orrock, you rang a bell at an apartment building south of Grand and on the west side of the street."

"You're kidding, aren't you? That's not funny."

"Andy never called or texted when you didn't show?"

"He never did either. I figured he must have had an emergency."

"Why didn't you call or text him?"

Orrock gave a hands-up shrug.

Pretty lame, Pete thought.

"How about your signals with Anderson Vining? Did you also get them crossed?" Martin asked.

"I don't know any Anderson Vining." Gordon said, rearranging himself in the recliner.

"How about Don Vining. Do you know him?" Martin asked.

"Can't say I do."

"Do you own a gun?" Pete asked.

"No."

"It's pretty cold these days. Do you own a down jacket?" Pete asked.

"No. They make me look bulky. My wife won't let me have one."

"Show us all the closets where you keep your jackets, coats, hats, gloves, etc.," Pete said.

Gordon led them back through the living room, passing alongside his wife again, and to the foyer. He opened the door, permitting Pete and Martin to see the contents. It held a lot of wool coats and one down jacket. The down jacket was mint green.

"Do you have any other jackets?" Pete asked.

"We hang all of them in here."

"We have a few questions for your wife," Pete said.

Gordon rubbed his cheek. "Follow me."

The three men walked back to the living room, and Gordon introduced Pete and Martin to his wife, Irene.

Irene half lay and half sat on the couch. Her legs rested on an ottoman, while her hands rested on a round, protruding stomach.

"This won't take long, Irene," Martin said. "I have a few questions for you. Where were you last Saturday night between 7:00 and 11:00?"

"I was home all day. It would take a stick of dynamite to get me out in this weather." Irene smiled.

"How about your husband?"

"He was here with me."

"The whole time?"

"Yes. You were, weren't you dear?" She smiled at Gordon.

"Yes, dear."

"Is your husband directionally challenged?"

"For sure. He gets lost more than anyone I know."

THIRTY-EIGHT

Pete and Martin hurried from Burnsville to HQ, to the extent road conditions permitted. They arrived just ahead of Megan's parents.

Megan's exotic oriental looks came from her mother. Dr. Keiko Dawson stood barely five feet tall, had small hands and feet, and beautiful, delicate features. Megan's dad, Bruce, was average height. Just shy of handsome, he had caramel-brown hair and hazel eyes.

Pete had insisted on this meeting with the Dawsons to determine their whereabouts on Saturday night. He met with Megan's mom, while Martin met with her dad. Before Pete could ask anything, Dr. Dawson opened with, "Megan has always been so insecure. I think she gets picked on at school, but she refuses to talk about it. We've worried about her the last few years, but never thought she'd run away."

"Kids can be cruel," Pete said. "Did you talk to Child Protection?"

"No. We decided to come here first."

Megan's mom said she and her husband were at a neighbor's birthday party last Saturday night and got home about midnight. Pete obtained the neighbor's name and phone number. He exited the room, saying, "I'll be back shortly. Please call Child Protection to get Megan's address."

Before calling the phone number, Pete got Bruce's alibi from Martin. It matched his wife's. Thank God for cellphones. On a good day they meant not having to wait for someone to get home from work. He reached the neighbor and got the same answer for where Keiko and Bruce spent last Saturday night.

Weston York now topped their agenda. "What would you say the likelihood is that Anderson won't have clued Weston in by the time we reach Weston?" Pete asked.

"Unfortunately, zero to none."

"The thing is, unless one of them can come up with another explanation, we know either Weston or Anderson was outside the girls' building Saturday night."

En route Pete tried again to reach Anderson's girlfriend. After the call, he had two strikes. Not looking good for the home team.

Weston York's middle-class neighborhood in West St. Paul was a far cry from the home of his father and brother. He lived in a compact, two-story brick, saltbox house in a neighborhood populated with much of the same.

Illuminated rooms inside the home added optimism as the two investigators approached Weston's address. Before getting out of the car, Martin grabbed his stocking cap out of the back seat. A polar vortex was settling in, and he wanted to be prepared in case Weston was less hospitable than his brother, who'd barely let them in the front door. Walking up the driveway, they passed a car on par with Donald's, a ten-year-old Nissan Altima.

On the way, Martin began sliding his feet, rather than stepping from foot to foot, after nearly losing his footing twice. Seeing Pete wasn't fazed by the icy driveway, he decided he should get boots like Pete's. Good enough for work and good on ice.

Both Weston and Anderson must take after their dad, Martin thought when a man resembling Anderson answered the door. Martin introduced himself and Pete.

The man didn't appear surprised to have the police at his door. When asked, he identified himself as Wes York.

Wes invited them in and led the way to the family room. The carpeting was worn but clean, and the room was sparsely decorated with Goodwill treasures or imitations. The light-gray walls held one painting, resembling the offerings at starving artists' sales.

"Where were you last Saturday night between 7:00 and 11:00?" Martin began.

"At Mom's. She invited me over for dinner."

"And you stayed until eleven?"

"We're both night owls and love to play canasta. I remember when she first taught me. I used to complain that she never let me win." Wes smiled and shook his head. "She's so competitive. It didn't matter I was an eight-year-old kid."

"Who else was there?" Martin asked.

"No one. It was just Mom and me."

"I understand you sometimes borrow your grandfather Donald Vining's car," Martin said.

"Who told you that? Anderson?"

"Can't say."

"That son of a bitch."

"We didn't hear it from him."

"Oh?"

"You borrowed the Camry last Saturday, didn't you?" Pete said.

"No."

"Are you aware of the penalties for lying to us?" Pete warned.

"I'm not lying!"

"Besides you and Anderson, who has access to the Camry?" Pete asked.

"Just Anderson, Grandpa, and me."

"Look, Wes," Pete said, "We reviewed the footage from the street camera down the block from where you were parked for an extended period of time on Saturday night. It sure looks like you. I know it isn't your grandfather behind the wheel."

"I spent the whole time with Mom, except when I went outside. I had to talk to someone on the phone."

"How long were you outside for that call?" Pete asked.

"Maybe fifteen minutes. Maybe twenty."

"Maybe enough time to get downtown and back," Pete said.

"Not while complying with the speed limits."

"Any speeding tickets on your record?" Martin asked.

Wes shrugged.

"So you drove around while talking. Makes sense. Too cold to sit in the car without starting it. Where did you go?" Martin asked.

"Nowhere. I sat in the car in Mom's driveway the whole time."

"What time did you go out to your car and back in the house?" Martin asked.

"I have no idea."

"Do you remember with whom you spoke?" Martin asked.

"Of course."

"The call must be listed in the recent calls on your cell. Check it," Martin said. "And while you're at it, see how long the call lasted."

Wes pulled the cell out of his pocket. After several swipes he looked up and said, "I made the call at ten to ten, and it lasted nine minutes. Seemed longer. Maybe because it was so cold, huh?"

"Or maybe because you didn't go back inside immediately, huh? Did you?" Martin asked.

"Did I what?"

"Did you go inside as soon as you completed that call?"

"I'm not sure. I may have sat there awhile."

"Does the Camry start better than your car after sitting in frigid temperatures for hours without being started? Is that why you borrowed it last Saturday?" Pete asked.

"No, I had *my* car!" Wes's face advanced toward scarlet.

"Have you talked to your mom since Saturday?" Pete asked.

"No, it's only been a few days."

"Call your mom," Martin said. "I want to talk to her."

Wes dialed the number and handed his phone to Martin.

Meanwhile, Pete put the questioning on hold.

Wes's mother agreed with him. She said Wes was with her until at least eleven o'clock Saturday night, they played canasta, it was just the two of them, and he drove his Altima.

Martin asked about how long Wes was gone when he went outside.

"Maybe five minutes. He had to take a call. He's hiding something from me. Let me know if you figure out what."

"When's the last time you spoke to Wes?"

"We haven't spoken since I saw him on Saturday."

Martin disconnected and handed the phone back to Wes.

"We have a positive ID on your grandfather's car sitting outside an apartment building in St. Paul last Saturday night," Pete told Wes. "We'll get to the bottom of this."

Wes frowned and ushered them back to the front door.

THIRTY-NINE

Pete tried reaching Anderson's girlfriend a third time.

Martin sat tight while he did, waiting to hear their next destination. This time, good fortune inched in their direction. Heather answered the phone. Pete explained who he was and asked what she did last Saturday night.

"I fixed dinner for my boyfriend Anderson," she said.

"What's Anderson's last name?" Pete wasn't taking any chances.

"Vining."

"Did you do that at his place or yours?"

"*Ah*, mine."

"What time did he arrive?"

"Seven."

"What time did he leave?"

"*Umm,* a little after eleven."

"Did you go outside at all during that time?"

"Why no."

"Are you aware of the penalties for lying to me?"

"No?"

Pete crossed his fingers and said, "Incarceration, for starters. Do you want to change your story before it's too late?"

"Yes," Heather sighed.

"Were you with Anderson Saturday night?"

"Yes. He arrived around 9:30 or 10:00."

"And it might actually have been as late as 10:30 or 11:00?" Pete asked.

"I suppose. I wasn't watching the clock. I was reading."

"Did you meet at his place or yours?"

"He came over here."

"How long does it take you to get to downtown St. Paul?"

"Ten or fifteen minutes, except during rush hour."

"Why did Anderson ask you to lie to me?"

"I don't know," Heather whined.

"Thanks for your help. Do *not* tell Anderson you spoke with me."

"You want me to lie to him?"

"If necessary."

"But he's right here."

"Tell him not to leave. If he does, I'll have no choice but to put out a BOLO (Be-On-the-LookOut). He'll have every cop in the Twin Cities looking for him. My partner and I will be there in ten minutes."

It surprised Martin to see the Camry parked on the street in front of Heather's apartment building. He wondered if Anderson would buy his grandpa a new car if the Camry died before he did. He had no doubt Anderson put more miles on the car than Donald.

Anderson answered the door. A woman, presumably Heather, stood on his heels.

"Get your jacket and come with us," Pete said.

"Where are we going?"

"Your place for starters," Pete said.

Anderson left them standing in the living room. He returned a minute later, wearing a navy and red ski jacket, and followed Pete and Martin out the door.

"Ride with us," Pete said.

He rode in the back seat with Anderson.

The only sounds en route to Anderson's home were the usual moans and groans emitted by a car taxed to the hilt by this weather.

Pete and Martin escorted Anderson to the door and waited while he unlocked it. When they followed him inside, this time he took them further than the foyer. He led them to a great room with hardwood floors. A large screen TV hung on one wall, and a pool table stood on the far side of the room. Anderson sat in a leather recliner and looked up at the two investigators.

Pete found a plaid overstuffed chair.

Martin spotted its twin.

"Before we begin," Pete said, "I assume you know you're already guilty of obstruction of justice. As a result, we can haul you in if we choose. Hence, I recommend you start telling the truth, rather than compounding your problems. Besides you and Weston, who has access to your grandfather's Camry?"

"As far as I know, just the three of us."

"We checked the street camera footage," Pete said. "Saturday night, someone drove your grandfather's Camry to an apartment near Selby and Grand. We know the Camry turned onto that street and parked for an hour, give or take. We know from the footage the driver is not your grandfather. Weston has an alibi. What were you doing there?"

"Maybe someone else, someone I don't know about, has a key."

"Okay," Pete said, "list all of the possibilities."

"I don't know. Grandpa would know better than me."

"We covered that last time we spoke," Pete said. "We've been patient, but we aren't about to spend the night listening to you spin tales. If you weren't driving the Camry, why did you ask Heather to lie to us?"

Anderson stood. "I've got to go to the bathroom. I'll be right back."

Reviewing his options, Pete thought.

When Anderson returned, he sat for several seconds without speaking. Pete decided to help him out. "Since you think others may be using your grandfather's car but can't name them, we can help. We'll haul the car in, and Forensics will go through it top to bottom. They'll fingerprint every surface and find fibers from every fabric that was ever in that car. Then they'll take all your grandfather's clothes to determine which of the fibers are attributable to him. They'll do the same with your clothes and Weston's. You, your grandfather, and Weston will be fingerprinted, and they'll get a DNA sample from each of you. It's a rather convoluted process, but if it clears you, it'll be worth it, right?"

"Okay, I admit it. I was there Saturday night."

"Why did you go there?" Martin asked.

"I was looking for a guy."

"The guy's name?" Martin asked.

"I don't remember."

"Why were you looking for him?" Martin asked.

"I wanted to ask him a question."

"What question?" Martin asked.

"Where I could find JD."

"Why did you want to know that?" Martin asked.

"I was told to find him and slip one hundred dollars to a blonde girl who'd be with him."

"What's her name?" Martin asked.

"I don't know. All I know is she's blonde."

"Lots of people at Crashed Ice. How were you going to recognize JD?"

"I'd seen a photo."

"So you got the answer, left, and found JD and the blonde girl," Martin said.

"No, I didn't." Anderson shook his head. "I wanted to find the girl and give her the money, but it had to wait. You saw the video. You must have seen I was wearing the ski jacket I wore tonight. After sitting there for an hour, waiting for the guy to return to his car, I was frozen. I couldn't even imagine going downtown, trying to find a parking space, walking for blocks and blocks, and possibly not even finding her. Instead, I came home. It took me hours to warm up."

"How did you know how to find a guy who knew where to find JD?" Pete asked.

"I was given the address and told to be at that apartment building by early evening. Once there, I was supposed to watch for any guy driving up with a young girl and going upstairs with her. I was told to wait until the guy came back and ask him that question. I did as instructed, only I got there later than I intended. I was lucky enough to pull up right behind a guy who went into the building with a young girl. I got out of the car and tried to catch them, hoping to avoid sitting there waiting. I pounded on the door. Either they didn't hear me or they ignored me."

"Who asked you to do those things?" Pete asked.

"My dad."

FORTY

"When did your dad ask you to find JD and the blonde girl at Crashed Ice?" Pete asked.

"I don't know," Anderson said. "Some time on Saturday."

"Look at your phone," Pete instructed. "I want the exact time."

Anderson checked his phone and said, "It was 1:32 Saturday afternoon. Is that exact enough for you?"

Pete obtained Donald Junior's phone number and asked, "Why didn't he ask you to do it the easy way? Why not just go to the apartment and give the money to the blonde?"

"Does she live there? If so, how would he or I know when she's home? Maybe he thought one trip, even if it took some time, was better than a dozen or more failed attempts. After all, each trip would take about an hour."

"Where is your dad right now?" Pete asked.

"I already told you. He's in Florida."

"You're positive about that?" Martin asked.

"Absolutely positive. Mom is there with him. I talked to her Saturday and today when I called Dad with some tax questions."

"We'll give you a ride back to Heather's, Anderson," Pete said. "That way you won't have to jockey to retrieve your grandfather's car."

Anderson nodded.

"Before we go, how late does your dad stay up?"

Anderson hesitated, then said, "Until 11:30 or later. He watches the 11:00 p.m. news. He rarely goes to bed before it's over."

"Okay, call him and hand me your phone. Then hang tight while I speak with him—and don't say a word—or else."

After identifying himself, Pete watched Anderson's face as he told Donald Junior, "I spoke with your son Anderson. He said you were here last Saturday. It's hard to understand why anyone would come up from Florida during this cold stretch."

"I haven't been there since October. I never return before winter ends. It would take something earth-shattering to change that."

186

"You called Anderson Saturday afternoon. Why?"

"I don't remember. We speak frequently."

"You asked him to do you a favor. Does that ring a bell?"

"No. He does lots of things for me."

"This favor has to do with a blonde girl and one hundred dollars. Remember?"

"No, I sure don't."

"I thought Anderson was lying. My partner and I are arresting him. Thanks for helping us clarify things."

"Wait!" After a long pause, Donald said, "I have a lot of irons in the fire. I don't remember asking Anderson to do that, but I can't guarantee I didn't."

"You told Anderson where to wait to determine how to reach this girl. Why did you name an apartment building in Crocus Hill?"

"I don't know anything about Crocus Hill."

"But you know about Amber."

"Who?"

"The blonde girl who lives in the apartment building where you had Anderson waiting."

"Sorry, I don't know what you're talking about."

"You can guarantee you haven't been in Minnesota since October?"

"Yes. That I remember."

"Unless you want to leave Anderson holding the bag, I suggest you do your best to remember your conversation with him on Saturday. Now let me speak with your wife."

"Sorry, she isn't here."

"What's the number for her cell?"

Pete memorized the number—just in case, handed the phone back to Anderson, and told him to dial the number. Anderson rolled his eyes and did as instructed, then handed the phone back to Pete. No one answered, so Pete left a message, identifying himself, asking for a return call *tonight*, and providing his cell number. Then he pulled out his notepad and wrote down the name and number.

"I doubt you'll hear from her tonight." Anderson smiled. "My guess is she's asleep."

"Anderson, where'd you get the money to give the girl?" Pete asked.

"Dad said he'd reimburse me."

"Good luck collecting it, if he can't remember anything about it," Pete said.

"Early-onset Alzheimer's. I've seen other signs."

Mighty nonchalant about such a devastating diagnosis, Pete thought.

Exiting Anderson's home, Pete saw a lot of illuminated lights in the neighboring homes. "Take Anderson back to Heather's," he told Martin. "One of their neighbors is a friend. I want to drop by and say 'Hi,' since I'm here. I'll watch for your return."

Anderson might call the neighbors if he knew what Pete was up to. Pete smiled because Anderson couldn't do that while in the car with Martin. That bought Pete some time. Consistency prevailed as he met with these people. Donald Junior *always* went to Florida for the winter, and no one had seen him since early October. Two neighbors had contact information for one of Don's best friends in Florida and shared it. Unfortunately, since Florida is on Eastern Time, Pete wouldn't call tonight. The good news was he had enough people to question to keep him going into and out of homes until Martin returned.

When Martin got back, he slid into a welcomingly warm car.

On their way to HQ, Pete said, "Thus far we can neither prove nor disprove Anderson's current story. If the neighbors I spoke with can be trusted, and if the Florida friend we'll contact tomorrow agrees, Don hasn't been in Minnesota. He could only have done it by proxy."

"If he did it by proxy and Anderson didn't exercise the proxy, who did?"

"That's the million-dollar question. That's why face-to-face is so much better. Do you think Commander Lincoln would have approved a round-trip ticket for me to meet face to face with Don Junior?"

"For you to meet with him, not for us to meet with him?"

"I was willing to sacrifice my schedule to keep from inconveniencing you and your family."

"Friends like you are hard to come by, Pete. I feel truly blessed. I sure wish we could find Mr. Illinois. Why is he hanging out around that apartment building? Do you think he killed JD and is now looking for one of the girls to get her out of there? He must know that without JD those girls can't manage financially."

"Not without help, unless they start selling their services on the street." Pete shook his head. "Speaking of the girls, I wonder how things went with Megan and her parents. We haven't heard anything. I'm trying to believe that's a good thing."

"Ditto. The early signs were positive. Hope nothing happened to change that."

During the trip to HQ, Pete called The Crooked Pint. The manager should be there, and he still wanted to know if the restaurant had one or more security cameras. It could disprove or substantiate the alibis for Ella's brother and father.

The good news was the manager was there, and they had a security camera. The bad news was the camera hadn't worked for years.

"You're welcome to come and check for yourself," the manager said.

And if we do, you'll make sure it isn't functioning by the time we arrive, Pete thought but didn't say.

FORTY-ONE

The two investigators took advantage of the invitation from the manager of The Crooked Pint. They drove right to the restaurant to check on the operability of the security camera.

As the manager said, it didn't work. They'd probably never know how long that had been the case. For now, they had nothing to gain from spending untold hours determining that, so they returned to the original plan and drove to HQ.

"JD had received texts from two phone numbers that didn't appear in his contacts," Pete said. "They turned out to be his mother and his ex-fiancée. We have no idea of the relationship between him and his contacts. I have mixed emotions about calling all of them. What do you think, Martin?"

"You and I agree face to face is far superior to a telephone conversation. It's especially true in a situation like this, when we know nothing about the link between JD and these people. What do you think about attempting to find addresses for as many of JD's contacts as possible? Home phones are becoming uncommon, but many cell numbers are listed on the internet. Meanwhile, we can continue attempting to untangle the lies we're hearing from Anderson and his dad. We need to figure out which is lying—if not both."

"Excellent idea, Martin. There's no need for both of us to sit here doing this. Would you like to go home? I'm sure Michelle and the kids would love to see you."

Martin glanced at his watch. "Thanks for the offer, but it's ten o'clock. The kids are both in bed, and I'd be surprised if Michelle isn't asleep by now. Besides, it will take half as long if we both work on it. That way we'll both have a chance at getting a decent night's sleep."

By today's standards, JD had few contacts. That was consistent with what they'd thus far learned about him.

The two investigators spent almost two hours searching the internet for addresses. Colleges and universities were among the most generous sources of information. By the time they'd completed their search, they had addresses for almost 70 percent of the contacts. By all indications, they could also reach his current or former barber, doctor, dentist, and lawn service.

"Do you suppose JD owes one of them a lot of money, and that was the motive?" Martin asked.

While getting ready for bed, Pete thought about his grandma. That wasn't unusual. She was always close to the forefront in his thoughts. He decided to go see her before going to HQ tomorrow. She was always up at 6:30. Thinking about her schedule, he shook his head and smiled. It was always the same. Grandma ate breakfast while listening to the morning news on the radio, then read the newspaper. Before she did anything else, she washed the dishes. Next, regardless of whether or not she planned to go out or have company, she put on makeup and dressed in a nice dress or pants suit. She always looked fit to host the president or have an audience with the pope.

Tuesday morning, Pete started in the usual way—with a four-mile run. Thanks to his familiarity with the local venues, he knew of a trail that would suffice despite slippery roads and sidewalks. The snow-covered shaded trail permitted running. As his feet sank into the snow, it reminded him of running on a sandy beach. He laughed thinking about running on a sandy beach in all these clothes.

He loved running, and his day felt incomplete without it. Running gave him a chance to stretch his long legs and loosen his muscles. He delighted in being outside, enjoying the scenery and wildlife, and breathing the fresh air—even when the temperature was in the teens or twenties. He settled for the treadmill in his basement when the temperature hung in the single digits or colder. After several days on the treadmill, he relished days like today. He always experienced an emotional high from the satisfaction of accomplishing this daily ritual. In addition to the physical pleasure that came with running, he was determined to derail, or at least delay, middle-age spread. So far, so good. He was also intent on remaining in shape for the rare but ever possible foot chase after a suspect.

After completing his run, he dashed from the garage into the house and back to the bathroom. He shaved, showered, and sped through breakfast, then headed for Grandma's. Right on schedule, he'd be there in time to join her for coffee, while she ate breakfast. Pete smiled every mile. Pulling up and catching sight of her living-room window, a sick feeling in the pit of his stomach erased the smile. He should be able to see at least a hint of light escaping her dining room. He parked and ran up the stairs to her third-floor apartment two at a time. He couldn't wait for the elevator. Never did. Inserting the key she'd given him, he turned the deadbolt and opened the door. The apartment was pitch black. "Grandma?" he called anxiously.

The sound of that smooth, silky baritone brought a smile to his grandma's face. "I'm here, Pete," she answered. "I've never heard anything sweeter than the sound of your voice."

Relieved to hear her, Pete stopped holding his breath and raced into the bedroom. After praying every inch of the way, he found her on the floor at the foot of her bed. Dropping to his knees, he carefully gathered her in his arms and blotted away a tear with his shoulder.

"What happened, Grandma?"

"I was getting my slippers. My leg turned, and I went down. It was the strangest thing. I tried to get on my hands and knees so I could get up, but I couldn't. I can't put any weight on my right hip."

"Are you in pain?"

"It's not bad."

"I don't dare give you anything, in case doing that creates an issue with what the hospital wants to do. Hold tight. I'll call 911."

Pete told the operator he thought his grandmother might have broken her hip and saw her wince when he said that. In reaction, he grasped her hand. It was warm. That reassured him.

The operator said to stay on the phone until the ambulance arrived. He explained he couldn't do that. He had to take care of his grandmother. The operator ignored him and continued asking questions. Pete disconnected and said, "An ambulance will be here shortly. Is there anything I can get or do for you in the meantime?"

"Having you here, Pete, is all I need. What brought you over at this hour?"

"I missed you and decided a visit before work was a great idea."

"Or maybe you're psychic?"

"All I know is, I'm so glad I came. Glad you didn't have to lie there any longer. I love you, Grandma."

"I've never doubted it. You know I feel the same way about you."

Pete heard the sirens and gave his grandmother a protracted, warm hug. When he heard pounding on her apartment door, he yelled, "Coming."

While the ambulance crew checked his grandmother and took her vital signs, Pete called his mother. "Mom, I found Grandma on the floor. I'm afraid it could be a broken hip. The ambulance is here. I'll ride to the hospital with her. Hang on a minute. Let me find out which hospital."

"Grandma, which hospital does your doctor use? Regions?"

"Yes, dear."

"They'll take her to Regions. See you there."

Despite Pete's best effort, the ambulance crew wouldn't let him ride in back with his grandmother. He had to settle for keeping the driver company. En route he texted Martin, explaining why he'd be late.

The ambulance crew maintained radio contact with the hospital, so they were expecting his grandmother. As Pete feared, x-rays showed her right hip was broken and required surgery. That necessitated conferring with an orthopedist. Thankfully, they didn't have to camp out in the ER, waiting for that meeting. Pete felt cold and asked his grandmother if she was warm enough. He suspected not. Her hand was no longer warm. She already had two blankets, but Pete saw her shivering. He turned on the light and requested more blankets. Before long she was transferred to a private room.

Pete spent the next hour holding his grandma's hand, visiting with her, and catering to her needs. He told a nurse she hadn't eaten since last night. The nurse said she couldn't have anything until they decided if and when to operate. He followed the nurse into the hallway and asked if there was any reason they couldn't do surgery.

"Are you her healthcare agent?"

"No, but she's capable of making those decisions herself."

"In that case the orthopedist will discuss it with her."

"Any idea when we can expect the orthopedist?"

"No."

Pete thanked her for her help, *or lack thereof*, he thought, and returned to Grandma. She looked drowsy. Pete took her hand again and told her to sleep if she could.

"We'll have plenty of time to talk later."

He worried it might be wishful thinking. If they operated, could she withstand the anesthesia?

He was still sitting alongside the bed, holding her hand when his mother arrived. Seeing her, he held an index finger up to his lips, then met her in the doorway. He whispered what had happened and gave her a status report. She took the chair he'd pulled up tight against the bed to be as close as possible.

Pete walked out in the hall and called Martin.

"How is she?" Martin asked. "Are you okay?"

"I'm fine. I'm at Regions. It looks like Grandma broke her hip."

"Oh, Pete." The words overflowed with sympathy.

"My car's at her apartment. Can you pick me up? I'll explain when I see you."

Pete disconnected and returned to his mother and grandmother. His grandma appeared to be sleeping.

Pete bent over his mother and whispered in her ear, "Martin's picking me up. I assume they'll do surgery. Let me know as soon as she's scheduled, okay? If they decide against it, please let me know."

She nodded. Her eyes were red and puffy.

"Love you, Mom," he said and kissed her cheek. "Talk to you soon."

On the way to pick up his car, Pete told Martin about his morning.

FORTY-TWO

Aware of Pete's attachment to his grandma, Martin said, "I hope things go well and she's soon back on her feet, Pete."

Pete nodded and sighed. He looked deflated.

"I called the watch commander, Pete. Mr. Illinois returned last night. When the officer stationed outside the girls' apartment did as you requested and tried to get the driver's name and address, he took off, tires spinning. The CR-V slid all over the road. There wasn't time and the roads were too slippery to take chase. The watch commander was sure we'd want to know. I asked to have a BOLO issued for the CR-V."

"Great. It may take a little time, but now we can talk to the driver. See you at headquarters," he said as he got out of Martin's car.

The first thing Pete did after reaching HQ was call Don Vining Junior's wife. She hadn't returned his call. He again failed to connect and left a second message. In addition to requesting a return call ASAP, he said he had a few questions that could keep her son out of jail. A stretch? Maybe yes, maybe no.

As soon as he hung up, he found the number for Don's Florida friend and tapped it in, hoping the friend was home. Due to the delay since speaking with Junior, the friend's veracity was questionable. Even so .... When a man answered, Pete identified himself and said, "I understand Donald Vining is your friend. By any chance did you see him last Saturday?"

"Yes, he and I played eighteen holes."

"I envy you. We're ass deep in snow."

The other man laughed. "Why do you think I came south?"

"Where do you golf?"

"We almost always play here at Hale Plantation. We can drive our golf carts to the course. Great arrangement."

"Is that where you played last Saturday?"

"Yes, why?"

"What time did you finish?"

"It was almost one o'clock. It's slow when the weekend golfers are out. I wish they'd take up tennis and leave golf to those who are serious about it."

I wonder how often he shares that opinion with the weekend golfers? Pete thought.

"What did you do after you finished playing?"

"We went into the bar, so I could celebrate my victory."

"Did Donald celebrate with you?"

"He wasn't exactly celebrating. He had to buy."

"What time did you get home?"

"It was almost 4:00. Don's wife was furious. He'd promised to do something or other," he laughed, "I didn't hang around to hear details."

"Did Don get a phone call while you two were together that day?"

"You mean like notifying him he'd won the Publishers Clearing House sweepstakes?" Uproarious laughter. "No, we don't take our phones to the golf course. It's extremely impolite and inconsiderate. I won't golf with anyone who takes their phone. Nothing is important enough to justify it."

If Don called Anderson at 1:32 that afternoon, he must have had his phone and ducked out long enough to call, Pete thought.

He disconnected and shook his head. He couldn't imagine spending a day, much less the winter, with a guy like that. Comparatively speaking, the snow and subzero temperatures seemed inviting.

Pete looked at his watch, then hurried and checked the airline schedules from Gainesville to Minneapolis. "It would have been tight," he told Martin, "but Donald Junior could have flown up and gotten here in time to be our man."

"We better hit the road. Alyssa is expecting us. I don't want to be late. I'd be surprised if she slept last night. She's pretty nervous about this meeting."

"Yeah, poor kid. Not to change the subject, but why is it every time the temperature gets above single digits, it snows? At these temperatures the chemicals they put on the roads are far less effective."

"Glad you're driving." Pete smiled.

"I hope Alyssa's mom is at Ella's or at least nearby," Martin said as they neared Ella's home.

"At this rate, the roads could be pretty nasty before long."

"Hey, Martin," Pete said. "Did you see Marty this morning? I was wondering how he's acting after you took away his cell."

"Michelle rolled over when I got in bed. I asked about it. She said he's taking it surprisingly well. Found out for myself this morning. I thought he might be giving us the silent treatment. He isn't. He's acting like nothing's changed. I know he's a really good kid, but this amazes me. If I was in his place, I wouldn't be taking it this well."

"I'd say you're a lucky guy Martin, but luck has nothing to do with it. It's known as good parenting. I hope to do that well with my kids."

The weather forecast was spot on. It started snowing as Martin pulled out of the parking lot at headquarters, and the white stuff fell with a vengeance. Alyssa had asked that Child Protection not attend this meeting but be on standby if she changed her mind.

Pete felt apologetic when he discovered Barbara Gilbert and her friend had arrived at Ella's before them. Thankfully, Ella's mother had taken the day off. Knowing Alyssa would want privacy, she'd taken Barbara's friend shopping on Grand Avenue. Hearing that, both investigators hoped the woman's kindness would help protect them both if the roads got worse.

Ella answered the door and led them to Alyssa. The girl and her mother were engaged in small talk when the two investigators joined them. Alyssa smiled hopefully when she saw Pete and introduced her mom to him and Martin, saying, "Mom, these are the policemen who rescued us."

The four of them settled around the dining-room table. Alyssa took her mother's hand before beginning. "Mom, I'm so sorry I ran away." Tears began welling up in her eyes and in her mom's as well.

"I'm so stupid. I thought life would be great if I made all the decisions. I know now you were doing what was best for me. I didn't realize it when I got on a Jefferson Lines bus. I had all these dreams about what it would be like. I couldn't have been more wrong. As soon as I got off the bus in Minneapolis, I began doubting myself. I had no idea what to do next. I had enough money for food for a few days, but not if I had to pay for a place to stay." Alyssa blew her nose and wiped her eyes. Then she resumed holding her mother's hand.

"This is the bad part, Mom. I hope you don't hate me after I tell you. If you do, I understand. If you never want to see me again, I won't blame you."

Questioningly, Barbara glanced from Alyssa to Pete to Martin, then back at Alyssa, who closed her eyes and bit her lip.

Pete wished he had a way to make this and the coming months and years easier for Alyssa. For every kid finding herself or himself in her predicament.

After several seconds she opened her eyes and looked at her mom. "I thought I was the luckiest person when I walked out of the bus depot and a man started talking to me. He took me out to dinner. He wanted to know all about me. He offered to help. He said I could stay at his house."

Barbara gasped.

"I know, Mom. I know it was stupid. My first reaction was NO WAY! But he was so convincing. He *promised* he wouldn't touch me if I didn't want him to. I believed him." Alyssa broke down sobbing.

So did her mom. Taking a few steps, her mom moved behind Alyssa's chair, bent over, and gathered her daughter in her arms. The embrace and the crying continued for a few minutes, then Barbara returned to her chair and reached for and held her daughter's hand.

Pete waited until Barbara was seated before speaking. He didn't want to interrupt. Then he said, "Barbara, you should speak to the people in Child Protection. This problem has reached epidemic proportions. People like the man who victimized Alyssa are pros. I think you already know, but in case you don't, you can't blame Alyssa."

"I could never blame her. I blame myself. I drove her to it."

"No, Mom. It's my fault." Alyssa leaned over and kissed Barbara's cheek. After a pause she continued. "I have to tell you what happened, Mom. He forced me to be a prostitute."

Once her mother succeeded in closing her gaping mouth, she said, "But Alyssa, why didn't you run away?"

"I couldn't without putting you and Dad and Garret and Madison all at risk. JD told me he'd force Madison to be one of his girls if I left. And he said he'd kill the rest of you, Mom. I couldn't risk it. I love all of you so much."

This time Barbara leaned over and kissed Alyssa's cheek.

Pete stood. "I think the two of you need some time alone. Alyssa, you have our business cards, and you and your mom know how to reach Child Protection. Please take advantage of what they offer. You have a brave, unselfish daughter, Barbara. She looked out for the other girls in JD's clutches."

"I'll second that on all counts," Martin said.

"I hope the girls will be okay," Martin said after they walked out of Ella's house. "It's bound to be a long, difficult road."

"Their chances improve markedly if they don't try to do it alone. Working in Alyssa's favor is the fact she seems both resilient and strong. My money's on her."

FORTY-THREE

The half dozen accidents Martin crawled past on the way back to headquarters painted a graphic picture of how much road conditions had deteriorated in the last hour. The return trip took more than twice as long as usual.

"I'm glad conditions weren't like this when we left," Pete said. "Alyssa would probably have been at wit's end. I wonder what's happening with Grandma."

Pete decided not to wait to hear. He pulled out his cell and called his mom.

"I'll call you right back," she whispered. "The doctor's here."

Pete didn't put the phone away. He did say a prayer.

"What's up?" Martin asked.

"Waiting to hear. Will soon know."

Silence filled the car until Pete's phone vibrated.

"The doctor scheduled surgery for four o'clock this afternoon," Pete's mom said.

"I'm worried about Grandma."

"I know, Pete. We both are. Mom's vital signs are good. The doctor's confident she'll come through the surgery just fine."

"Will they use general anesthesia?"

"That's the plan."

"I want to see her before they administer the anesthesia. Do you have any idea what time they'll start prepping her?"

"I suggest allowing some leeway and arrive between 3:00 and 3:30."

"I'll do my best. How are you doing, Mom?"

"Okay. It helps to know the plan. Mom's sleeping a lot. Your dad will be here around noon. I'm expecting your sister this afternoon. She's rattled, but she'll be fine. Frankly, Pete, I'm more concerned about you."

"Is Grandma awake now?"

"No. She was while the doctor was here but drifted off again. I think the trauma is draining her energy."

"Understood. Barring a catastrophe, I'll see you around three."

After disconnecting, Pete tapped in the phone number for Don Junior's wife. Before he connected, Martin's cell vibrated.

Martin glanced at the screen while handing his phone to Pete.

"I'm calling regarding the BOLO Sergeant Tierney requested for the Honda CR-V with the Illinois plate," the watch commander said. "A state trooper spotted the vehicle on I-94 and turned on lights and siren while following him toward the Wisconsin border. The driver, Kenneth William Lamberton, accelerated right after the strobes went on and lost control. He spun out, bounced off the guard rail and into another car, then was hit by two other cars."

"How long ago did it happen?" Pete asked.

"It's been an hour or a little longer."

"Where's Lamberton now?"

"At Regions. He wasn't wearing a seat belt. I understand he's pretty banged up. No word yet on his condition."

"Thanks for the info," Pete said, disconnected, and told Martin, "They found Mr. Illinois. He's at Regions. Let's go."

"Is this a case of, 'If Mohammed can't go to the mountain?'"

"I'd never be quite that arrogant."

Martin dropped off Pete off at the ER entrance and went in search of a parking space.

Pete went to the check-in desk and explained for whom he was looking. The woman paged a charge nurse. When the nurse arrived, Pete showed his ID and badge and asked about Kenneth Lamberton.

"I'm not allowed to say. HIPAA, you know."

"I know. I'm a police officer investigating a murder and need to speak with him. Where can I find him?"

Martin arrived in time to hear that much.

She walked around behind the desk, tapped a few keyboard keys and said, "He's on 4 North. Check at the nurses' station."

Pete and Martin followed the terrazzo-covered hallway to the closest elevator, got off on the fourth floor, followed the signs to 4 North, and spoke to the aide at the nurses' station. They found Lamberton's room after following several jogs in the hallway and saw the cop stationed outside his room.

"Hi Matt. How's it going?" Pete asked the uniformed officer.

"Slow, but I can't complain. I'm not freezing."

"How's Lamberton doing?"

"Sounds like he's pretty doped up, but I understand he'll make it. It was a dumb move, in light of road conditions."

Pete and Martin entered the room. Lamberton had a single room and a plethora of tubes. His eyes remained closed when the two investigators entered.

"Kenneth Lamberton?" Pete asked.

Lamberton took his time opening his eyes. "Yeah," he said finally.

Both investigators displayed their IDs and badges. Lamberton looked from their hands to their faces. "Don't you guys have anything better to do? I didn't pull over. Big deal. Why the hullabaloo?"

"We understand it was a mighty nasty four-car accident," Pete said.

"You're not suggesting it was my fault, are you?"

Much as they wanted to, Pete and Martin didn't call him on it.

"Where were you last Saturday night between 7:00 and 11:00?" Martin asked.

"I was home."

"Where's home?" Martin asked.

"Rockford, Illinois."

"Can you prove you were there?" Martin continued.

"I was with my wife. Ask her. She'll tell you."

"Were you home, or did you go out?" Martin asked.

"We stayed home."

"What did you have for dinner?" Pete asked.

"You want to know what I had for dinner on Saturday. Hell, I don't remember what I had for dinner last night, and that has nothing to do with me banging my head."

"You're often in Minnesota. Why?" Pete asked.

"Business."

"What business?" Pete asked.

"I'm an area representative for an insurance company. Do you have life insurance? With a job like yours, you shouldn't be without it, you know." Lamberton wagged his finger at Pete, then Martin.

"Why were you in St. Paul's Crocus Hill last night?" Martin asked.

"I was in the neighborhood and stopped to see a friend."

"You didn't leave your car, and no one joined you," Martin said.

"You know, this 'big brother' thing is getting out of hand."

"If you went to see a friend, why didn't you get out of your car?"

"Because I called after I pulled up, and she wasn't home."

"What's her name?" Martin asked.

"Esther."

"Last name?" Martin asked.

"Babbitt. If you're planning to check who lives in every apartment in the vicinity, you won't find her name. Her ex rents it for her. It's part of the alimony."

"What's her ex's name?" Martin asked.

"The last name is something like Carver. I don't know his first name."

"What's Esther's phone number?" Pete asked.

"I'll give it to you, but you'll be wasting your time. She won't answer an unrecognized number."

"No problem," Pete said. "Give me her phone number and address."

Kenneth provided the phone number and said, "I don't know the address. I just know how to get there. She's in Unit E."

"Where does Esther work?" Pete asked.

"At the Apple store at Rosedale."

"How long has she worked there?" Pete asked.

"I don't know. I met her there."

"When was that?" Pete asked.

"Last summer."

"So you went to see Esther, discovered she wasn't home, and took off when a cop walked over to your car?" Pete asked.

"I never saw a cop approach my car. Why would they hassle me?"

"Then why did you accelerate so much you were all over the road?" Pete asked.

"I have no idea what you're talking about." Lamberton wiped his face on his gown.

"Why didn't you pull over this morning?" Pete asked.

"I was sure they were after someone else. I even looked at my speedometer. I was well within the speed limit. I was just trying to get out of the way. I should sue the State of Minnesota to replace my car and pay my hospital bills."

"A trusted source told us you know JD St. Peter," Martin said.

"The name doesn't ring a bell." Lamberton shrugged

"He's a pimp," Martin said. "Does that help?"

"No way."

"Do you know Don Vining and his son Anderson?" Pete asked.

"No, I don't know either one," Lamberton said, and fidgeted with the straw in his water glass.

"I understand you're a friend of Danny Jackson," Martin said.

"Who?"

"Danny Jackson. He manages a restaurant in downtown St. Paul."

"What restaurant?"

"The Hub," Martin said.

"I've heard of it but never been there, and I don't know anyone named Danny Jackson." Lamberton took a drink of water, then opened and closed his tray.

"Does your wife know you were in an accident?" Martin asked.

"Yes, I called her."

"Is she coming here?" Pete asked.

"Yes, but she can't leave until after work. She won't get here until ten or eleven at the earliest, depending on the roads."

FORTY-FOUR

Pete and Martin stopped at the nurses' station and asked if there was any chance Lamberton would be released before eight tomorrow morning. He was told, "It's highly unlikely, but I can't rule it out."

The two investigators returned to Lamberton's room, and Martin asked the officer stationed there to give him a heads-up if he heard mention of releasing Lamberton.

"How long do you think Lamberton rehearsed? Or is he that good on his feet?" Pete asked Martin as they stepped in the elevator on their way back to the unmarked car.

"First, he wasn't on his feet. He was flat on his back. Anyway, he's had good reason and ample time to plan and rehearse his answers."

"Yeah. I hate it when that happens. There are so many disjointed pieces, Martin. Is there a connection between Donald Junior and his son Anderson, Samuel Ulen, and Lamberton? If there is, does it have anything to do with this case? What about Danny Jackson, Larson and Percy Henderson, and Ted Acton? We can't disqualify any of them."

"Lamberton's wife could be an important contributor," Martin said. "That interview has to be face to face. Unfortunately, we can't meet with her before midnight."

"Here's the problem," Pete said. "I'm not certain JD's being a child trafficker provided the motive. Due to the information available to us, that's where we've concentrated our efforts. But Danny said JD didn't repay a substantial sum. Money is a common motive. Along those same lines, he said JD had been gambling. Was JD hooked on gambling? Or was he blackmailing someone or being blackmailed? If the latter, suppose he stopped making payments."

"Forensics wrapped up their search at his house. If, like most people these days, he'd gone paperless, what we'd need wouldn't have been there anyway. Getting a search warrant to access his bank information requires a convincing argument. One we don't have. Considering what we have, most likely the judge would accuse us of being on a 'fishing trip.' She or he, of course, would be right. Where do we find that one little piece of information that will bust this case wide open?"

"Before we do anything else, Pete, I have a recommendation I think you should give serious consideration."

"And that is?"

"Lunch. I'm just thinking of you. You aren't likely to have much of a dinner—if anything at all."

"Do you have a place in mind?"

"How about Keys again? It isn't far; they serve breakfast all day."

They followed Martin's recommendation. As soon as they'd placed their orders, Pete said, "How about an update on Michelle, Martin? I can see you're stressed."

"That sucks, Pete," Martin sighed. "She's had a rough couple of days. The doctor told us several times that there'd be ups and downs along the way. But I let myself believe the worst was behind us. Now she's barely functioning again." Worry lines creased Martin's forehead and the corners of his mouth.

"I'm so sorry, Martin. Do you think she did something that caused a setback?"

"No, not for a second. She's too afraid to take chances." Martin played with his silverware. "She's still taking the supplements and resting whenever she can. It's been three weeks since we started our new diet. You know, Pete, any diet is hard to stick with. Now that the benefits of this one seem to have evaporated or at least gone on vacation, it's even harder."

"I understand, but you have to concentrate on the good days. If you and Michelle stay the course, they're sure to outnumber the bad and become the norm. Find strength in that. Keep your eye on the prize."

Martin nodded. He knew Pete was right.

"Tell me about the diet again," Pete said, taking a bite of his everything omelet—his go-to meal when he and Martin ate at Keys.

"Well, right now it's high on protein with very limited carbs. Lots of leafy vegetables. No sugar. No gluten. Nothing out of a box."

Pete knew Martin, hence exactly how he felt about it.

"You'd probably like it, Pete. It's not very different from the way you usually eat. It's radically different from the way I usually eat ... and like to eat. It certainly doesn't include this stack of hotcakes with a side of bacon." Martin shook his head.

Pete laughed and watched Martin take a big bite of buttermilk pancakes soaked in syrup. "Does eating the things you like when you're away from home help?"

"I don't know. It doesn't seem to. Sometimes I crave sweets and carbs when I get home. Sometimes it's almost easier on my days off, when I don't get a break from the diet."

Pete rubbed his upper lip. "You know, Martin, there could be a moral to that story. Some of the doctors who push low-carb diets say if you stick with it, it gets easier as you go along. You might consider giving it a try, but I won't watch over your shoulder. It's up to you."

"Glad to know I won't have to start sneaking food when I'm with you." Martin rolled his eyes.

"Definitely not. I'll say one more thing, then I'll shut up about your diet. It could make you feel better, a lot healthier, even extend your life expectancy."

Martin smiled. "You sound like Michelle. On the bright side, even though I don't follow the diet all the time, I'm losing weight. And Michelle's thrilled. I have to admit I like that side effect. I just hope Michelle doesn't like it so much she wants me to eat this way permanently. As far as her health is concerned, we should be able to start easing up on some of the restrictions over the next month or so."

"That's something to look forward to, and I noticed you're shedding pounds. I thought it was the stress."

"Probably a little of both. Ahh for the good old days." Martin blew out a long breath.

"Tell me, Martin, is Michelle worth it?" He smiled.

"You know she is. Thanks for reminding me."

"We still haven't heard from Donald Vining Junior's wife, Martin. It's hard to know how to interpret that. There really are so many possibilities."

FORTY-FIVE

"In light of the reception we received from Mrs. Vining's husband and son, you aren't surprised she's ignoring your requests for callbacks are you, Pete?"

"No, actually very little about this job surprises me anymore." Pete called her again and found her infuriatingly consistent. He moved her down several notches on his list of priorities. By now, Donald had plenty of time to influence her answers, if she was malleable, and he had no way of assessing that. Hence anything she said was highly suspect.

Shortly before 3:00, Pete left for the hospital. "Cut out early, Martin," he said on his way out the door. "Tomorrow will probably be another long day. Enjoy dinner with Michelle and the kids." The fact Martin could enjoy being home for dinner but probably wouldn't enjoy the food struck Pete as soon as those words passed over his lips.

Martin wished him and his grandma all the best and said, "Before I hang it up, I'm going to attempt to determine if Esther Babbitt lives in apartment E in the girls' building."

"Good idea. Let me know the outcome."

Pete parked in the ramp and hurried to his grandmother's room, anxious to have at least a few minutes with this dear woman who meant so much to him and held a very special place in his heart. Why was he so worried? Was this a premonition or a normal reaction to major surgery on a ninety-year-old? Thoughts of her flooded his mind as he ran to the elevators. He was so caught up in these thoughts that he nearly failed to recognize the man entering the parking ramp from another elevator. Punching several buttons, he tried futilely to reopen the elevator doors. The mechanism ignored him. Despite being driven to solve this case, to solve every case, he stayed on course to Grandma's room. Questioning Gordon Orrock had to wait.

When he reached his grandmother's room, his mom, dad, and sister Sarah were there with her. "Any update on the time?" he asked no one in particular.

"We haven't heard anything yet," his mom said.

"Since Pete's here, if it's okay with everyone, I'm going to run some errands," his dad said. "Please keep me posted, and if you need anything let me know." Then he kissed his wife, hugged Sarah and Pete, and left.

"Did you have a chance to call Aunt Beth and Uncle Gil?" Pete asked his mom, referring to her sister and brother.

"Yes, I called them shortly after I arrived. I called again when we learned they'd do surgery and had an estimated time. They're both worried and want to be kept updated."

"Mom, Sarah," Pete said, "I hope it's okay if I want a few minutes alone with Grandma."

"I'd have been surprised if you didn't." His mom smiled, nodding. "We'll get something to drink. If they come for her before we get back, please text."

"Wait a minute!" Sarah stood and got in Pete's face. "You found Grandma and had time alone with her until Mom arrived. It's my turn, thank you very much."

Grandma cringed. She looked like she wanted to cover her ears.

Pete wasn't shocked by Sarah's pronouncement, even though she'd just spent hours with Grandma. It was patently Sarah. He wished he'd done something earlier to derail this. Rather than wasting precious seconds lambasting her, he said, "Please text when you finish. I pray we both have the time we need." *Hint, hint!* he thought.

Pete and his mom left Sarah and his grandma, then walked the hallways, waiting to hear from Sarah.

"I'm sorry, Pete," his mom said. "Sarah's probably stressed out, and you know Sarah. She's always been a take-charge person. She's only six years older than you, but for years she spent more time telling you what to do than I did. You thought you had two mothers. She told you what you could watch on TV, when it was your nap or bed time, when it was too soon for you to get up, and when you could have a snack or a cookie. She even tried to influence the kids you played with. I should have done a better job of putting my foot down." Pete's mom shook her head. "It seemed the more I told her you were my responsibility, not hers, the more she told you what to do."

209

"While Mom slept," Pete's mom continued, "Sarah challenged the advisability of Mom having surgery. Then she lectured me about permitting Mom to return to her apartment and resume living alone

She threw out all kinds of statistics, supposedly proving both were bad ideas. I, of course, had no statistics to throw back at her. Finally when I'd heard more than enough, out of exasperation I told her Mom is an outlier. I think I got that term from you." Angie smiled, went up on her tiptoes and kissed Pete's cheek. "I told her I would not take away Mom's independence unless and until it was proven imperative."

"She seems to think I'm too old to make rational decisions, at least about Mom. I tried to explain that Mom is the only one with the authority to make these decisions, at least until she demonstrates she's unable to run her own affairs. I was so glad when your dad arrived."

"I'm sorry, Mom. I know this is difficult, and Sarah's making it worse. Grandma has a healthcare directive, doesn't she?"

"Yes, thank goodness."

"Did she name you as the agent in her directive?" Pete thought he knew the answer, based on his mom's answer to the previous question. Unwilling to assume anything, he held his breath.

"Yes."

Pete blew out a long breath.

He and his mom discussed the post-hospital plans. If his mother had any doubts about the outcome, she carefully masked them. "Mom will be released in two or three days. Thankfully, she has long-term-care insurance. It includes in-home care. Tomorrow I'll start working to set up around-the-clock care. I know there are companies that screen their staff and will handle the scheduling. I'll insist on interviewing anyone they want to send. If she's available, Sarah can help. You, of course, are welcome also if it fits in your schedule. But don't worry. I know you're busy with a new case. We'll manage."

"I have faith. If anyone can do it, it's you. I'm serious, Mom. Please don't let anything Sarah says cause you to doubt yourself."

Pete's mom stepped closer and hugged him, holding him tight for a protracted period. She found comfort in his presence and his strength.

"Remember, Mom, I'm with you on this. If you want me to tell Sarah to back off, I will. She has no right to make any of the decisions that lie ahead or push you to do what she thinks is best."

"I know that's not her intent. The problem is, she's sure she knows a lot more than I do about these things."

"And she got the expertise from reading a few books or talking to friends? She has no professional or personal experience. I know whatever you and Grandma decide will be best, Mom. Please don't let Sarah intimidate you."

Pete and his mom were walking toward his grandma's room. As they turned a corner, they saw Sarah approaching. Thankfully, Sarah didn't hear him.

"Your turn, Pete," Sarah said.

Pete hurried into the room, bent over and gave his grandma a long, warm hug. Then he pulled a chair up tight against her bed and held her hand. Before he could say anything, she said, "I'm so glad you had time to talk before they put me under. I believe I'll be fine, but I have a few things to say ... just in case."

"Pete, you're a wonderful blessing. I treasure every minute we've spent together. There was a special connection from day one. From the time you were a baby, every time you saw me, you reached for me and wanted me to hold you. It didn't matter who else was in the room. It touched me deeply. You've always been kind to me and considerate of my feelings, even when you were a teenager. I've always felt complimented that you habitually take time out of a busy schedule to be with me and take me places. You have greatly enriched my life. I'm so thankful for you."

"Don't get me wrong. I love Sarah. She too holds a special place in my heart. But it's not the same. I also love your cousins, but they live on both coasts and I rarely see them. I'm not complaining. That's just the way it is."

"There's something I want to tell you, Pete. Something I want you to have. There's a square tin box in the second drawer from the bottom of my dresser. It contains the medals your grandpa was awarded during World War II. I want you to have them. I know your grandpa would want that too. Do you have your notepad and a pen? I'd be surprised if anyone challenged you taking them, but just in case. I'd never forgive myself if you didn't get them."

Pete pulled out his notepad and pen and gave both to her.

She wrote a note with meticulous penmanship, despite being almost flat on her back, signed it, and handed everything back to Pete.

"Thanks, Grandma," Pete said. He tucked the notepad away for safekeeping, then bent and kissed her. "I hope you've never doubted how much you mean to me and how much I love you, Grandma. Thanks to you, my life has been so much richer. You more than anyone helped me get through the loss of Andrea and our baby. You helped me believe things would get better with time. I have so many wonderful memories of our times together, starting with when I was a small child and spent time with you and Grandpa." Pete brushed away a tear.

"I've learned so much from you. I learned to roll with the punches. I learned to appreciate little things. I learned how to age gracefully ..., but I'm not planning to need that for quite some time." He smiled. "I saw how to love selflessly. Still working on that one. I discovered having more stuff doesn't bring happiness ... that any happiness derived from stuff is fleeting. Throw in self-confidence and stick-to-itiveness for good measure. And that's just for starters. I'm planning to learn so much more. I'm planning on giving my kids plenty of opportunities to learn from you."

"Speaking of which, Pete, I'll be at your wedding, and I won't be in a wheelchair or trailing a walker. I'll be walking straight and tall."

"I have faith, Grandma. In fact, I've already picked out a dance partner for you."

"Great." She smiled. "You know I love to dance."

FORTY-SIX

In the waiting room Pete, his mother, and Sarah endured the three-hour surgery. Pete spent most of the time praying. He believed in prayer. He believed his prayers could bring his grandma through when she otherwise wouldn't survive the surgery. If there was any chance, even the smallest morsel of a chance, he wanted the prayers to be there for his grandma. He wondered if people can ever be prepared to lose their grandparents and decided the answer was an emphatic no.

His mom drifted off a few times. Pete knew he'd interrupted her sleep this morning. She, unlike her mother, wasn't an early riser. Sarah spent much of the time working on crossword puzzles and playing spider solitaire on her phone.

A little after seven the surgeon came to the waiting room, looking for the family of Jacquelyn Schmitt. Pete, his mom, and Sarah stood for his report. "Jacquelyn is in recovery. As soon as she regains consciousness, she'll be returned to her room. She came through it amazingly well—even for someone a decade her junior. She's a real trooper. You need to make arrangements with a nursing home or rehabilitation facility for her recovery. If you need help, the hospital social services staff will be available."

All three joined Pete's grandma, waited for her to regain consciousness, then accompanied her to her room. They stayed there for more than an hour. Pete's grandma spent most of the time sleeping.

"Sis," Pete said, "why don't you head out? You've had a long day. Mom, you too. I know you're tired, and tomorrow will be another long day. If it's okay with everyone, I'll stay here with Grandma tonight. Or we can take turns, if that's what the two of you want."

"Let's discuss the plans for the next two nights tomorrow," Pete's mom said. "I'm dead on my feet. If I'm back by seven, Pete, will that suffice?"

"It'll be perfect. See you then." Pete held his mom and kissed her, then did the same with his sister.

Sarah walked out the door with their mother but returned a few minutes later. "Pete, you know Mom is being unrealistic, don't you? Grandma needs to go to a nursing home." Her volume was increasing.

Pete put an arm around Sarah and ushered her into the hallway. "Sarah, I don't want Grandma to hear you. Did you discuss this with Mom?"

"Yes. I don't know why she won't face the facts. Grandma's future is in a nursing home."

"Why?"

"She's ninety. It'll take a long time to recover from this surgery. She'll never be as strong as she was before the surgery. She can't live alone anymore."

"And you're basing those conclusions on?"

"The experiences of my friends with their grandmothers."

"How do you think Grandma will react to a nursing home?"

"She'll get used to it. They have all kinds of activities she'll enjoy."

"Do you think Grandma should have a voice in this?"

"Of course not. We know what she'd say."

"And that's exactly what I say. Until we discover she's incapable of staying in her apartment with in-home care, let her be."

"Pete, you have no idea."

"If we're talking experience, nor do you, Sarah. If you don't have anything else, I want to get back to Grandma."

Sarah spun and stomped away ... as best she could on a terrazzo floor.

Pete spent the night in a chair alongside his grandmother, holding her hand. He was awake more than asleep, and he filled the hours listening to the bleeping and clicking of the myriad of monitors—thinking about the current investigation.

His mom arrived a few minutes before seven.

Pete told her the night was uneventful, made sure she was set, and hurried to his car. He had to get home, shower and shave, and return to Regions. And he had to accomplish all of that by eight o'clock or a few minutes after.

FORTY-SEVEN

It was a rare day when Pete didn't start with a four-mile run. This was one of them. He anxiously awaited a chance to interview Kenneth Lamberton's wife. He hoped she'd voluntarily tell the truth or that strategically applied pressure would force her hand. All the way home and all the way back to Regions Hospital, Pete thanked the Minnesota Transportation Department and the Ramsey County and St. Paul Streets Departments. He knew many other jurisdictions wouldn't have the roads so passable after yesterday's snow. If he lived elsewhere, he might not have had time to clean up before meeting Lamberton's wife.

As soon as he got home, he texted Martin, asking him, "Can U pick me up @ HQ @ 7:45? If problem, come 2 Lamberton's room or see you at HQ when finished. BTW Esther Babbitt?"

Pete checked the text that arrived while he was in the shower. It was from Martin and said, "C U at 7:45."

Pete finished getting ready, grabbed a granola bar, and headed out the door. He parked and was outside the main HQ entrance by 7:40. Martin arrived a minute later. On their way to Regions, Pete told him about seeing Gordon Orrock yesterday. Martin told him about Esther. "No one answered the buzzer for apartment E, so I buzzed Eleanor. She came to the door. I asked if she knew who lived in apartment E. Of course she did. I have to look up the name. It isn't Esther Babbitt. The woman in that apartment is in her eighties and doesn't work at the Apple Store or any other store at Rosedale."

"Good job and great timing, Martin."

They caught an elevator and reached Lamberton's room by 8:00. His wife wasn't there. Neither was Lamberton.

"Do you know where he is, Mark?" Pete asked the new officer stationed outside Lamberton's room.

"They wheeled him away an hour or more ago."

"Do you know if his wife arrived last night?"

"Yes. She slept here in a chair last night. She's getting breakfast."

Pete called her cell. He wasn't sure, but thought people weren't supposed to use cellphones in at least some departments in hospitals. *It's a bad idea if you're having an MRI,* he thought and smiled.

"Is this Mrs. Lamberton?" he asked when a voice said, "Hello?"

"Who is this?"

Pete identified himself.

"Ken Lamberton is my husband, but I go by my maiden name, Ellsworth."

"My partner and I want to talk to you. We'll come to you. Where can we find you?"

"My husband told me about the two of you. I'm in the cafeteria and almost finished. I'll meet you in Ken's room."

"Please, stay there. My partner and I could both use a cup of coffee. How will I identify you?"

"I'm wearing a white turtleneck and a bright-yellow sweater."

Pete and Martin entered the cafeteria and scanned for a yellow sweater.

"Right there," Martin said as Pete spotted her. They headed for her via the coffee bar and cash register.

"We stopped at your husband's room before I called you," Pete said. "He wasn't there."

"I know. There's blood in his urine. They took him to imaging."

"I understand he travels frequently to the Twin Cities," Martin said.

"Yes, I'm surprised at the frequency. I think he's here as much for pleasure as for business. He went to school in the Twin Cities and still has several good friends here."

"Have you met any of them?" Pete asked.

"Yes, occasionally he brings me along."

"I think we've met some of them as well," Pete said. "What are their names?"

"You should ask Ken."

"Was Ken on his way home when he was in the accident yesterday?" Martin asked.

"Yes. I was so concerned when he didn't arrive. I worried I might have lost him. Unfortunately, I have a knack for worrying."

"When did he come to Minnesota?" Martin asked.

"Sunday afternoon."

"And where was he Saturday night between 7:00 and 11:00?" Martin asked.

"Home with me."

"Are you sure about both of those answers?" Martin asked.

Pete took a sip of coffee and watched Ellsworth's reaction over the rim of the cup.

"Yes, he left when I went to meet with my mystery book club. We met at one o'clock."

"I'm not saying you're lying, but I want to make sure you know if you lie to us you could be charged with obstruction of justice or worse, Ms. Ellsworth," Pete said.

"You could have fooled me. It sure sounds like you're accusing me of lying. I'm *not*." Ellsworth glared at Pete.

"We might be willing to believe that if you tell us the names of Ken's close friends who live here," Pete said.

Ellsworth rolled her eyes and said, "Fine! Ken, Sam Ulen, and Don Vining are inseparable."

"How about Gordon Orrock?"

"The name isn't familiar," she said, looking at her watch.

A cloud of skepticism descended on both investigators.

"We need some time alone with your husband," Pete said.

"No problem. I need to get a hotel room. I'm *not* spending another night in that chair."

"I know what you mean," Pete said. "I spent last night in a chair just like it. My grandmother broke her hip and had surgery yesterday."

The chill she cast off warmed a few degrees. "Really? In this hospital?"

"No, she's in United," Pete lied. He calculated the risk as zero to none since they had different last names, but wouldn't risk it. "Let's see if Ken's back in his room."

Pete and Martin walked into Ken's room with his wife.

"Oh, ahh, did you meet in the hallway?" Ken asked, straightening his sheets and rearranging his hospital gown.

"No, Ken, they found me in the cafeteria."

"Really." It was a statement, not a question, and Ken said it without expression.

"She was very helpful," Pete said.

"Really," Ken said in the same expressionless voice. "Sweetheart, why don't you get a hotel room and get some sleep?"

Ms. Ellsworth walked over to the bed, kissed her husband, and asked if he was sure it was okay if she left.

"I'm sure I'll be fine. I feel better now. Go take care of yourself for a change. I'll see you later."

After Ms. Ellsworth exited the room, Pete said, "We have some additional questions, Mr. Lamberton."

"I don't think my doctor would approve. I'm feeling really sick. I could be having a heart attack."

"You're hooked up and they're monitoring your vital signs," Pete said. "If there was something to worry about, a nurse would have come through that door almost before you felt anything."

"I'm not taking any chances," Ken said and pushed the button, turning on his call light. A nurse arrived in a minute or five, and Lamberton said, "I'm feeling terrible. Is it a heart attack or a blood clot? What can you do for me?"

The nurse walked to Ken's side, felt his forehead, and looked at the blood pressure monitor. "Tell me exactly what you're feeling," she said.

"I just feel sick all over."

"He'll probably feel a lot better after he talks to us," Pete said. "It could reduce his stress." *Or put it over the top.*

"I don't think that's a good idea, nurse," Lamberton said.

"This is very important. Could even be critical," Pete told the nurse.

"We have to respect the patient's wishes."

"Even when there's a police officer stationed outside his room?" Pete asked.

"Please understand my position. If I permit you to stay and something happens, it could mean my job."

"I don't want to put you in that position. I do want you to know I'm sure he's doing this to avoid speaking with us."

The nurse shrugged.

Pete said one last thing before leaving. "Keep one thing in mind Mr. Lamberton. This might be your only chance to cut a deal."

With that, he and Martin walked out the door.

"Wait!" Lamberton shouted.

FORTY-EIGHT

Pete and Martin were on their way to the elevator when Lamberton called out to them. Pete looked at Martin. The two men shrugged and returned to Ken.

"What kind of deal?" Lamberton asked as the two men entered his room.

"That, of course, is up to the judge," Pete said. "Maybe a reduced sentence, maybe probation. Whatever it is, it's better than what you'll get if you continue playing these games."

"Okay, sit down."

Pete and Martin pulled the two chairs closer to the bed, but nowhere near as close to the bed as Pete sat to his grandmother's.

"Where were you last Saturday night, Ken?" Pete asked.

"I already told you, and I told you the truth. I was home in Rockford."

"You were in St. Paul on Sunday and Monday. When did you come here?" Pete asked.

"Sunday afternoon."

"I know you know who JD St. Peter is," Pete said. "Why did you go to the building where he rented an apartment for his girls on both Sunday and Monday nights?"

"I wanted to know if they were okay. I heard on the news what happened at the Crashed Ice competition. If I was right and that was JD, I knew they'd need money. I couldn't support them, but I wanted to help them."

"I hear you went to school in the Twin Cities and have several good friends here," Martin said. "What are their names?"

"I'd rather not say. I'm sure they had nothing to do with this."

"Do you want to help yourself or don't you?" Martin asked.

"Do you have any idea what it would do to my wife to learn I've been sleeping with an under-aged girl? It will destroy her, to say nothing of our marriage."

"That's not why we're here," Pete said. "Our job is to determine who murdered JD St. Peter. Did you ever see him? Would you recognize him if you passed him in the street?"

"Not a chance. It was all arranged over the dark web."

"How did you find him and his girls?"

"Through a friend."

"What's that friend's name?"

Ken sighed and stared at his hands. After a long pause, he said, "Don Vining."

"When's the last time you saw Don?" Martin asked.

"September or October. I can't give you an exact date."

"Any chance he was here last Saturday?" Martin asked.

"He *hates* winter. I'd be amazed, but I can't rule it out." Lamberton used the sleeve of his gown to dry his face.

"Do you know his son Anderson?"

"I've met him. I wouldn't say I know him."

"When's the last time you saw Anderson?" Martin asked.

"I have no idea. I would've been with his dad, so it had to be before last October."

"Did Don get either of his sons involved with the girls?" Martin asked.

"If so, he never told me."

"Did he get Gordon Orrock involved?" Martin asked.

"Who?"

"Gordon Orrock," Pete said. "I understand you're friends."

"I don't know where you got that idea, but it's incorrect."

"Your wife said ...," Pete said.

"She was mistaken."

"But Ken," Pete objected, "I saw Gordon coming out of your room yesterday."

"You're wrong. Unless he works here, if you saw him coming out of a room, it wasn't mine."

It was worth a try, Pete thought.

"Oh, Don, why did I listen to you?" Ken moaned, closed his eyes, and blew out a long, slow breath. "I really am feeling sick now. Please get a nurse." He looked scared.

Pete and Martin did as Ken asked.

Once in the privacy of an elevator holding only the two of them, Pete asked, "What do you say, Martin? Do we start with Ulen, Vining, Vining, York, or Orrock?"

"*Hmm*, should we flip a coin?"

"I have another idea. Anderson Vining sat in front of the girl's apartment building Saturday night. No doubt he lied to us about the reason. How about starting with him?"

"Well, when you frame it that way ...." Martin smiled.

"With any luck, Anderson will be home. Wes should be at work, so if we don't find Anderson, we'll work our way to Ulen via Orrock."

"I'm trying to think of a way to ensure they're home. Do you remember in which course we covered that?"

"I think it was Detection 101," Pete chuckled.

"If we don't find Anderson, Wes, Gordon, or Sam, we'll hop a plane for Gainesville, Florida?"

"I think you should take that trip, Martin. I'll stay, catch up on the paperwork, and attempt to get you off the hook with Commander Lincoln."

"So selfless."

On the way to Anderson's home, Pete called Anderson's mom, again. This time his call went right to voicemail, and the message concluded by stating her mailbox was full. He couldn't leave another message.

Anderson Vining wasn't home, but he answered Pete's call. "We have a couple more questions. Where can we find you?"

"Uh, this isn't a good time. How about tonight?"

"That won't work. It's advantageous for you to rearrange your schedule. We're at your home. How soon can you get here?"

"Seriously, I'm tied up all day."

"Where are you?"

"In meetings."

"Location?" Pete persisted.

"I'm telling you, I can't be interrupted."

"You have two choices, Anderson. You can be at your home in fifteen minutes or see your face plastered all over TV, asking anyone who sees you to call Crime Stoppers."

"I'm on my way. I'll be there as fast as I can."

Pete disconnected, and Martin chuckled. "I don't remember doing it that way in Detection 101. Do you think I was taking a bathroom break?"

Martin kept the engine running during much of the wait. Both investigators exited the unmarked as a car pulled into the Vining driveway. They stood alongside the car as Anderson opened the door, looking irritated.

"What's this all about!" he yelled.

"As I said on the phone," Pete said, "we have some questions. We can stand out here or go inside. It's your call."

"Follow me," Anderson snapped and led Pete and Martin into the house and to the den. All three men took the same chairs they used during their last meeting.

"We know you didn't wait outside the apartment building to learn where to find JD and a blonde girl—a girl he was trafficking," Pete said. "Why were you there?"

"I'm telling you, that's the truth!"

"Stand up and put on your jacket," Pete instructed.

Anderson did as Pete said.

"Now turn around and put your hands behind your back," Pete said.

"Are you crazy?" Anderson screamed. "Why are you arresting me?"

"If for no other reason, for lying to us," Martin said.

"*Wait*, give me a chance," Anderson whined.

"One more chance. That's it," Martin said.

All three men sat, and Martin repeated Pete's question, "Why were you parked outside that apartment building last Saturday night?"

"I had to find out where to find the girls' pimp."

"Why did you want to know?" Martin asked.

"Because Dad wanted to know."

"He was in Florida. Why would he want to know?" Martin asked.

"For a friend."

"Why did that friend want to know?" Martin asked.

"I have no idea."

"What's the friend's name?" Martin asked.

"All Dad told me was a friend of his wanted to know. He didn't share the name."

"So you passed the information on to your dad's friend, Gordon Orrock," Martin said, grasping at straws.

"Gordon Orrock? Have you met the guy? He's too soft to go out in

222

weather like we had on Saturday. I'm amazed he doesn't winter in Florida or Arizona. I gave the information to Dad."

"When did your dad fly in?" Pete asked, attempting to blindside Anderson.

"Huh?"

"He's here, isn't he, Anderson," Pete said. It was a statement, not a question.

"If he is, it's news to me."

FORTY-NINE

Martin drove to Gordon Orrock's home in Burnsville while Pete called Don Vining. He hoped Vining wasn't on the golf course again. When Vining answered, Pete said, "I never heard back from your wife. Let me speak to her."

"She's at the mall. Shopping is her middle name."

"I don't believe you, Don. I left two messages requesting a return call and never heard from her. Now her voice mailbox is full. It's impossible to leave a message."

"Par for the course. She's not a detail person. I'm not sure she ever listens to messages. In fact, I'm not sure she knows how to access or delete them." Don chuckled.

"Make sure she calls me today. Understand?"

"Sure. No problem."

"It will be a problem if I don't hear from her today."

"I'll tell her."

Switching to a conversational tone, Pete asked, "You don't golf on Wednesdays, Don?"

"Not until after noon. Wednesday is women's league. Trust me, you don't want to golf behind them."

Arrogant SOB, Pete thought but refrained from sharing his opinion. Instead he said, "Remember our conversation on Monday, Don?"

"Yes."

"And remember you said you wanted Anderson to give one hundred dollars to a blonde girl who is being trafficked?"

"Wait a minute! I never did that, so I sure wouldn't have said it."

"JD was trafficking this girl, Don. We accessed his records. You're one of his johns."

"No way!"

"Amber or one of JD's other girls can identify you, Don. Are you going to cooperate or continue making it worse for yourself?"

"Okay, I know who JD and Amber are. I felt sorry for Amber and wanted Anderson to give her some extra money. She couldn't take money directly from me."

"But she could take money from Anderson when she was standing next to JD?"

"I expected Anderson to be creative."

"You know, Don, I'm amazed when a guy like you puts his son's neck in the noose and walks away."

"I don't know what you're talking about. How could I be doing that just by asking Anderson to give the girl money?"

"Was it a tag team event, Don?"

"Huh? What do you mean?"

"This wasn't about money, was it? You know one hundred dollars wouldn't have been enough to help this girl. Who wanted to know where to find JD, Don?"

"Look, I just wanted to give Amber a little cushion."

"And you thought one hundred dollars would suffice."

"Yes."

Pete was getting nowhere, and that wasn't likely to change while they were twelve hundred miles apart. *Apparently, there's safety in distance as well as in numbers*, he thought and resorted to Plan B, at least for the time being.

"Make sure you're available for the rest of the day, Don. When I call, make sure you answer. Do you understand?"

"You're speaking English, aren't you? If so, I understand."

They were halfway to Burnsville by the time Pete disconnected. Pete filled him in on the other side of the conversation with Donald Vining, and minutes later, they reached Orrock's home. Pete attempted to remain optimistic when Orrock's wife answered the door. "Good morning, Mrs. Orrock. We're looking for Gordon."

"He ran out for a few groceries. I'm expecting him back shortly. Would you like to come in and wait for him?"

Pete thanked her, and she led them into the living room. They made small talk until Gordon returned.

"I'm back," Gordon called out as he entered the back door that led to the garage. "They had your favorite coffee cake. I bought one for you, sweetheart."

"The two police officers you spoke with on Sunday are here, Gordon."

Pete heard the back door open. He jumped out of the chair and ran into the kitchen as Gordon started to shut the door behind him.

"If I didn't know better, Mr. Orrock, I'd think you're avoiding Martin and me."

"No, I have more groceries in the car. Never mind, that can wait."

"I'm happy to help you carry them in."

"Thanks. I'll take care of it later. What can I do for you?"

"We have some additional questions. I'm sure you'd like privacy. If you like, we can do this at headquarters."

Gordon walked into the living room and told his wife, "I'll be tied up for a while, sweetheart. The groceries are still in the bags. Sorry."

"No problem. I'll put them away. Thanks for the coffee cake, honey."

Gordon bent over and kissed her, then led the way to the den.

In keeping with a pattern familiar to Pete, all three men settled in the same chairs they'd previously occupied. "I understand you solicited help from Don Vining last Saturday," he said.

"I'm confused. Can you be more specific?"

"First," Pete said, "you know Don Vining, don't you?"

Gordon nodded and busied himself pulling pills off his sweater.

"And you asked Don to tell you where you could find JD St. Peter at Crashed Ice last Saturday. Didn't you?"

"I don't know anyone named JD."

"You may not know him," Pete said, "but I'm sure you know at least one of the girls he'd trafficked. How did you find out about JD's girls?"

Gordon's head dropped. He sighed and said, "I don't remember."

"Don Vining was the conduit, wasn't he?"

"I don't remember." Gordon continued checking the front and sleeves of his sweater, intently searching for and removing the pills. "You do remember Ken Lamberton, don't you? He deeply regrets allowing Don to get him involved with those girls. How about you, Mr. Orrock?"

Gordon repeatedly rearranged his bulk in the recliner, then pulled up his sleeves. Finally Martin interrupted the silence, saying, "Gordon, we know you were involved with those girls. If you insist, we can have them point you out in a lineup. Is that what you want?"

Don grimaced and slowly shook his head. "No, please don't."

"We also know you were looking for JD, their trafficker, Saturday night at Crashed Ice. Weren't you?"

Gordon concentrated on the blank TV screen and said, "Like my wife and I told you, I was here all night last Saturday."

"In other words, Irene's complicit," Martin said.

Gordon rubbed his forehead and stared at his feet. "Irene is a good, honest person."

"A good, honest person who would risk jail time to protect the man she loves?" Pete asked. "Too bad you won't even be in the same prison. She won't be able to visit you. Go put cuffs on Irene, Martin. Gordon and I will join you as soon as I get the cuffs on him."

"Wait, please! Irene drifted off while watching TV. She didn't lie. She didn't know I left, and she was still dozing when I returned."

"Why did you want to find JD?" Pete asked.

"I wanted to talk to him."

"So you found him and talked to him?" Pete asked.

"No. It was too cold. I never found him. I turned around and came home."

"The part about it being cold is true, Mr. Orrock," Pete said. "The rest is not. If you confess, we may be able to help you cut a deal."

Gordon sat silently, staring at his hands and biting his lip.

Martin and Pete waited him out.

Eventually Gordon said, "I need to go to the bathroom. It can't wait."

Martin followed him into the bathroom—just in case he intended something drastic. When Gordon finished, they returned to the den. Gordon moved at the pace of someone walking the plank.

"How did you know where to find JD?" Martin resumed.

"A friend."

"We need that friend's name," Martin said.

After a protracted pause, Gordon said, "Don Vining."

"What happened after you learned where to find JD?" Martin asked.

FIFTY

"I'd parked in a downtown ramp, waiting for JD's location. I worried that it took too long, afraid he might be gone. I left my car and walked up to the cathedral."

"And once you got there?" Martin asked.

"With all those people, it took a while. I finally found JD. He held onto Amber and another young girl for dear life. That's how I knew it was JD."

"And?" Pete prodded. He needed details to ensure Gordon's truthfulness. He might take the fall for someone else.

"JD had dressed for Antarctica. The girls had dressed for a Florida winter. JD's doing, of course. I saw Amber shivering. Her lips had actually turned blue. That infuriated me! How could anyone treat another human being that way?"

"Because of the way JD set up his business," Gordon continued, "that was the first time I knew where to find him. I went there to talk to him—to reason with him. I wanted to get him to stop hurting the girls and thereby hurting me. Seeing his total disregard for Amber and the other girl, I realized that thinking I could reason with him was ludicrous. The girls meant nothing to him. I knew there was just one thing I could do for the girls ... and for me. And I did it." Gordon licked his lips. Then he bit his lower lip and rearranged himself on the recliner.

"And?" Pete asked.

"Can I get some water? My mouth is so dry, I can barely talk. There are paper cups in the bathroom. I can get it there."

Pete left Martin with Gordon. He found the bathroom and the paper cups. When he returned, he handed the cup to Gordon and repeated the question.

"I'd spotted JD from a distance. I made a wide circle around him and walked up behind him. Before I reached him, I gripped the gun in my jacket pocket."

"Then?" Martin asked.

"I walked up tight against him, faking a stumble to get close without raising the suspicions of those nearby, and I shot him in the back. I know shooting someone in the back is a chicken move. Even so, that's what I did." Gordon sniffed and ran an index finger under his nose.

"In other words, you went to Crashed Ice intending to kill JD," Martin said.

"No! I intended to talk to him, not kill him."

"And it takes a gun to talk to a guy like JD?" Martin asked.

"No, but I'm not exactly an imposing figure. A gun can drive home a point when words can't. I took it as a prop. I only wanted to talk."

"This might be believable if the gun didn't have a silencer," Martin said.

"Say you're JD and at Crashed Ice. Say a guy points a gun at you. In a crowd, are you more likely to believe him if the gun has a silencer to cover the sound?"

"Why didn't you settle for making your point with your prop?" Martin asked.

"Like I said, there was no use. It was obvious the girls meant nothing to him. They looked so cold. Forcing them to stand out there dressed that way was criminal. I know. The fact he trafficked them was also inhumane. And it was criminal of me to buy their services. But seeing Amber that way put me over the edge. I realized words would never suffice with a guy like JD. I can't imagine ever thinking they would."

"So you did it for Amber?" Pete asked.

"I did it for Amber. I did it for me," Gordon broke down. "I felt trapped. I couldn't believe I'd taken advantage of this young girl. Not just once, but on a regular basis. I hated myself for doing it. What kind of loser, what kind of creep, what kind of a piece of shit would do it with a beautiful, young girl—a child?"

"Each time I did it, I promised myself it was the last time. But each time I had another opportunity, I jumped at the chance. At first, I hated my friend for hooking me up with JD, then I realized he didn't force me the first time or any subsequent times." Gordon wiped his tears away with his hand. "It was like an addiction. When I wasn't with Amber, I thought about being with her, wanted to be with her. You have to understand. I love my wife. This has nothing to do with her. I can't even say sex with my wife is lousy. It isn't."

"I know being with an under-aged girl is repulsive. That was my immediate reaction when I met Amber. I have a granddaughter her age.

I didn't realize that was what I was getting into. When I saw Amber, I turned to walk away. She came up behind me and put her hand on my shoulder. She told me not to leave. I don't even know what else she said. All I know is I stayed, and I've regretted it ever since. Don't get me wrong. I'm not blaming Amber either. I have no one to blame but myself. I am so sorry ... for Amber, for killing JD, for everything. I hate myself for being so weak." Gordon rested his head in his hands and cried quietly, back shaking.

"The last time we met with you, you said you didn't have a gun," Pete said.

"I found the gun on the web and bought it for one reason. I'd already gotten rid of it before you asked."

"What did you do with it?" Pete asked.

"There's still open water on the Mississippi River. I dropped it off the Wabasha bridge."

"And the down jacket?" Pete asked.

"I told the truth about Irene's reaction to my having one. I bought it Saturday and left it in the car. I put it on Saturday night and donated it to Goodwill on Sunday."

Pete stood.

Gordon dried his face on his sweater and went to his wife. He held her tight and told her he was being arrested. He said there was no need to hire an attorney. He intended to plead guilty. He didn't mention the crime. He concluded by whispering in her ear, "I'm so sorry, sweetheart. I hope you'll eventually be able to forgive me. I know I don't deserve it. Please never forget I love you. I always have and always will."

Martin drove.

Pete rode in back with Gordon.

It was a silent trip. All three men felt weighed down.

The two investigators escorted Gordon to the Ramsey County Jail and waited while the detention deputy booked him.

Before leaving, Pete told the deputy he wanted Gordon put on suicide watch.

FIFTY-ONE

"This was my first vice-related case," Martin shook his head. "Solving it feels good, but it doesn't outweigh my concern for the girls. It seems like an uphill battle for all four."

"My first too. I'll take homicide any day. Gordon eliminated one trafficker, but that's barely a start. There's some consolation in knowing with help from the FBI and vice, four johns will pay. Even so, what lies ahead for the girls weighs me down. Putting a more positive spin on it, Anderson and Wes may think long and hard before following in their dad's footsteps."

"JD's murder seems like destiny, Martin. There were so many opportunities for Orrock's plan to fail. He recognized Alyssa. It sounds like she's the only one he knew. Had she not been there alongside JD, Gordon couldn't have found ... and murdered him. Anderson was late in getting to the apartment building. He got there just in time to see Jessie go in with Ulen. Megan was already there. Had Anderson arrived a few minutes later, he wouldn't have known Ulen was a john. He'd have been too late to learn where to find JD—unless Alyssa or Ella came who knows how much later? It would have been at least another forty-five minutes. He might well have given up before then.

Pete and Martin shared the paperwork. After they'd completed a significant portion of the necessary reports, Martin headed for home to spend some awake time with his family.

Pete shared their findings with the St. Paul PD representative on the FBI's Anti-Trafficking Coordination Team and the St. Paul PD's Vice Unit. He found some satisfaction in knowing Don Vining wasn't home free.

Alone in his office, he put his feet up on his desk and texted Katie: "It's a wrap. Depressing outcome. Would love 2 c u. Available tonite?" He'd barely hit send before his phone vibrated.

Katie's text said: "Yes! Want to come over tonight and relax? Any other ideas? Call. Now is good time."

Katie answered, saying, "Congratulations. Sorry it was such a downer. Is that because of the person who did it?"

"Yeah. Too many hours dealing with criminals like JD and his murderer. I'm trying to concentrate on the fact a child trafficker is off the streets, and four girls can now begin putting their lives back together. Worried they may not succeed."

"How tired are you, Pete? I know you've been working a lot of hours. I thought maybe I could fix dinner. Then we could go see your grandma."

"I'd planned to go see her now. I'll check with Mom and see how it's going. We could both drive to Regions after dinner, and I could spend the night again. That will give Mom a good night's sleep. I know it's been another long day, and she'll need sleep. I've got a few things I have to wrap up at headquarters. I also want to check on Doc. Will it work if I arrive about 6:30?"

"Whenever you arrive will be perfect! I love you."

"Same here, Katie. One question. If I'm lucky enough to find Doc, are you okay with me inviting him to our wedding?"

"Of course. Please do."

Pete smiled, glad to have Katie in his life. He spent time tying up loose ends, then cut out. Before going to see Doc, he stopped at Regions to check on his mom. He found her and his dad talking softly while Grandma slept.

"Pete, does this mean you solved the case?" His dad smiled.

Pete nodded. It was hard to smile about this one.

"The anesthesia has taken a lot out of her," his mom said. "I understand that's common, especially for someone her age. She ate only a few bites of breakfast and fell back to sleep. The same with lunch."

"Mom, you look exhausted. Here's my plan, subject to change if something else works better for you. I'll stay a short time, go to Reaching Out in search of Doc, and join Katie for dinner. Then she and I will come here, and I'll spend the night with Grandma. How does that sound?"

"Wonderful." She reached out and grasped Pete's hand.

"I should also have time to help with the arrangements for Grandma. Just let me know how I can help."

His mom's expression relaxed, and she smiled. "Oh, Pete, that would be great."

"So glad, Pete," his dad said. "Your mom could use your help in keeping Sarah at bay. She means well but doesn't seem to understand or accept these decisions aren't hers to make."

Pete's grandma slept through his visit. Before leaving, he hugged his parents, then walked over to the bed and kissed his grandma lightly on the forehead.

Her eyes sprang open. "Pete!" a soft voice said. "Did you just arrive?"

"Actually, Grandma, I was just leaving, but I'll be back in a few hours."

"Wish I'd known you were here. How dare I sleep through one of your visits?"

"You need the sleep to heal, Grandma. We'll talk later. How about 6:30 tomorrow morning, over coffee?"

"Isn't that how this whole thing started?"

"No, that's when the resolution of the problem that occurred beforehand began."

"I have you to thank for that." She smiled.

Pete bent over and kissed her again. "Get some sleep, Grandma. Katie and I will see you soon."

Pete drove home, changed into broken-in jeans and a quarter-zip shirt, then drove to Reaching Out, hoping he'd succeed in connecting with Doc.

FIFTY-TWO

All the way to Reaching Out, Pete thought about his friend. He couldn't comprehend how homeless people withstood these bitter temperatures. A few weeks ago, during a bitterly cold stretch ushered in by a polar vortex, he'd offered Doc a place to stay. After a firm rejection, he'd resorted to buying Doc some extra clothes and blankets. Knowing Doc, the majority of those items were distributed to his homeless friends. After parking he ran around multiple ice patches to Reaching Out, thinking all the way, *Please be there. Please be there.*

A few late arrivers moved along the counter getting food when he ducked inside. Most people had their food and occupied the tables, eating and talking. Doc wasn't in line, so Pete scanned the room. There was no sign of Doc, but Pete saw one of his friends.

Stew saw Pete and raised a hand in greeting. Pete smiled and walked to Stew's table.

"I know, you're looking for Doc, right?"

Pete nodded.

"He's in the bathroom. That's his tray." Stew pointed at the tray directly across the table.

"How are you coping with this weather, Stew?"

"By reminding myself spring will come. Always does. I'm getting soft. On the worst nights, I resort to a shelter."

"How about Doc? Is he doing that?"

"Why don't you ask him? He just came around the corner." Stew pointed with a flip of his chin.

Doc was a very private person. Pete doubted he could get any straight answers from him while in this location. When Doc sat down, Pete noticed his friend remained true to the moniker his friends at Reaching Out had given him. He still resembled Doc in Snow White and the Seven Dwarfs. Not his height, but definitely his face and eyeglasses. Pete thought the name fit for another reason. Doc was obviously well-educated. Might even have a PhD or doctorate.

"Pete, to what do I owe the honor?"

"The weather."

"Tell me you're not still on that crusade."

"I'll never lie to you, Doc."

"At least I find a measure of consolation in knowing that." Doc smiled and shook his head.

"Looks like you're almost finished, Doc. Can I walk you at least part way to your destination?" *Wherever that is. Still living under that bridge?*

"Part way, perhaps."

Pete followed Doc out the door, then moved up alongside him and the two men headed east toward the heart of downtown St. Paul. On the way, they passed several Reaching Out patrons. Pete waited until they left everyone in their wake before saying anything. Then he opened with, "The weather remains treacherous, Doc. Have you found a more hospitable place to hang your hat?"

"And abandon my friends? I can't do that. I look out for them and they for me. It's a symbiotic relationship."

Pete knew from speaking to people in social services that this sentiment was common amongst the homeless. Many would rather sleep outside, under a bridge or wherever they'd established themselves, rather than leave their friends or endure the rules and sleep in a homeless shelter. "I'll bet some gloves, wool socks, warm boots, stocking caps, blankets, and a jacket or two will make that relationship warmer. What do you say? Can we run over to St. Vincent DePaul and see what they have to offer?"

"In Minnesota in January, never turn your nose up to added warmth. That's my philosophy." Doc smiled.

Doc followed Pete to his car, and Pete drove the short distance to the St. Vincent de Paul thrift store. Based on past experience, Pete didn't offer to take Doc to Penney's or Macy's, because Doc railed at such extravagance.

Once inside, they found enough things to fill the five large, reusable bags Pete brought, plus a heaping armful of spillover. Pete hoped the sheer volume would cause Doc to consent to a ride most of the way to the place where he spent his nights. The last time they'd done this, Doc permitted Pete to get just close enough to narrow down the location. The second benefit would be more time to speak with this friend who had him so puzzled. He couldn't understand how this highly intelligent man became homeless—or why he remained that way.

Will tonight be the night? He hoped so.

Loaded down with a dozen pairs of wool socks, a like number of thermal-lined gloves, turtlenecks, wool sweaters, a down jacket, three stocking caps, and a pair of Klondike boots that Doc put on before they walked back outside, they headed to the checkout. Before paying, Pete added a dozen wool blankets.

"Thanks, friend," Doc said as they walked to the car. "My friends love it when I go shopping with you. Tonight will feel like Christmas."

"I also have this for you," Pete said, pulling out a GO TO card that provided rides on all city busses and light rail trains. "There's a one-hundred-dollar balance on it now. I wrote down the card number and will call every few weeks to check the balance. Whenever you get below fifty, I'll bring it back up to one hundred."

"You shouldn't, Pete. You're too kind. You've paid me handsomely one hundred times over for the paltry help I provided in solving Brad's case."

"I disagree, but that's not why I'm doing this, Doc. I'm doing this because you're my friend. I just wish you'd let me do more. I'd also like to see more of you. The fact my schedule is often unpredictable makes that difficult. We could set a date and time, but I might have to cancel at the eleventh hour. And getting word to you would be difficult."

"You're a good person, Pete. My schedule too is quite unpredictable. I rarely know in advance what each day will bring. I enjoy the spontaneity."

"But you sometimes plan ahead, don't you, Doc?"

"Occasionally."

"I want you to reserve a date for me. Katie and I set the date. We're getting married on May 26th. We're hoping you'll come. I know it can be uncomfortable going to a wedding when the only people you know are the bride and groom. I spoke with my family. They'd like you to join them and sit at their table. You won't have to be alone, trying to find a way to melt into the walls."

"That was very thoughtful. Does the fact I'm invited mean its casual dress?" Doc smiled.

"I'll wear a tux, but what the guests wear will run the gamut. Anything goes. Also I'd like to take you shopping for whatever you'd like to wear. If you want a Ralph Lauren suit and silk tie, it's yours. If you prefer khakis and an oxford cloth shirt, that's what we'll get."

"How about a sequined suit coat, if I decide to go as Liberace?"

"If you want to go as Liberace and can find the sequined suit coat, I'll buy it. Does that mean we can rely on you to play the piano for the wedding? Do you know 'Here Comes the Bride'?"

"Playing the piano used to be so relaxing. I haven't played in more than a decade, and I think these digits are now too arthritic to play."

"Do you miss playing?" Pete asked.

"Actually, I haven't thought about it in a long time. But now that you mention it ....

"Someday will you trust me enough to tell me what caused your life to change so radically?"

"It isn't a matter of trust, Pete. Most of the time, I succeed in pushing the memories far enough to the periphery that I'm not forced to face them head on. Talking about it would bring those events center stage. I don't relish the thought."

"What if talking about it helped you pull your life together and start fresh?"

"What makes you think starting 'fresh' is preferable to what I have now?"

"I hold you in the highest regard, Doc. Judging strictly from the person with whom I've dealt, I believe a lot of people benefited from the former you. I'm sure your friends are benefiting from the current you, but I also believe a lot of people could benefit from the recaptured you. Whether you move forward or stay right where you are, I want my kids to get to know you."

Pete saw tears welling up along Doc's eyelashes. *This had to have something to do with a kid,* he thought. If he knew Doc's real name, a little research would probably tell him what. Although more difficult, he knew research would also reveal Doc's actual name. Respect for Doc kept him from doing either.

Katie watched out the picture window in her living room, waiting. She smiled as the car drove up, and Pete sprinted up the steps. Once inside he said, "It smells great in here!"

"It's the new perfume I'm trying."

"*Eau de* cabbage roll?"

"I didn't realize you're a connoisseur of fragrances."

"You have so much to learn, Katie." Pete looked into her deep-blue eyes. "And lots of time to learn it."

He cradled her in his arms and ran a hand through her thick, short, light-brown hair. They stood that way for a couple of minutes. He found comfort in her closeness. He always did. But after the last four days, it helped him feel grounded.

"Thanks, I needed that," he said as he let her go. "You're a treasure, Katie."

Katie smiled up at him. "Your last case, huh?"

Pete nodded. He looked drained.

"I'm here for you, Pete."

Over dinner Pete brought up their wedding. "Do you feel like too much of this is in your lap? Am I being unfair, relying on you for too much?"

"Oh, oh. Does that mean you and Martin have been talking about the wedding?"

"Yes. That led to a discussion of what remains on our to-do list."

"Currently," Katie said, "everything's on schedule. I'm working out some final details on the locations. You've accomplished everything on your to-do list until we finalize the guest list and address invitations. I know your schedule's often packed. If that's the case when the time comes, I can handle the invitations for you. No big deal."

"It would be a big deal, Katie. You have a full-time job."

"True, but I don't work sixteen- or twenty-hour days." She squeezed Pete's hand.

"If that's the way it plays out, I'll make it up to you."

"You'll make it up to me every time you arrive home safely, Pete."

He leaned over and kissed her. "By the way, I did work on one thing this week. It's actually a post-wedding thing. I spent some time on the Parade of Homes. Found a few places and layouts I like. The problem is, they're not for sale. I'm doing my best to change that."

"Don't tell me you're again doing drive-bys and questioning anyone whose house appeals to you?"

"Guilty." Pete laughed.

"Don't worry, Pete. We can live in your home or mine. Mine is small but will suffice until our first child comes along. It'll all work out."

Pete was relieved. Despite Katie's assurances, he'd continued believing it unfair to ask her to live in his house ... the house Andrea had selected and decorated. Andrea and their unborn child had died almost four years ago, when a drunk driver T-boned her car. Nonetheless, could Katie really feel comfortable there? Could it feel like home to her? He didn't want to risk it. Until he met Katie, he hadn't been able to move on and really start living again. He felt grateful that a case introduced them, they accidentally crossed paths a year later, and the rest was history—a history filled with happiness.

He asked Katie how she was doing with the venue and whether she had dreams of a destination wedding.

"That's out of the question, Pete. It's unlikely your grandma would or could go. She'd be heartbroken. I know she says she has no favorites. I also know you're her hands-down favorite grandchild. I see it every time she sets eyes on you. Her face lights up. She glows. Did Martin bring that up?"

"Martin loves digging for details. He's trying to decide what color tux he should rent. I told him chartreuse."

"You didn't," Katie laughed.

"Well, I didn't tell him it was my choice, I said it was yours." Pete smiled.

"I assume he trusts my fashion sense."

"We'll find out. I saw Doc tonight and invited him."

"I'm glad. I'd like to see him again. It's been awhile. Has he opened up?"

"No, he clams up every time I broach the subject of his becoming homeless. But I'm not giving up. I'd love to help him get his life back on track."

"Your definition of on track or his, Pete? It may sound crazy to you, but he may want to keep things the way they are."

"If so, that's his call. But I won't be satisfied until I know that's the case. What if there's something I can do to make his life better?"

After cleaning up the kitchen, Pete and Katie left for Regions.

Pete's dad was gone, but his mother was there when they arrived. This time his grandma's eyes were open. She smiled when he reached her door. She'd been watching for him.

"Pete, Katie!" She needn't say anything else. In combination with the smile, that said it all.

Katie walked over to her bed and kissed her forehead ... right after Pete.

"Want to hit the road, Mom?" Pete asked.

She nodded and said, "That would be great."

Pete walked her to the elevator, giving her time to share any information. Turned out there was no news. Grandma was doing well. No surprises.

Pete and Katie spent the next hour visiting with Grandma. She wanted to hear all about their wedding plans.

When Katie got up to leave, Grandma took her hand. "I'm so happy Pete found you. I couldn't have done a better job myself. I'm looking forward to dancing at your wedding, and I'm anxiously awaiting my great-grandkids."

After Katie left, Pete's grandma told him, "She's a lovely girl, Pete. You'll have a good life and make each other happy."

Again Pete slept in a chair pulled up tight against her bed, and again he held her hand all night.

She found comfort in that. So did Pete.

FIFTY-THREE
Five Years Later

Katie walked outside to Pete, holding out a letter, as he and their four-year-old, Teddy, played catch in the back yard. "It's from Alyssa Gilbert. The name rings a bell, but I don't know why."

"She's from that trafficking case Martin and I worked right before our wedding. I've wondered about them."

Teddy moaned, "Oh, Daddy, don't stop now!"

Katie offered, "How about if you two keep playing, and I read it to you? The twins are sound asleep. They'll sleep for at least another hour, and I have the baby monitor with me."

Dear Mr. Culnane,

It's been so long, and I wanted to let you and Mr. Tierney know how Ella, Megan, Jessie, and I are doing.

I returned to Virginia, Minnesota, with my parents and started counseling, sometimes with my mom too. I got permission from my high school principal to return to school, and I struggled through the rest of sophomore year. But I caught up enough to finish the year with my class. During junior year, I applied to St. Kate's. Now I'm far enough from home to feel independent, but close enough to go home if I want. St. Kate's is a small college and a caring environment in the middle of the city. It feels safe. I'm working on a degree in electrical engineering. I love it and I hope to build better electric cars.

My relationship with Mom is really good. She's like a trusted friend and sounding board. I can talk to her about anything. I still haven't told anyone else about what happened with JD back then. I told my friends I was with my cousin in Colorado and came home because I was homesick. I still feel pretty ashamed. I still want to find a way to talk about it with my little sister Madison so nothing like that ever happens to her. I've told her about some bad things that can hurt a kid her age. I want to protect her. I've stayed in some contact with the other girls at least once in a while, so here is an update:

Ella found some real helpful healing by singing! For years before meeting JD, she was too self-conscious to join her church choir. But her mother convinced her to join that choir and she found a couple new friends there too. The choir director was super impressed by Ella's beautiful voice, and she became the choir's featured vocalist.

She finished her junior and senior years in high school by testing into the Post-Secondary Enrollment Options program at Inver Hills Community College. So she got college credit at the same time, which she then transferred to the University of Minnesota to work toward a double major in music and theater. She works at the Chanhassen Dinner Theater, and they love her voice too. I think she's doing okay.

Unfortunately Megan began drinking heavily. I think she's an alcoholic. Her parents tried everything to get her into rehab, counseling, etc., but she went back to drinking every time. In tenth grade she met a boy who was sorta like JD, and she got pregnant. She went to an alternative school until she was sixteen but then dropped out, married the boy, and had another kid. Thankfully, her parents finally succeeded in helping her escape the abusive marriage. Megan and her two kids live with them. They pay for her counseling and provide day care for her kids. Megan is now a junior in high school. She says she wants to be a nurse. She says that goal helps her stay away from alcohol. I hope she'll be okay. Her kids are cute.

Jessie enrolled in an alternative school for the rest of her sophomore year. Her brothers were so happy she was home. They are super tight with Jessie, and they look out for her. She went to all their practices and games for the rest of high school. Jessie's school counselor convinced her she'd feel right at home at the University of Wisconsin, Madison. So far she likes it. She continued to fight for the causes and issues that matter to her, such as the Enbridge pipeline, bullying, and racism. She's majoring in political science, and plans to run for state representative. She door-knocked for political candidates. She already has a grassroots organization in place and commitments from numerous volunteers. I think she'd be a good politician.

That's about it for now. Thank you for everything you and Mr. Tierney did to help us.

Warm regards,

Alyssa Gilbert

"I'm so glad they're doing that well," Pete said with a smile.

Katie nodded and said, "Hey, don't forget Doc will be here at 6:00. The steaks are thawed. You can have some time alone with him while you barbecue."

ACKNOWLEDGMENTS

My thanks to Mark Kempe, retired investigator, St. Paul Police Department; and Don Gorrie, retired chief investigator, Ramsey County Medical Examiner's Office. Any errors in those areas are the result of my misinterpretation or misapplication of the information these people so generously shared.

Thanks to Tara Kennedy, Allison Dean, Andy Pieper, Pat Harper, Chris Smith, Pam McCord, Jen Smith, Ethan Smith, Ellie Smith, and Suzanne Donnell for their research assistance.

Thanks to Ruth Krueger, Rick Winter, Deb Harper, Tara Kennedy, Arlene Carpenter, and Marly Cornell for sharing their proofreading and editorial expertise; and Christopher Smith for being quick to share his time and computer expertise.

HOTLINES

Brittany's Place/180 Degrees, St. Paul, MN
Shelter and programs for girls under eighteen who are victims of or at risk of sex trafficking or exploitation
- 651-287-4801 (for immediate help/referral to shelter)
- 180degrees.org/brittanys-place.html
- https://ysnmn.org/ (to check immediate availability of shelter/services for sexually exploited youth)

National Sexual Assault Hotline 1-800-656-HOPE

National Human Trafficking Hotline 1-888-373-7888
    or text 233733

Domestic Violence Hotline 1-800-799-7233

National Suicide Hotline 1-800-273-8255

LGBT National Help Center 1-888-843-4564
    or http://www.glbthotline.org

Other books by S.L. Smith

Blinded by the Sight
Running Scared
Murder on a Stick
Mistletoe and Murder